LEAF, WATER AND FLOW

Praise for *Leaf, Water and Flow*

'A tale from Naxal country meets a protagonist in search of a novel. The intrigues of revolutionary violence are punctuated by the author's concerns about the craft. With this disturbing document of the ultra-left political movement, Avadhoot Dongare cements his place among the powerful new voices in Indian fiction.'

Ashutosh Bhardwaj

'The novel is put together by stitching together various characters, constituents of the society and episodes. The thread that is used for sewing together these pieces is not any plot, but the helplessness of the weak. Here and there, this thread comes to the fore and becomes starkly visible during the episodes of human deaths ... the question that springs up involuntarily in his consciousness is, "Who is responsible for this lethal state of affairs, for their deaths?"'

Loksatta

'The reader is repeatedly shaken with the realisation that art is artifice. So much of the novel is actually about the act of writing it with the author figure collecting parts and pieces from here and there that the final result is an ever-mutating work. Demanding the reader's time and attention even as its tone and tenor change with each chapter, this is an intensely rewarding read. ... Nadeem Khan's remarkable translation captures the changes in cadence across chapters and uses various Englishes for different characters as a reflection of the original novel's attempt at embracing "varied voices with their dialects and also the dialectics of their surroundings" in Marathi.'

Areeb Ahmad, *Hindustan Times*

'The novel undertakes a roller-coaster journey, meeting and navigating individuals who are trapped in a Maoist conflict. There is an element of fable too when an Egret appears and schools the narrator on the prevalence of violence in the human world. We meet an author who is in search of a novel. Nadeem Khan's translation is excellent ... His translations are like a transparent glass-pane—not just to the words of the original but also to the context, tonality, situations, dialogues, mode of narration ... *Leaf, Water and Flow* is a cerebral novel focusing on the interiorities of a nation's fault lines. It is a book of ideas, meant to be digested. Slowly.'

Umesh Kumar, *The Book Review*

'It takes fiction to make us see the world in ways we can scarcely imagine. The connectedness of things in the scaffolding of power comes to the forefront in Avadhoot Dongare's extraordinary Marathi novel—a word that can scarcely do justice to this creation that loops back on itself and brings the reader into its page by closing the space between them and the text ... Nadeem Khan dances alongside the Marathi in English, matching it move for move with his dexterous translation. A reminder of what fiction can be in all its glory.'

Arunava Sinha, *India Today*

Longlisted for the JCB Prize for Literature 2024

LEAF, WATER AND FLOW

— A NOVEL —

AVADHOOT DONGARE

TRANSLATED FROM THE MARATHI BY

NADEEM KHAN

RATNA BOOKS

HARPERPERENNIAL

An Imprint of HarperCollins *Publishers*

First published as *Paan, Pani Ni Pravah* in Marathi in India by
Prafullata Prakashan, Pune 2015
First published in English in India by Ratna Sagar P. Ltd. 2023
This edition co-published in India in 2026
by
Harper Perennial
An imprint of HarperCollins *Publishers* India
Cyber City, Building 10-A, Gurugram, Haryana-122002, India
www.harpercollins.co.in
and
Ratna Sagar P. Ltd.
Virat Bhavan, Mukherjee Nagar Commercial Complex
Delhi 110009, India
www.ratnabookseries.wordpress.com

2 4 6 8 10 9 7 5 3 1

P-ISBN: 978-93-6989-636-3

Printed and bound at
Nutech Print Services Pvt. Ltd.

FSC
www.fsc.org
MIX
Paper | Supporting responsible forestry
FSC® C195953

This book is printed on FSC® certified paper
which ensures responsible forest management.

HarperCollins *Publishers*, Macken House, 39/40 Mayor Street Upper, Dublin 1, D01 C9W8, IrelandDublin 1, D01 C9W8, Ireland

To

Harchiri
and
mother and father

Contents

Author's Note

In the specific case of this narration, a Marathi author could try and embrace varied voices with their dialects and also the dialectics of their surroundings that were more rooted to their geographical cultural environment. These voices the author might have heard in the real world or in his imagination. Does an English rendering of the narration take away from this attempt at being genuine to the rootedness of the voices? The author does not wish to claim anything. In any case, theoretically, claims have already been made that a translation can never remain altogether true to the roots of the original text. The author does not wish to commit himself to such theoretical claims either. A translation is an attempt in a certain direction, which often appears uncertain. Writing, too, is an attempt in a certain and more frequently uncertain direction. It is easy to say that these attempts may never reach the destination that was secretly desired. If the original Marathi novel tries to embrace various voices, it means that it tries to translate those voices into a narration that is written and published in the form of a book. That book has now been translated into another language. As the author was alive when the English translation was being done, he tried to intervene in certain areas that he deemed necessary. There are not many such areas, but they certainly require this note of confession.

Avadhoot Dongare

Thus begins

The letters of the Marathi alphabet begin with अ (a) and end with ज्ञ (jnya). At least that's how they are taught in schools. At least that's how they've been taught till now. At least that's how they've been taught for some time in the past. And that's how they were taught to the author. The author begins and ends with his language, which makes him अज्ञ, which is the Marathi word for 'unknowledgeable'.

I have no intention of deceiving you. So I thought I'd better put it straight right in the beginning.

For the rest:

You are great. You are knowledgeable. You understand everything: history, civics, geography, science, mathematics, economics, all the subjects. All the information. All the knowledge of the world that exists or doesn't. Where history begins and ends. Where art begins and ends. Where science begins and ends. What existed before. What will happen in the future. You know all of this. You rule over the entire world. You are the superpower. You are the wise citizens of this world. It's a gathering of learned citizens that spreads everywhere. A flow.

But for all that, you would certainly be a human being. Even if you are not any of the things mentioned in the paragraph above, you are still a human being. I mean, there is no possibility of your being an egret or a bulbul or a buffalo or a lapwing or a teak tree or a banyan tree or a mango tree or a stone or a pen or a brick stove. So the treachery that has already happened out of being born a human being, if there is no remedy for correcting that, what does one do?

Even if this question sounds self-wounding, it doesn't matter. Let's move on with whatever it feels like. This question may have occurred to you or it may not have; you may agree with it or you may not; but let's move ahead together nevertheless. Hope you don't mind that? Doesn't matter if you mind it too, but shall we move ahead together? See how you feel about it. Do you mind if the novel comes along too? You have the choice. No tension at all. Don't say somebody may say something or such stuff. If you feel it from the heart, let's move ahead.

Prologue

One

There is this path in the interior of Ratnagiri. It is a dust track – red, hard earth. In the summer it gets dusty, and when the wind blows, the dust blows with the heat. No such dust during the monsoon and winter. In winter, the air is heavy; but the cold, as such, is just the Ratnagiri kind. The rains, by comparison, are something else altogether. It is cold during winter, but not all that cold. Summer is sweaty, but not really hot. But the rains clam you up proper. The water makes a tremendous sound and attacks from all directions.

There isn't any crowd on this by-path. There is this slushy kind of lake here. You may see occasional white lotuses there. There is moss everywhere all the time. Some egrets visit that water body once in a while. There is a well there too, but it is quite lost amid all the weeds and shrubbery surrounding it. Lined with stones gone black, it's not a pretty well to look at. There doesn't seem to be much water in it either. When it rains, you can see some mysterious water deep down inside.

One side of this path has pretty dense, wild vegetation – a profuse tangle of trees. There are some teak trees, standing erect. These teaks are not bent and twisty like the coconut trees beyond. They shoot straight up. A dense litter of crisp leaves below.

One such teak leaf fell in the still, clear water of a puddle down there in that red earth. The sunlight had preceded it, but when the leaf floated in, the rays got on top of it. White leaf. Small compared to the other big leaves that had fallen around it. Its veins are quite clear, its edge is rough. The upper edge dips into the water such that it is difficult to separate the leaf from its reflection in the water. There is a muddy twig next to it. A leaf sometimes gets caught in a channel, arrested by a stone or a piece of stick, or something. But here the water was still. And since there hadn't been any rains, it lay stagnant, and now this leaf resting peacefully on its surface.

Which of those trees could this leaf have belonged to? Could it have fallen off because the tree's need for it was over? Could the tree have caused it to fall? Why did it fall exactly where it had fallen? When would it have sprouted on the tree, and how long would it have stayed there? When did the process of dying start with this leaf? I didn't have an answer to any of these historical questions. But I saw that leaf fall on the water. That sighting was definitely something I possessed, and I don't think I have any sense of guilt about it.

Teak wood is strong, very strong. This leaf that carries some of the strength of that wood lies in front of me, waiting for death. There are not many teak trees on this path. There are about as many here as in that wild patch there. And they are fine. Nobody has got after their lives yet. There is still plenty of space around here. The leaf fell on a spot in that place, and I stood close by. We were quite close. I got closer. The leaf looked beautiful, lying in that still water. For the sake of that leaf, I would have wanted to stand alongside those trees. But I was not a tree, so I couldn't stand there beyond a period of time. So, after some time, I went home.

Came home. The flat where I stay measures 525 square

feet, and it is in a two-storey building. Whether somebody else had stood there before the building came up, and whether a similar teak leaf had lain there then, how can I know? The leaf that I saw falling into that puddle of still water and lying there, that, of course I knew. It had become obligatory for me to look at that leaf till so long as I could see it in that water every time I passed by.

The leaf had turned whiter with all that sunlight falling upon it. If I looked at it unblinkingly, it would create illusions at the upper edge. Could be that the sun and the water were playing tricks. The edge seemed to appear and disappear. I was watching one single teak leaf with both of my eyes, of that I was sure.

What if I fell dead right next to the leaf this very moment? People would gather in a little while. Going by the history of the path, they may think it's some drunk lying there. But by and by, they will know that it is a dead human being. A little more by and by, there'll be quite a crowd gathered round. Still later will come the relatives and the neighbours. Then they would be bound to dispose of the body at the assigned place. There would be some chatter alongside. They would have got to know from the doctor, meanwhile, how the death occurred. Whatever information is gathered, the disposal of the body will happen at the hands of other human beings, that's certain. It's not as if this is exactly how it will happen, but the chances are strong. Once dead, you can only assume, so this can only be an assumption.

But the path that this leaf's death takes is different. Nobody has gathered here. Just I and a few words alongside. Don't feel like speaking in spite of possessing words. So I went home. Pulled out a notebook from a wooden shelf. Rested the tip of my pen on the first line of the first page and decided: I would not let this leaf's death go waste.

What does it mean?

It means that this was probably an escape route. What can I say with any certainty? I was seeing the leaf finishing off every day. I had these words for company. No people had gathered around. People surely will gather when I die, for some time at least, some people at least. They have no option before them, really. A corpse has to be disposed of, like it or not, so people will gather. People gather when people die. People gather even while people are dying. People also gather to kill people. Even otherwise, people gather. Otherwise means: for interactions related to the act of living. If an example has to be given, it can be of this place close by on the other side. There used to be some four-five shingled houses there that were ready to collapse. A year back, a two-storey building was erected at that place. There are many more families living there now. There were two jackfruit trees at the edge, which are now inside the compound of the building. There were three-four betel nut trees, which have now disappeared. That was a good place for people to live in. People gather, then, for the sake of living.

Or people gather there at the shops on the Gokhale crossing, for buying various things. There are these two alleys that move towards the Gokhale crossing: Maruti lane and Ram lane. There used to be a small mosque on Maruti lane; it has now transformed into a white building with black panes. In Ram lane, there was a red stone temple with a shingled roof for Lord Ram. It has now transformed into a marble temple with a spire on top. People gather there too. These alleys are on one side of the main road. There, on the other side, is the State Transport bus stand. If nowhere else, here at least people gather in large numbers. Further down the main road, there is a weekly market every Saturday, and there they gather in hordes. Such numbers never gather in the lane where the leaf fell.

People don't assemble at the death of a teak leaf. Why not? Probably because the dying of a leaf is a trivial thing. So, why do people gather? What do they do after gathering?

People/groups/society – people who investigate do investigate where, when and how it all started. I cannot do it. I just know how to write stories. This is my limitation. I am searching for things within my limitation. You may call it a limited research project. Or a research flow. The beginning of this flow of writing would have happened somewhere far behind. Which page of which notebook, I can't remember. Don't know how many pages were turned either because the pages are not numbered. But I love this work of searching through pages. Sometimes I run into a new page, some other times an old, fragile page reappears. Some pages turn into nice, small stories, some into big ones. The pages right now are filling up with some big stories. I too, for convenience, give them the name of a novel. I can even see a link running through them. I went on joining page to page and got my first novel, and a second one joining the first novel, and now this third one is linked to the earlier two. This is a triple Preface to the novels that will follow. Good if they get to be written; if they don't get to be written, good too. If ever somebody wants to search out an address for this place, these pages will be useful. There will be a big web created out of all these pages, and I will be dead by then, like this leaf. At least I can hope so.

It's this habit I have of collecting these pages. Well, calling it a habit may be distancing myself from it a bit. These pages are just there with me, like my nose, like my belly. It's because of these stories that I noticed the teak leaf in the first place. I was alone, and the leaf was alone too. It was dying, I was alive.

People and all, groups and all, society and all, well, they keep changing. Are there conflicts on account of these changes? Do people die in these conflicts? Are they killed? If I can get flustered by the death of a leaf, am I not going to be flustered by the death of humans? The words that gather at my getting flustered, it's possible for me to get these words on paper. In fact, I really have no other alternative. When their stop arrives, they disembark, willy-nilly. And a story gets woven out of them, automatically. The flow stops for the nonce, and the leaf in the water gets visible, the whole of it. That leaf is the novel.

Two

Call it an arrow shot from a bow, call it a bullet shot from a gun –

A sentence shot out:

Not a leaf moves without their permission.

Leaf. Page. Sheet.

Who said this? When?

What leaf? From a book or from a tree? History or geography?

Whose permission? Theirs or theirs, this sarkar or that sarkar?

Subject

'What's the subject of the story/novel?' people ask. Difficult question to answer. Some ask this question merely to while away the time, that's evident. But some others, it appears, do ask with all sincerity. That's when some words spring out that may pass for an answer. But when writing, words cannot just tumble out; they get dealt out in careful measure. So, for a person like me, all that's barely possible is to try and write down the answer to the question: what's the subject of this novel?

An honest answer is: the subject of this novel is not something that can be expressed in brief.

If the subject had occurred like a flash and could have been articulated with felicity, wouldn't I have gone on and earned a degree in it? The highest degree available? Wouldn't I have pasted the subject on a board and thundered out a lecture on it? But because that is not possible, I sat down to write the subject, and all that has come to my head is these stories. It's only through these stories that we can form some estimate of the subject of this novel.

One

Look, this is a big hotel. 'It's not called a hotel, idiot!' Okay, it's a big restaarent. 'It's not pronounced "restaarent", dumbo;

it's pronounced "res-tah-ron".' Well, all right, this is a 'res-tah-ron' in a good-sized city of Maharashtra. Now if you go on chanting 'res-tah-ron', it puts you in mind of the guys who use the wus-tah-raw, a razor, at our Arun Hair Cutting Saloon. So even if someone insists on calling these refreshment houses 'res-tah-rons', it feels so much better to call them hotels. So, well, this is a hotel with fifty odd tables laid out. And you get a wide variety of dishes here, mostly south Indian. Also, batata vada, misal pav and such like. Good, high-quality, tasty dishes. On an average, we may say, people who come here run up a bill of at least 150 bucks per head. There's no maximum here. It could easily be Rs 500 per head, or even more. That's exactly why, appended to its name, 'Ruchaayee', the tag-line reads, 'Your Palate, Your Purse, Our Dishes – Come in, Please'.

While we were talking about this hotel, the information regarding the hotel/restaurant/'res-tah-ron' mess-up arrived courtesy of Mr Nene. Mr and Mrs Nene go to the hillock nearby at 7:30 a.m. in their small four-wheeler called Nano. They park their car at the gate, climb up the hillock, and on their way back, go into this hotel, sweat-soaked, at 8:30 a.m. Here, they help themselves to either idli–sambar or cheese–chilli dosa or cut-dosa or appa and a cup of coffee per head. Then they head homeward at ten.

Right now they are tucking into appa, dunking it in some green chutney with great relish. As always, the fan next to them covers their sweaty bodies nicely in its sweep. While we were talking about the hotel, whatever information this Nene guy gave us on pronunciations, he gave exactly the same information to his wife when sitting inside. He doesn't use abusive words like 'idiot' and 'dumbo' when addressing his wife, so minus those abuses he told her, 'It's not pronounced

"Paris", it's "Puh-ree", "Puh-ree".' His son left to take up a job in Austria a year back and since then, Nene has become extremely pronunciation-conscious. There's a reason for this too. Even if Nene does not disclose it in public, it's important to record it here. When the son got this offer in Austria, he informed the people at home. With great enthusiasm, Nene called up all his relatives and spread the word. 'Varad is going to Australia, y'know? Such-and-such is the package. Three-year programme,' and so forth. He posted the information on Facebook too: 'My son...flying to Australia...' After all this was done, the son came and told him that he was going to Austria, not Australia. Well, this flustered Nene and he tried to get out of it by holding the spellings alone responsible for all the confusion. Then he suddenly remembered about Austria. He had read somewhere that Austria was the first place Hitler had invaded during the Second World War. 'Aah! Yoorope!' he said. 'It's not Yoo-rope, Dad,' the son shot back, 'it's Yoo-rup, Yoo-rup.'

Since then has Nene become extremely alert and finicky about pronunciation and spellings. Otherwise, bloody hell, he never had run into this kind of a problem in so many years of service. These days, however, the pronunciation of various words forms the staple accompaniment to the Nene couple's breakfast. Today's breakfast was held on Paris. Now, before the two step out and chuck a few more abuses at us for keeping a watch on them, let's disappear. Heck, you'll say, so what the devil happened in this story? Well, all that happened was that the Nene breakfast was conducted on the subject of the pronunciation of Paris, the capital city of France, being 'Puh-ree'. What else can one say about Nene's breakfast, huh?

Two

It could be because they know that people get to know the caste by the surname and draw conclusions from it, or it could be because of a need for overall social security, but the family that lives in the neighbourhood of the hillock, originally Khilare, has been using the surname Bhosale for the last few generations. A rising star of this family, Rajesh has lately made the family mightily proud by clearing the exams for PSI. Rajesh will join the state service as police sub-inspector and will fight to bring about positive changes in the present state of affairs, said his neighbour Dinkarrao Kamble during a programme organized by the neighbourhood to felicitate Rajesh.

For the first two years, Rajesh will have to serve in Gadchiroli district. After that, maybe, he will be able to get himself transferred to this side. Rajesh is fully prepared to accept the challenge of working in the most backward district of the state. As a consequence of the four years of efforts he expended to get into the central and state government services, after all the classes he has attended and the lectures he has heard, Rajesh has begun to feel a sense of attachment to the country. Staying within the confines of the Constitution drafted by Dr Babasaheb Ambedkar, he will fulfil the responsibility of serving the country in the area of administration. This Rajesh believes, as do the other members of his family. Rajesh has always possessed energy and enthusiasm. Now that he has gained the fruit of success, the other youngsters of the neighbourhood need to keep him as their ideal, Dinkarrao Kamble had advised on the occasion that day.

Rajesh's mother is so overcome with emotion that – oh,

don't even ask. The boy has made them proud. Rajesh's father drives a rickshaw. Meaning, he simply has to. His elder brother works at a call centre. He, too, has to. That is why Rajesh could take the competitive examination and make the family proud. The circumstances of Rajesh's family, in fact, are no longer desperate. The brother's salary has allowed them to set the house up properly. Besides, with the brother having got married a year back, there is now a daughter-in-law in the house, so there is a helping hand now to run the household. Thinking about the difficult times they've waded through has churned Rajesh's mother up far more than it has affected his father. Her eyes have brimmed up too. The curry today is likely to be sharper with all that saline water getting in. *Hey, maavshi, what's cooking today?* Chicken. *Arey, wah!* Rajesh's mother is a home bird. She has to be. Rajesh truly has turned all the hard work of the family into gold, Dinkarrao Kamble declared while speaking on the occasion.

Rajesh has bagged the PSI job, true, but he may well be taking exams for higher posts, looks like. May try for a Class One officer's post, likely. He has the ability for sure. No harm trying at least for a Deputy Collector's position. Should give it a shot, Rajesh seems to have decided. Since Dinkarrao Kamble didn't have any information on this, he didn't make any mention of it during the occasion.

What Rajesh's wife-to-be, Rani Jadhav, had to say on this subject comes later in the novel. Rajesh's wasn't a love marriage. His family chose the girl. Rajesh got married within a year of landing the PSI's job, and Rani entered his life. It's a great name, Rani, thinks Rajesh. What does Rani think?

Three

Even though Babasaheb was the chairman of the drafting committee of the Constitution, he had to face a great many tensions during the process of drafting. That's exactly why in 1949, during the debate in the Constituent Assembly, he had said, 'On the 26th of January 1950, we are going to enter into a life of contradictions. In politics we will have equality and in social and economic life we will have inequality. We must remove this contradiction at the earliest possible moment or else those who suffer from inequality will blow up the structure of political democracy which this Assembly has so laboriously built up.' These details do not come from the author of this novel; they come from Shridhar Hasure. The present political dispensation in India has reached a point of explosion, he believes. Shridhar so loves reading books that he devours whatever he can lay his hands on. He was a full-time worker of the Bahujan Samaj Party (BSP) for two full years. He left it five years ago. With age creeping up, he had to settle down, so he acquired a BEd degree and became a primary school teacher. That led to his marriage too.

Movements are all finished and there's darkness now everywhere, believes Shridhar. If this is what he believes at age 35, what is he likely to believe at 50 and what then at 75? Difficult to say. Well, anyway, he had a son a year ago, so he is looking after his family now in this darkening world. But he is forever restless. As a result, he has roped in three-four of his friends and together, they bring out a little magazine. The mission of this magazine is to create a ferment on the caste question. A thousand odd copies are brought out. He finds no intellectual engagement in the regular work; it's all turned dark out in the world, besides. So what does one do at a time like this? Shridhar's answer to this question: bring out little magazines and keep the reading going. Ranging from our own Comrade Sharad Patil to Antonio Gramsci of Italy, Shridhar's mission of consuming it all continues with sufficient sound and fury.

All this increases his feeling of being surrounded by darkness. But while Shridhar suffers from this feeling of envelopment, his friends don't and, therefore, things carry on. Besides, the confidence with which his friends can talk on the public platform, Shridhar, despite reading far more than his friends, just cannot. Well, actually, he has won a number of big-time awards in public speaking contests. But that was when he hadn't felt that darkness was descending. Now he does, hence the problem.

There's a road running along the hillock that leads to a suburb, which is where Shridhar lives in a house for which he pays five thousand rupees as rent. In the company of his books, his wife and son, Shridhar searches for a way out of the world upon which darkness has descended. He senses he has the company of Dr Ambedkar and Karl Marx in this enterprise. And he regrets, on a daily basis, that his routine work is not of the intellectual kind. It could well be the consequence of this that for any event whatsoever, Shridhar always has some book or the other to which he makes reference. For instance, the average number of dalit women getting raped every day is 4.3, so what's the point in crowing about the first lady President and all? Shridhar can start such statistics-backed arguments even in the year 2013. Shridhar attends innumerable lectures, reads innumerable books, and thus the day passes and night arrives, and he waits for the next day to dawn.

Shridhar has a very distant cousin by the name of Sayali. Shridhar has been a worker of a political party, so has been

Sayali. In fact, she still is. But because a ban has been placed on her party, and because the mission of the party is to establish a communist society in progressive steps by acquiring power through armed revolution, Sayali cannot work openly. She is a member of the party, nevertheless. Since an entire chapter has been devoted to her, let's not discuss her here. And Shridhar and Sayali are not very closely connected either. Even though the two have independently enjoyed intimacy with a vague thing called a movement, and even though they are distantly related, there is no connection between them. How is that?

Well, this is how. There is this boy whom Sayali has not yet married but has been with for at least two years, and will live with for the rest of her life. His name is Ajay. He is currently in jail. Ajay worked for the same party as Sayali. He visited the jungles on account of his work. That was why the police arrested him, and right now he is still in jail. Which jungle and why, the reader may well want to know. Well, that comes later. For now, it's enough to say that the party that Sayali and Ajay are connected with – the Communist Party of India (Maoist) – has thrown armed roots in the Bastar jungles of Central India. It's from here that it spreads to various parts. Bastar is in Chhattisgarh, but the jungle spreads across the neighbouring states of Odisha and Maharashtra. The names, of course, are a human imposition, but trees–animals–rivers–vines have their own presence everywhere. One can see the armed presence of this party across some parts of the Gadchiroli district of Maharashtra. The charge against Ajay is that he has visited these places. Such incidents become sensational news stories. One outcome of these sensational stories was that whatever little connection Shridhar had with Ajay and Sayali, he severed it completely. The friendship that had developed between Ajay and Shridhar over some time came to an end. That's how it has been with Shridhar. Bonds are suddenly created in movements like these, and bonds suddenly snap, can anyone know why and how?

Four

Even if people fail to identify Vijayendraraje Jadhav's caste from his surname, they can do so from his first name, and he doesn't feel small on account of that, so no problem. On the contrary, out of a sense of pride for his caste, Vijayendraraje alias Vijay wears a heavy gold bracelet round his wrist, and embellishes the cover photo of his Facebook profile with a collage of pictures of himself and Chhatrapati Shivaji Raje Bhosale. It can be said that generally Vijay reads a booklet or an article every couple of months. Vijay is very alert on caste matters. It's through these booklets that he gets details on the great conquests his caste has made till date; and whichever caste he belongs to, Maratha or whatever, the caste that is considered superior to his, Brahmin or whatever, well, this superior caste urgently needs to be neutered, this the booklets make abundantly clear to him. Even more than these booklets, Vijay draws nourishment from small recorded clips, Facebook and blogs.

The hillock that we have talked about above, there's a mall on top there, and the land on which the mall stands belongs to Vijayendraraje Jadhav's father. Getting a measure of the property that the Jadhav family owns is beyond our ability. An uncle of Vijayendraraje Jadhav is a corporator and belongs to a political party. What else Vijay should do beyond getting married is not a matter for worry. For the present, he goes for classes that prepare him to take the exams that are necessary for getting into a high post in government service. He got his Master's degree four years ago. Vijayendraraje also keeps doing various small courses. His name can be found on the rolls of programmes on journalism, spoken English, and such like. On the third of last month was his birthday, and for the first time, a big flex banner was put up on a street corner near where he stays, offering good wishes to Shri Vijayendraraje Jadhav on his twenty-ninth birthday. This is an important development. Placing on record the hope that this important event will continue to happen every year, we conclude, after expressing our gratitude to Shri Vijayendraraje Jadhav.

Five

The audience stepped out of the I-Max multiplex on the hillock after watching a particularly violent movie with 3-D goggles, a movie based on a battle that took place 2500 years ago between the Greeks and the Persians (now Iranians). Sword running right through the head, ships telescoping into each other and killing people in heaps, a steaming hot sex scene with a white woman and a hulk of a man getting into strange contortions, blood squirting straight onto one's clothes, the audience stepped out coated all over with this spine-tingling experience. It was difficult to know what went on in the audience's mind as they stepped out after getting thus conditioned in the air-conditioned atmosphere. They were laughing and chatting; some of the girls were straightening their clothes, a few boys were stretching their arms, a few couples were having cold drinks, a few families were getting into their cars; some were peering into their mobiles, some others were busy watching others. Point to note: in spite of the quantity of blood that rained upon them from all three dimensions, not one carried the slightest trace of it on his/her person. After all the tossing each other around that the fair woman and the wicked looking hulk (looking wickeder with the beard) had done during their high-voltage sex, no trace of that exercise could be spotted on the audience. Even if they were given a close and careful inspection, not a drop was to be spotted on their person: not blood, not water, not nothing. The audience comprised people belonging to different castes and creeds. The tickets cost 250 rupees. And the movie was 3-D. There is a dialogue in the movie. The Greeks get into a heated argument while talking about the Persian invasion, when their leader admonishes them, 'Stop screaming. We are not any street mob, we are a democracy.'

The audience stepping out of the multiplex would return home down the roads that belong to a sovereign, secular, socialist, democratic republic. They were above a certain social level but belonged to different economic strata, and would use different modes of conveyance too. But the road they would all use was the same – the tarred reality that stretched out before them all for all to see. Sovereign, secular, socialist, democratic – these are not the words that have originated in the mind of the author of this novel. They are mentioned in the Constitution of India.

Six

If you were to run into Virang as he stepped out of the restaurant that the Nenes have their refreshment in before they go home, and who lives in the same colony as Nene's, and if you were to say something about Shridhar – his views on caste and stuff, he would respond with a snort. He would say, 'Where do you see caste issues mattering these days?' Although Virang is 27, there is no pressure on him from his people to begin earning his own money. The clothes that he wears, the food he eats, the footwear he puts on, the two-wheeler he drives, the sunglasses he sports, the big multiplexes he goes to, where international film festivals are organized – no doubt ever seems to creep into Virang's head about how all these things reach him. He watches movies in international film festivals; he even talks about making an international picture, sorry, film. What do we understand from all this?

For example, just the other day he came out of that lovely short stone building after watching a German film. The name of the movie was *The Tin Drum*. The movie deals with the period when a person named Adolf Hitler came to power in a European country called Germany. There is this boy named Oscar who was born in the beginning of this period, and as a small boy he moves around the house carrying a drum. Whether it was because of the childishness he observed among the elders at home, or because the overall distaste for growing old arrived a little early, the boy goes to the staircase that leads down to the basement. He has firmly convinced himself that he does not want to grow old, no way, no way, and he jumps off the top of the staircase. Then hospital and all the running around. From then on Oscar remains frozen at age thirteen. Oscar remains frozen there while Germany gets ground to dust under Hitler's leadership. From the viewpoint of the people around he progresses in age, but he remains the same height, just the same. Well, this is a quick summing up of the movie. There is plenty else, of course. And certainly there is plenty more in the novel on which this movie is based.

But if you were ever to ask Virang about the movie – 'hey, how's the movie' – he'd say, 'Oh, it is an interesting film. You must see it.' This is Virang's response after every single film he watches. And if you were to ask whether the movie was based on some novel, 'Yes, oh yes!' he'd say. (And he'd give you the name of the original writer with the original pronunciation.) If one keeps visiting a certain place regularly over a period of time, certain things keep falling on one's ears; that's how it was with Virang. There would, of course, be no sense in asking Virang whether he had read the novel. Because who the devil wants to read a 500-plus page novel? He may stretch himself to the extent of buying a European Nobel prize winner, but reading all that stuff? Come on, who wants that headache? And the company in which Virang moves around, the benefit of this moving around is that one gets to form a decent idea of the stuff without reading anything at all, to the extent of even talking on it. Besides, if you run into a page on Facebook dealing with the writer or the novel, click the 'Like' button, that's it. Talking too becomes easier. So that's how it is then. You very likely know the proverb: The vocal ones can sell dust; the silent ones can't even sell gold. Okay, let's move on, these premises are not for shooting off proverbs.

Making conversation with Virang is difficult. For example, there was this short, darkish little girl sitting on a culvert, trying to read aloud news from an English newspaper. She was a high school student. Her name is Smita, and beginning from a village in Gadchiroli, she has studied her way through Allapalli and reached this city. If you know even a bit of English, you would know that this girl sitting on the culvert trying to read the news was doing it wrong. Virang knew it too. His question: 'Why do people do this silly stuff?' He won't shoot this question at the girl directly, so you are supposed to ask. Got it? Why does she do this? Now, you try telling this to Virang: 'Look, people come from different circumstances. Money, clothes. Even the Marathi here is spoken differently, so that hits the self-confidence hard. Then there is the English language hitting you from all sides, and that puts paid to whatever little self-confidence is left. The girl, therefore, is trying to learn English.'

'Pshaw! Why should self-confidence get hit because of language?' is what Virang would ask. You feel like giving an answer to this question? Do, if you really feel like it. I don't. It was tried once, and you know what he shot back with great self-confidence? This: 'Confidence comes out of language? Pshaw!'

The English paper the girl was reading was quite poor stuff. The girl, perhaps, may not learn English beyond a certain point, or perhaps she may too. Whatever she makes (or doesn't make) out of life, let's keep this aside. But looking at the poignant circumstances in which she is struggling with language, what should a person feel looking at her? This question just doesn't occur to Virang. Even if this question were spelt out, it wouldn't register with him.

Life is meaningless, career and stuff are all hogwash – it's only these kinds of basic things that he still finds interesting; and he talks about these things at his usual haunts with his usual friends. When he finds somebody striving specifically towards a specific goal, Virang has a set response for such a person: 'Pshaw!' But then brushing his teeth in the morning, or not brushing them out of fashion and setting off, driving 10–15 km on his motorbike, eating, taking a former girlfriend for a spin to the hillock, smoking, watching movies, watching plays, talking about them, these too require specific efforts; knowing this neither makes him cool nor confuses him. His 'Pshaw!' comes out like he has answers to all questions. When we last met, he was assisting some old acquaintance of his who was directing a Hindi movie.

Seven

Among the people from whom Virang picks up information on a novel or a movie is a 42-year-old person named Ayan. Ayan is highly educated. He is an engineer from an institution of good repute, and has got himself some higher degree too from some foreign country. People like Virang are his Facebook friends; besides, the two of them also run into each other at the screening of one foreign movie or the other. Usually, Ayan has read the novel on which the film is based, and there is conversation. The details then spread to a number of people. A lot of details on a lot of subjects reach a lot of people courtesy of Ayan. Paintings, movies, literature, ranging from European to Marathi – Ayan delights in a lot of things. And considering that he gets a salary of seventy-six thousand rupees per month, he can comfortably indulge in these delights, and he does that beautifully. Besides Marathi and English, he knows German. He knows there is no palpable link between a person's self-confidence and language per se. But he also knows with great clarity that circumstances can be different; so if he were to see Smita there on the culvert, reading her English newspaper, he wouldn't come up with 'Pshaw!' And even if, from the perspective of the people around, he has built a successful career, he knows that there is nothing much to a career beyond bread and butter. Besides, he doesn't even feel that he should do something to move forward. After all, with all the movement, how much forward can a person move on this round-and-round spinning earth? That's why, other than paintings, movies or literature, he doesn't make any special effort towards anything at all. And when he sees people from his company trying to move ahead, he feels immensely disgusted. It has reduced somewhat lately, but earlier the disgust used to be immense.

But Ayan knows that the circumstances of the people in his company and those of Smita on the culvert are different, so he wouldn't 'Pshaw' it away. He would at least try to understand. In Smita's case, at least, he would certainly try to understand. It's not as if he would behave this way all the time. When depressed, as he is sometimes, he would ignore, but he wouldn't say 'Pshaw' for sure. Ayan has read a great deal, so he is aware of a few things. He is also aware that many things remain beyond one's comprehension. That makes him feel low, true. But he never insists that just because he feels disgusted, everybody else should feel disgusted too.

Well, since we are talking about Ayan, we must talk about the hillock too. It's not as if the only link between him and the hillock is that he goes to the multiplex there if there's a good movie running. He makes it a point to visit the hillock on the last Sunday of every month, without fail. There is a part of the hillock that remains the kind of place that a person like him would want to visit. The sun sets so sadly or so beautifully every evening. Like so many others, he wants this place to remain as it is. But, of course, things do not always happen the way one wants them to. The chances of this place staying the way Ayan wants it to are almost zero.

Eight

Smita has opted for the science stream and is about to go into Std XII. On the first page of her Mathematics notebook, you will find the following lines:

Zindagi mein dukh hain sahney ke liye
Lekin jhoojhnaa hai sukh ke liye
(There are sorrows in life for one to bear

But the struggle to attain joys has to go on)

Smita has adorned this page with a few flowers here and a few stars there with a sketch pen.

Smita's native language is Madiya, and she also knows Marathi and Hindi, Hindi being a little more intimate. Now she believes the most important task for her is to learn English, and she goes into all sorts of painful contortions to be able to do so. If she has to move ahead in the world, Madiya is going to be of no use to her, and while she had thought earlier that Marathi would be important, she now thinks that it isn't of much use either. As for understanding English, she has been making noteworthy progress. When she first landed in the city, she was jolted. She had never crossed the limits of Gadchiroli before. Within Gadchiroli town, the hassle of travelling by bus doesn't exist at all. Travel within the town is by shared rickshaw, that too, from Indira Square to the Municipality complex. So no bus travel there. And for out-of-town travel there's the State Transport. So for Smita there was no routine of daily bus travel. She didn't have many such habits, which she is trying to get into little by little. Among the many habits she is trying to form is her daily efforts at English. After all this, she does squeeze out time for making entries in her diary about her experiences. She loves to write down her thoughts about her native place, as also about the people there. But the diary is very private. She hasn't shown it even to the few close friends she has. She could be carrying plans in her head of using her diary entries for some other writing some day. People from outside often visit her place of birth and write some stuff on it, and their writing is quite superficial, Smita feels. That's why she loves to write about her area, even if it's just in her diary.

Smita's native village is a place called Pittekasa. 'Pitte'

means bird and 'kasa' means a deep depression in a river. There was also this person by the name of Pitte. He would go to the river bank to hunt birds. Would catch fish too. One day he went fishing and got drowned, and that's how the name Pittekasa came about, goes the story. Smita so much wants to write all this down. She will write when she writes, meanwhile let's look at a true incident.

Smita had set off, for the first time ever, with two of her friends to take a round of the mall on the hillock. Just to see what it looked like from the inside. It was not at all within her means to buy anything, of course. Merely a spin inside and then out. She was slightly ahead of the others, so the security chap stopped her with 'Where?' That flustered Smita. Her friends were stopped too. But because Smita was a little ahead of them, he addressed her. Smita was flustered. There were so many people drifting in and out, and she alone was stopped. Her confidence wavered. The confidence of her friends wavered too. Smita returned to the hostel. It was a critical moment. She hadn't said anything and thus avoided further humiliation. There wasn't anything to say. She couldn't have managed it either. You know the proverb, don't you? The vocal ones can sell dust; the silent ones can't even sell gold.

Nine

Udayendraraje, alias Uday, and Nandkishor, alias Nandu, attend the international film festival every year. As for the movies that are screened in the multiplex on the hillock, they don't miss them – ever. They watch all the movies they want to watch and accomplish another mission alongside – watching international girls. Uday is not as affluent as Vijayendraraje. After three years of working, he has bought himself a 60,000-rupee bike. He has a job that helps him save some money after meeting his expenses. His family does not own vast stretches of land. They do, but not on the same scale as Vijayendra. That is why Uday has to work at a tin-pot firm. Nandkishor, aka Nandu, is an assistant professor at a tin-pot college. Just like every year, Uday and Nandkishor arrived at this international festival. They decided to watch a Marathi movie and went in.

The movie was based on a play by a Marathi playwright. Uday didn't know who the playwright was and he found the film boring. Nandkishor went off to sleep. In spite of finding the movie boring, Uday did not go to sleep because next to him sat a very fit Australian girl. He began chatting with her. From his earlier experiences at international film festivals, Uday has learnt that it takes far less confidence speaking in English with a native English speaker than it does when speaking with an Indian. Even if there are errors, nobody stutters and stammers – not we, not they. So Uday speaks with abandon. He began talking with this Australian girl with such abandon that before the two knew it, they had walked out and up to Uday's bike. By the time Nandkishor awoke, Uday had disappeared with the white girl.

The white girl had no hesitation in getting onto Uday's bike. Uday that way is nice and tall and all, so on this issue there was no reason for his confidence to run short. So, riding on this confidence, he took the girl to a chicken restaurant. They chatted there for two hours. Bemused at what Uday would have chatted about with the Australian girl for two hours, Nandkishor sat in AC comfort, looking through the programme to decide which movie to watch next. During the chat, Uday got to know that the girl was making a movie herself. She had already made three-four short films, and she was to leave for home in two days. Testing the possibility of creating some kind of chance for himself in these two days, Uday sat chatting with the girl. Then she said she would have to leave for her hotel. Uday's bike was there. She sat clinging to him closer than any girl had done before. Uday then dropped her close to that hotel with very shiny panes.

For Uday, this year's international film festival was the most exciting and rewarding of all. Within a matter of three-four hours, he collected enough fuel to keep many a dream running a long time. After this personal experience, Uday realized that the dreams peddled by Hindi movies can be so bloody brittle, and he became internationally satiated.

Ten

The one common element that runs through the above stories is the hillock. Even on a casual walk around the hillock, you run into these stories. There is a clangour of many such stories reverberating across the world today. Amid all this clamour, in fact, it has become difficult for an ordinary writer to write even one single story for a novel, say some people. Other than that, reading a story does not give you the feel of a walk, or of consuming appas, or of wearing gold bracelets; it doesn't provide light to dispel the darkness that has descended on a movement; a story read off a page or a screen cannot give the 3-D feel of blood splashing on your person. Does a piece of a novel carry the same price as a piece of land? Or take a plate of appas, or take a gold bracelet of 20 or 30 grams – would the price of a novel be the same? Again, if it cannot even start off a social movement, what is the use of the story, eh? Offering good entertainment, or presenting a political or sociological or aesthetic or civic analysis, even these functions appear to be beyond the power of this story. No information, no entertainment, so why have the story at all?

But if you have been able to tolerate this rather scattered, egretistic story and come reading so far, I assure you that you will want to go on reading beyond. And since we have told the above nine stories and are now telling this tenth story for the purpose of telling the reader the subject of the novel, the subject then is whatever has emerged from these stories. What further clarification can be given? The stories we have gone through may sound very generalized to some. You know how it happens? Sometimes even when one records things exactly as observed, they begin to look like generalizations. And if the characters in the stories come with their surnames, you would instinctively want to work out their caste and arrive at conclusions on the basis of your own caste; even if you belong to a caste that does not believe in caste, that is a conclusion too. The stuff we have put in these stories, we haven't written about people belonging to absolutely all the different castes that exist; we haven't written about all the people that exist within a single caste either. In sum, we took this round only to get a clear perspective of the subject matter of our novel. Whatever was observed that could help throw light on the subject matter of the novel was recorded. It's no more than that. Does this satisfy you?

The author managed to understand the characters in the stories a little. You, as a reader, would have understood them a little too, probably a great deal more. Bringing our understandings together and stitching up a whole, meaningful question, not being satisfied with looking at the stories as little bits and pieces, but balancing that single drop of water from the writer's eye on a teak leaf and storing it in a safe place, this is the job we will do through this novel. This job is the subject of this novel. The characters we have met in the above stories, we may not meet them all further ahead in the novel. But the group these characters belong to, the author is a part of the same group too, and this group certainly is a character in the novel. The writer will try to bring these small stories together to create a detailed picture of this composite character. The creation of this detailed picture will bring a lot of places into the novel, bring in all kinds of stories, bring in the jottings of somebody's diary; somebody's narrations will find a place here, and a little picture lost and found in somebody's notebook may be pasted there. The novel will be constructed with all these.

I hope some clarity has arrived about the subject. But after all this, somebody can still ask, why this subject? And on what grounds have the specifics been selected? Well, the author doesn't have a very clear answer to this either. But this much can be said. The author once saw a dead and decaying teak leaf drifting along. What answer would there be if the question were, why exactly that particular leaf? But the writer did see the leaf dying, and he felt something about it. His feeling whatever he felt, as far as he was concerned, was a story by itself. Quite in the same way, he saw some people dying too and he felt something. His feeling that something, for him, was a story.

Given the limited strength of the author, it would be difficult to hunt out the address of the teak leaf. But with men it's a little different. Their faces can be identified instantly and their addresses can be located; and hence, when humans are dying, writing their stories is work that's possible. People, of course, die of old age or of commonplace causes like accidents or such stuff, but the author began to sense that people were dying in a continuous stream on account of some cataclysmic convulsions too; and then searching for the cause and writing its story, well, that's routine for the writer. This novel, then, is that work; it's a novel about what this writer feels. It's not as if you should be compelled to feel the same kind of feelings. But if some part of these feelings percolates into your feelings, the novel can have meaning. Else you may as well give it the boot.

Bhaskar

Despite having seen the different-seeming stories above, Bhaskar is completely focused. Bhaskar: focused on a specific target.

If you pull out a page from a notebook and focus the sun's rays on it through a magnifying glass for sufficiently long, it catches fire, doesn't it? That's how revolution will be ignited, that page will burn to ashes, and a new page will arrive, feels Bhaskar. No point in doing this page-and-magnifying-glass experiment if there is no sun in the sky, or if it is cloudy, or if it is very early in the morning or very late in the evening. Bright sun rays are a must. It's the same with experimenting with revolutions. It is certain that the sun rises and sets on this earth, even if it does so at different hours. There is an identical certainty about a number of things related to the rising and setting of human societies, Bhaskar believes. Just as it is possible to set alight a piece of paper after ascertaining the intensity of the sunrays, it is possible to ignite a revolution by ascertaining the intensity of the social circumstances of the time. A magnifying glass is necessary for setting the paper alight; a political formation is required for setting a revolution alight. The fact is that a lot of the sun's rays converge to set the page on fire. Revolution too is basically ignited by a countless number of people coming together; what works as a magnifying glass here is the communist party.

The final name that Bhaskar has acquired for himself is Bhaskar. There is no point at all in trying to find out what his original name was. That the police will do, so let them do it. But why would the police want to do it? Because Bhaskar is an accused in two or three cases.

Bhaskar's story begins about sixty or so years ago. That was when he was born, that is, in the year 1951. His early years were like everyone else's, but as he grew into youth, he got drawn into the communist movement in India and has been a comrade there since. The Communist Party of India was established somewhere between 1920 and 1925. Bhaskar, then, was born twenty-five years later, so we'll skip that. Let's also skip a few more years beyond that. The Communist Party of India (Marxist) broke away from the Communist Party of India in 1964, and Bhaskar was not in the movement yet. But when matters flared up in Naxalbari in 1967, and later when the Communist Party of India (Marxist–Leninist) came to be established as a separate party in 1969, Bhaskar was there on the battlefield. Later, when the party disintegrated, broke into numerous splinter Naxalite groups, Bhaskar stayed with the CPI (ML) People's War Group in Andhra Pradesh. He was also there when the People's War Group joined up with a big group from Bengal–Bihar to form the Communist Party of India (Maoist) in 2004. The police caught him about three years later.

Right from pasting posters done in red ink on the road-side walls in Adilabad in Andhra Pradesh to marching around shouting slogans, Bhaskar was present in many such activities. He also got involved, obviously, with the demand for a separate state of Telangana that had been going on for many years. Recently, Telangana has become the twenty-ninth state of a country called India, and Bhaskar is living on. The question of why he should live has been resolved. He had this question to resolve in the very early days, but he had managed to earn an answer that had satisfied him then. Since then, he hasn't had to worry about this question. Why live? To do his bit for the creation of a communist society, he will openly declare to anyone now.

There are some details, however, that Bhaskar is not likely to talk about openly with everyone. Just the other day, a stupid journalist from an English paper had met him, to whom Bhaskar refused to give the details. This journalist was doing a series of articles on Naxalism for some magazine, and he had thought he could write an article on information related to Bhaskar. Bhaskar had gone to Nagpur on some work where he met this man. Bhaskar did not part with too many details about himself. He merely told the journalist that he had been in and out of jail for the past seven years; therefore, he was not too well up on the current state of the party. However, the journalist churned out an article that stretched to about 1500 words. Bhaskar read the piece and just laughed.

Bhaskar is five feet and seven inches tall, which is about the average height for an Indian male, but he is thin enough to appear much taller. He has salt-and-pepper hair and wears black-rimmed spectacles. He would have done well as a hero of the so-called parallel movies of the seventies along with Smita Patil. When seeing him for the first time, one would imagine that all his photographs would come out just black-and-white. They may be called black-and-white for convenience, but they are mostly ash-grey. That's Bhaskar described. Imagine the dusky Smita Patil in a light-coloured sari and a watch on her wrist, and you can fit Bhaskar perfectly by her side. An off-white shirt and dark-brown trousers. Even if this photograph is coloured, it is more likely to be remembered as black-and-white. But Bhaskar is not just a photograph, he is a real person.

People harbour funny, romantic ideas about being underground. They carry similar notions about being revolutionaries. Bhaskar has had plenty of experience in both areas, but he hasn't turned it into capital. In spite of not being directly connected with the underground areas of the movement right now, he can certainly have a great time by extracting all the surplus value out of the heavy basic capital he possesses in the communist movement. But he is not that kind of a person. There are plenty of others who are not those kinds of persons, Bhaskar laughs and says, which was why the movement took root and continues.

He has a special laugh, an open, straight laugh. There's no complexity in that laugh. His ability to laugh such a complexity-free laugh in spite of the turmoil that rages in the world is a major gain out of his political ideology, one should imagine. But when we speak of complexity-free laugh, we imagine computer smileys, and human beings don't laugh in the readymade smiley way, so that is a complexity in itself. Also, to be honest, even readymade smileys have their own complexities, so what can one say about human beings? Bhaskar's complexities never show on his face, not enough to be noticed. One may even say that he has no complexities that he is conscious of. But one can never say what complexities lie at the unconscious level, some people say.

As of now, Bhaskar consciously lives in a flat at Biyani Square in Amravati. It's barely four months since he has been released from jail. His wife teaches at an institute in Mumbai, though; so he will move to Mumbai in due course. The arrangements there are good. But before that, he wants some time to adjust to the free world, and talks about staying on for a few months in this Amravati flat that belongs to his wife. His wife Samidha used to teach at the Sant Gadge Baba Amravati University earlier, and before that she was in Nagpur too. She will teach now in this reputed institute of social sciences in Mumbai till she retires. She lives in the staff quarters there, but she can now buy a flat for herself a little distance away. That's when Bhaskar may shift to Mumbai, in all likelihood. Right now, though, he sits in the Amravati flat, ruminating his old memories.

His memories are quite vivid. For one, he remembers so many stories, he has so many of them lodged in his head that he can easily beat the first fifty in this game.

Here's an example. A battle had been fought at Telangkhedi near Nagpur in 1817. With the utmost casualness, Bhaskar can tell you how the British soldiers arrived from Achalpur and subjected the Bhosales' fort to gunfire and such things. He also remembers that Marx was born five months after the battle. So many such battles the British would have fought in India, and so many would have died, and so many would have been born after that. But remembering the details of a certain battle, and remembering the date of birth of a certain person to go with it, it's amazing. He doesn't make any special effort at remembering the details; it comes to him naturally. If there are efforts, they are towards reading about the details. Now, if you talk about these British battles, the *Economic and Political Weekly* had brought out a special edition on the 1857 uprising, and this edition had later been converted into a book. Bhaskar moved heaven and earth to procure this book. The book, very likely, would have been easily available, but he himself was not all that easily available. It took a full two years for the book to reach him. There were so many such books that Bhaskar had collected bit by bit and put together a personal library of about a thousand volumes; but when he was arrested, all those books just vanished. They disappeared in police confiscation. Among them went his edition of *Das Kapital* which was first published in 1867. But, of course, one can buy another copy anywhere.

We were talking about the details that sit in Bhaskar's head. But a listener may catch him on the wrong foot occasionally, and some of the details may not be correct. For example, in the flow of the conversation Bhaskar may say that even they, that is the Maoists, acknowledge the contribution of Tukaram and the other saint poets, and then veer to say that Tukaram was a radical and had even taken up arms. Well, an occasional blunder like this can happen – here, he thrust arms in the hands of the person who considered words as his only weapon. But not counting accidents of this kind, most of the details in his head are authentic.

Another peculiarity of Bhaskar is his extraordinary use of similes and metaphors and analogies. A novice listening to him is often so impressed that he instantly falls for Bhaskar's argument. Take the example of street signals, which Bhaskar uses to endorse the strategy of the Maoists. Street signals are as much for motorists as they are for pedestrians, and both can flout the signals with equal impunity. But motorists have the necessary strength, speed and ability to bang into someone, and except for an occasional serious accident, they get away with very little damage. If the pedestrian – with his lesser strength, lesser speed and lesser ability to hurt – also flouts the signal, he does so as a reaction to the motorist's action. At this point, Bhaskar's listener is very likely to come up with a few of his experiences, remarking how even pedestrians walk in the middle of the road, or that they obstruct passing vehicles. But Bhaskar has his answers ready. First of all, walking is the original activity, hence roads should be made primarily for this purpose; but they are actually made mainly for the convenience of vehicles, thus giving priority to the motorists. The motorist is more powerful than the pedestrian, so he will always have greater opportunities, in any case. The pedestrian runs the risk of dying if he comes in the way of a moving vehicle, so he is more likely to observe the rules, if only to ensure the security of his life. The motorist, however, does not need to observe such rules; in fact, he has a greater need to increase his speed, or such a need is manufactured. Advertisements are prepared for this purpose. Then he moves on to how the number of private vehicles is on the increase, and the subject keeps stretching and stretching. At the time of independence, the railways carried eighty per cent of the traffic, while today, they carry barely ten per cent because the system has been designed this way. Thus, Bhaskar is capable of coming up with great examples and irrefutable arguments. What he means is that when a pedestrian abuses a motorist, it is a response to the position that the motorist occupies in the system. In other words, the violence unleashed by the establishment creates space for violence in Maoist strategy, hence the counter-violence.

How can the listener, then, sit arguing against this kind of statistics-based and point-by-point presentation? There are the other kinds of experiences, though, where some people just tick him off and criticize him for arguing within the confines of a framework. This is what happened with a person who had come in his vehicle for a walk in the Amravati University campus. The topic popped up during a casual walk, and when the conversation veered around to the increasing number of private vehicles, Bhaskar rattled off the above thesis. Needless to say, the gentleman just drifted away from him.

Bhaskar goes for a walk to the Amravati University campus and does a three-kilometre round inside. The acquaintance mentioned above, it isn't as if they had really got to know each other. It was just that as the gentleman was stepping out of his vehicle, his spectacles had fallen close to Bhaskar's feet who had been walking past, and he had merely picked it up and handed it to him. It was after that that these two had exchanged smiles for the next few days when they crossed each other and maybe exchanged a word or two a couple of times. It was in the third meeting that the topic of vehicles sprang up; from then on the vehicle took a reverse on conversation, and stayed put on the exchange of smiles. Just hello-hi, no more.

Bhaskar has acquaintances all across Maharashtra. He's been to a large number of cities, and digging up acquaintances has been a part of his job. He has spoken Telugu since infancy, and Hindi, of course, he knows. His family hails from West Bengal, so he knows Bangla. He knows English and he knows Marathi. That makes it easy for him to widen his circle of acquaintances. He has written stories in Telugu and Hindi, some poems too. It's not as if he can write Marathi, but a couple of his poems had been translated into Marathi and published in a magazine sometime in the eighties. Under another name. As a result, he has Telugu, Marathi and Hindi-speaking people among his acquaintances. Well, actually, his Telugu-speaking acquaintances of earlier times are no longer in touch. He should go and meet them one of these days. In Amravati he has these three-four people he knows. Even here he has lost contact with the people he has known in the neighbouring localities. Must go and meet them too, he thought.

In the course of his walks in the University campus, there

was another person he made acquaintance with. A clerk in the bank on the campus, about thirty years of age. He was sitting watching a bird when Bhaskar spotted him. Bhaskar also got curious and turned. It was a bird called Haladya (golden oriole). They then turned towards each other and smiled, and that's how the acquaintance developed. This time it didn't finish off as it had with the motor guy. It deepened. When Bhaskar talks, his political thoughts seep through; that is inevitable. This was why, perhaps, his acquaintance with the clerk deepened, as the clerk too was thinking about those thoughts. And if ever Bhaskar ran into any person who was willing to consider thinking about those thoughts, then Bhaskar would try his damndest to turn him round; that was inevitable too. He went on feeding the youngster with the synopses of all the tutorials he had given. He told the boy that he had retired as a professor of Political Science in a Nagpur college and had come over to Amravati for a few months of relaxation.

Our democracy, whatever shape it is in, isn't it less hazardous? This was among the basic issues that were discussed. Bhaskar was a past master in punching fist-sized holes in such notions. He instantly pulled out his statistical weapon.

'Take a look at the latest elections for the Maharashtra Assembly. Look at the candidates from the commercial capital of the country. You would have read about them in the newspapers. Who was the poorest among the contestants?'

'I don't know.'

'It was somebody from the CPM, I forget his name. His assets amounted to something around fifteen thousand rupees. Do you know who was the second poorest?'

'No, I don't.'

'A gangster's daughter. Her assets amounted to more than 1.25 crore. If there is a millionaire among the poorest, what do you say about the richest?' But the young man had doubts. There would be some independent candidates, and there are bound to be some at least who don't have substantial assets.

'Yes, sure, there would be, but we are talking about party politics. That's why we have looked at only party candidates. And what about the people? How many would you find among the citizens of Mumbai with this kind of wealth? If you look at countrywide statistics, seventy percent of them have a daily earning of twenty rupees. Mumbai is the commercial capital of such a country as this. So, these millionaire contestants represent whom? Is this then a democracy that elects the people's representatives?'

The youngster didn't respond because he had no statistics with him. He had raised his question from the reading he had done on Russia and such other subjects. Another reason for his question was that, after all, India was the first country where the communists had come to power through the ballot. But he was merely a bank clerk. His statistics were related only to accounts. Besides, Bhaskar also told him, sorry, India was neither the first nor the only country. There is this European country called San Marino surrounded by Italy. It is recorded as the first place where the communists won an election to come to power. This had escaped the youngster's notice despite all his substantial efforts at reading and mulling over the subject. He checked on the internet later and found the reference to the country. Yes, all right, but even so, the elections and the politics of this country could not really compare with a country like India. So, okay, India may not be the first country, but his question still remained valid.

Statistics as weapons, all right, one could accept them,

but what about the weapons proper? Bhaskar and the clerk had had discussions on that too. 'It's not just about bringing temporary justice and developing closeness with the people,' held the clerk. 'It doesn't stop there. If you go on with your unrelenting use of weapons, it's going to be very difficult to put it back into the bottle. We see it everywhere, don't we?'

'That's true, of course,' Bhaskar responded, 'but America accounts for 35% of the total defence expenditure in the world. You think you have the courage to say this to the imperialist powers?'

'But considering that this information has reached you, somebody has talked about it, right?'

'But it also proves that merely talking about it is not enough. Nothing ever happens with people talking about it at the individual level. Merely chatting about the economic and armoured assault of the capitalist powers upon the exploited classes is of no use. There has to be a tit for tat.'

'Agreed. America hasn't reduced its spending after all the telling, and that may trigger a violent response anywhere, agreed. But what the Maoist Party has been doing as a policy here in central India, isn't that different? Something happening spontaneously is quite another thing. History has a number examples of such rebellions by the adivasis. But what the Maoist Party does as a matter of policy in this corner, how does it affect America? It's not as if it helps the adivasis either; only, the injustices visited upon them are used as an excuse. Injustices there are, of course, but instead of finding a remedy, the Maoists use them to set off a big conflagration, is what I sometimes feel. Injustices are removed sometimes, but in the long run, suffering is what the tribals get. Leave aside America, even the government here finds it easy then to get after them. Administrations say that there is fire, and instead of throwing water to douse it, they keep throwing in more fire, and then they are not even required to admit that they are the ones responsible for it.'

'The policies of the Maoist Party emerge out of a number of experiences and strategic needs. Don't look at the violence alone. There is a certain progression of history, and you'll get nothing out of looking at individual events. One has to find out what historical factor at which point is responsible for the event, and the communists are concerned with locating the obstacles and removing them. When the dominant class picks up weapons, weapons have to be used as defence against them. Any number of such events can be presented as examples. When the struggle related to the rates for gathering tendu leaves was in progress, the Naxalites had initiated the holding of a conclave at Kamlapur in Gadchiroli in 1985. At that time, the roads were blocked to prevent the activists from participating. The police are on record to have told some students that they could have their rallies and etc. in the cities, but they wouldn't be tolerated here. Out of such repeated experiences, weapons have to be used for self-defence.'

'I don't know whether I am expressing it right,' smiled the youth, 'but did you teach political science or Maoist politics?'

Bhaskar laughed, as always. The clerk took a little time. He looked at the birds flying past. Knowing well enough that not much would come out of it, he asked, 'I am not saying how a person should react to a certain situation, but, for example, there was this news the other day of how the Bodo insurgents in Assam slaughtered the tribals who had come to work in the tea gardens. Seventy odd people died. They had come from central India some time or the other in search of work. And now, the Maoists who claim to be fighting for the adivasis in central India also support the call of the Bodo rebels for an independent land. Both prioritize the use of weapons, but who dies? The adivasis. There were photographs in the papers the other day of the adivasis having pulled out their bows and arrows to protect themselves from Bodo assaults. Is there any comparison between their weapons? Who is fighting whom here? And generally, isn't it the same bunch of people that gets killed?

'The Bodo question is the outcome of the defective policy of the touts – the Government of India. The violence has emerged from that. It's the result of the government sending the army there with extraordinary powers. This woman who has been on a fast for the past fifteen years against these special powers, there's no response to her.'

'All that may be true, but who dies in the end? Wait, another example. The inclination towards terrorism that we see in the Gulf countries today...' Bhaskar butted in as the youth paused, 'It is a reaction to the capitalist policies of America. Earlier America had also supported...'

'Yes, of course. It's all right for you to say this while doing your analysis, but my question is: who suffers? And it's out of this reaction too that a hard-line religious organization like the Taliban takes birth, doesn't it? In other words, making sense out of violence emerging from reaction is one thing, but supporting violence as a matter of policy is quite another thing. Here's another piece of news: a similar terrorist organization slaughtered around two thousand people in Nigeria. An uncountable number of corpses were strewn around the villages. Some say two thousand, some say hundreds, even the figures are difficult to determine.'

'So, whose responsibility is it to bring this violence to a halt? The examples you have given, who poured the weapons in there?'

'I don't know many details about the weapons, but the guns on the logo of this Nigerian organization are Kalashnikovs; just read this yesterday. Saw the logo too, and then did some research to find out that Kalashnikovs are Russia-made guns.'

'The journey of weapons is not so simple. Who began it all in the first place, whose interests are involved now, what are their plans for the future, all these have to be studied.'

'Sure, so let's study that; but my question is who dies in all this? It's the local people there, isn't it? After this event, news comes from Paris of French cartoonists and others getting killed. Bad. Some ten people died in it. The news came with photographs and names. Again, there was a Muslim among those who died, as far as I can remember. Add to that, the police then killed the assailants. All of this has come out in decent details, at least. But the Nigeria thing didn't gain much exposure, although the deaths there were many times more. Anyway, how many died where is not the issue.'

'You depend a little too much on news. These are all churned out by the propaganda machinery. As you've just said, the Paris news was everywhere and the Nigerian one was not.'

'Yes, that may be so, and there are so many other killings that just don't figure in the news. But can that help us deny that it was the local Nigerian Muslims who died in large numbers?'

'Why deny? What happened was bad. But when you want to search for the causes, you will have to go to the roots of the imperialist capitalist system, and then we will know how it can be stopped. What do you think, on whom does the responsibility rest?'

'I don't know that, but at least a little bit of the responsibility rests on me, really,' said the clerk, without a smile.

'That is a bourgeois romantic viewpoint. Our sitting and chatting here makes no difference there. It's a war going on there, not chats. And these kinds of chats only strengthen the established order; they suggest the existence of freedom of expression. In a war, you necessarily have to stand for one side or the other; so if you have to chat, you have to take the side of justice,' said Bhaskar.

'But how can you say that? Shouldn't we utilize whatever space we have for expression?' said the clerk.

'You've heard of Slavoj Zizek?'

'No, who's he? The name sounds familiar.'

'Go to YouTube. You will find a lot of his speeches, books too, maybe. If I have one, I'll give it to you. Slovanian philosopher, making waves these days. There's a joke in his book about the time when Russia was ruled by Mongol chieftains. There's this Mongol chieftain riding through a farmland. The farmer and his wife are working there. The chieftain tells the farmer, "I am now going to copulate with your wife and you will have to help." "What kind of help, sire?" asks the farmer. "While I am copulating, you will have to keep your hands under my testicles so that they don't touch the dust." Well, the chieftain finishes his job and rides away. The farmer then begins clapping in glee. The wife snaps at him, "That man raped me so ruthlessly. You not only did not resist his efforts, but now you are dancing in joy as well?" At this the farmer laughs and says, "I removed my hand once in a while and let his balls touch the dust".'

The clerk laughed and said, 'You seem to be quite in agreement with the Maoists.'

'The space for expression that you talk about, it's just the satisfaction of letting the exploiter's testicles get dusty. The issue is of chopping off those testicles, not of my agreement,'

Bhaskar laughed back.

'I don't agree. Who this guy is I don't know, but this example is just flashy, at least to me. I am a little wary of these people who are identified as just philosophers and intellectuals. It's not enough for them to convey, they want to strongly convince people, is my reading. And why can't it be that all that you say is also reaching everywhere through the propaganda machinery that you talk about? All right, we'll let that pass. What I have to say is that suppose this space doesn't exist at a certain place, then shouldn't those who have this space work towards increasing its extent? But if priority is given to this policy of chopping, who is it that loses in the end? It's the common man, right? I may even go and say, "Okay, chop the balls." Or if somebody else says it in Delhi or Mumbai, they may get enough support too, but where does this talk create space for those who haven't got it? I've seen this in North Korea too, a single family monopolizing it there for years upon years. So, what communism has arrived? They may be anti-America, all right, but what meaning does this kind of alternative have? And even if we ignore the coloured versions of the media. Even so.'

Bhaskar didn't say anything. It happens sometimes, doesn't it? We are talking with somebody with great passion, and then suddenly there is silence; that's how it happened.

The clerk went on, 'It happens here too. Somebody from Delhi comes and says whatever he wants of this kind. But sixteen-seventeen-year-old boys with guns in their hands, do we let them die for the sake of the new order? We are not going to die with them; we are not going to live with them either. While we call globalization all kinds of names, these alternative talks too have gone and acquired a global authority, wouldn't you say?'

'Once imperial powers begin stretching themselves across the world, this is bound to happen. What's wrong with that?'

'But how does it make a difference at the local level? I talked to a few people in Gadchiroli, it occurred to me then too. That's why I felt quite the opposite: that we shouldn't be chatting this way. How can one talk so casually, at least in the matter of somebody dying? We live in one set of circumstances, and the other dies in another set of circumstances. It's all right, whatever else you may chatter about, but dying? Otherwise, I can instantly shoot off whatever I find morally proper, can't I? It's going to be nothing beyond one of the two sides being yours. But why should you talk merely for the sake of pulling people to your side?'

'Whom did you talk to at Gadchiroli?' asked Bhaskar.

'My wife's uncle works there in the city. I had gone over to see him and from there I visited a few villages. Talked to a few people there.'

'What did you feel?'

'They are not instantly forthcoming with their opinions, but they are tired of dying in this fashion, that's for sure. It's quite true that they have no love for the government, but does that mean that they should want to die for another government?'

'I won't talk more about this now, but there are certain things you can understand only after being in the Movement. They are not intelligible from the outside; they make sense only when you have had practical experience.'

'What's the use, then?'

'Talking to individual persons here and there isn't going to make you understand. It requires a proper analysis of the foundations of the entire system. Marxism is a scientific tool for this analysis. People live as a part of a certain system, and the issue is of changing that system. Different people have different opinions. This is exactly the strategy of the current democracy, but that's not true democracy. It's the democracy of the capitalist touts. It's the same at the global level, and that's the reason why there is a difference of opinion among the media regarding the Nigerian incident and the French incident, this at least you should understand. People won't even dream of the alternatives in the manner that you are suggesting.'

The clerk stayed quiet. It happens this way sometimes, doesn't it? We are talking with somebody with great passion, and then suddenly there is silence, that's how it happened. Besides, he didn't know anything of Bhaskar's history. Bhaskar had told him that he had retired as a professor of Political Science in Nagpur. So the clerk was talking to a professor when he was talking to Bhaskar. A number of professors would carry these opinions, he believed. It was also true that because of the friendly manner in which Bhaskar talked, he had begun to talk quite openly too.

They were talking here of this and that, and the 'hoop hoop hoop' sound came floating in from a distance. It was a coucal.

The bird, Bhaskar and that young man, the three of them coming together had created a kind of atmosphere for some while, one could say. When another person of Bhaskar's age came along for a walk a couple of times, the atmosphere appeared to change. This person, Sartaj Behl, was from Delhi and had written a few poems and novels in Hindi. When they ran into the young man once, Bhaskar introduced the two to each other. It happened that the youngster had read a few of Sartaj's poems on the internet. So, in spite of the acquaintance being new, it hadn't been difficult for the three to get into a conversation. This writer too held leftist views, and to add a little more to it, he had sympathy for the Maoist movement in India. In this regard, he has even expressed his opinions in press meets at Delhi a few times. All of this background the youngster would have known quite well.

That was why the youngster asked, 'What's the role of a poet?' For Bhaskar, this question from the youngster was not unexpected. From the numerous conversations he had had with him, he had made a fair enough estimate of the youngster; hence, he did not butt in. He had just introduced the two and a few formal statements later, the youngster shot this question.

Mr Behl said, 'As it is with a blacksmith, a goldsmith, or any other component of a society, so it is with a poet.'

'What a person does for a living, a poet does too. But what do you have to say about his work as a poet?'

Mr Behl and the youngster were meeting for the first time. Bhaskar's introduction had made the conversation easier, for sure. But a question of this kind right at the start of a conversation, well, it was a difficult beginning. Besides, all that Bhaskar had told Behl about the youngster was his name and his job. The youngster, of course, knew about Behl. Under these circumstances, then, how could any conversation get started suddenly?

However, Mr Behl said, 'Look, I am sure you know that I believe in the Marxist ideology.'

'Yes, of course. The question is in that context. If a poet is a Marxist, what should he do? The language that blacksmiths, goldsmiths, masons and engineers use, they use it in a manner suited to their profession. So, how does the poet use it?'

'The poet's work, the writer's work is related to emotions. He readies the people's emotions for revolution.'

'But if the people's emotions are not ready for revolution, what should he do then?'

'That's just what I've said: convince them about the importance of revolution, prepare them emotionally for the purpose, that's the job of a poet. I am a Marxist, and I have told you this right in the beginning. If you look at it from this ideological perspective, then you will know what I am saying. Poetry is not something that is divorced from other social activities. I think about what role poetry has in the development of a society. As somebody has said, a poet is someone who sits in the opposition.'

'Yes, but what I am saying is…like…for example, the Communist Party gave a call for a revolution in 1948, and the party workers got busy accordingly. You would know of Sharad Patil of Dhule?'

'Yes, I do.'

'So, he was instructed to organize a "rail roko" at Bhusaval. He went there. He collected the people on the railway tracks, delivered speeches, and so on. Okay, done. But the casual manner in which they dispersed after that indicates that they were not ready for any revolution. I don't know what Patil himself felt at that time, but he went there as a disciplined soldier of the party and did what he had been asked to do. His own ability to analyse a situation and to examine history, he utilized in a big way later. This led to differences with the party, and he had to walk out; but that happened later. In other words, he can be recognized as an expert in some subject or the other, and that, we can say is his work. Doing that kind of work is different. Would you say that the work of a poet-writer is different from this kind of work? Suppose a poet or a writer were present during the rail roko episode, what should he have done? Should he have expressed his understanding of the feelings of the people on the railway track honestly? Or should he have just observed discipline?'

'I don't know about the episode you are talking about.'

'But suppose we were to take it as an example?'

'If you sit looking at such individual cases, it will confuse things. You yourself say that Patil had the ability to analyse, which he used later. So, why he didn't utilize it when the call for revolution arrived – what do you think?'

'I don't know. I had read about the episode, so I gave it as an example. He may have utilized it too, but the instructions had arrived and he had wanted to observe party discipline, maybe.'

'That's what I'm saying. When the call arrives, criticism and self-criticism too can be a part of the internal processes of the party. A poet cannot be separated from this process. The individualistic perspective from which you think, we don't think that way.'

'No, it's not about individualism. Look, people have given words certain meanings, and poets utilize these words to express themselves. So, wouldn't it be more truthful if the poets acknowledge these debts to the people and be loyal to them? Whatever the party analysis, whatever the party discipline, if, instead of holding on to the party line, the poet were to understand the people's mind and express his understanding of that, if he were also to honestly express his agreements and disagreements, won't his work be more genuine? Even if he were a Marxist? Would it not be better for him to stay outside the party structure?'

'The way you are deconstructing the poet, we don't look at him that way. A number of Marxist writers were outside the party structure, and they still are. But what you are saying about the poet, it applies to everyone who uses language. Everybody does not write poetry, but if he merely gives expression to his thoughts and continues to behave likewise, revolutions will never happen. And the incident you talked about, the party line was at fault there, so I cannot say anything about it.'

Mr Behl owed allegiance to the later Marxist–Leninist Party line and the current Maoist Party line, and he said as much. So, he believed that the Communist Party of India and the Communist Party Marxist were not the vanguard revolutionary parties, and they are not so now. Hence he subscribed to the criticism that the lines adopted by these parties were faulty. Then the youngster gave the most recent example of Gadchiroli. His wife's uncle worked in the BSNL office in town, so he'd had the opportunity of visiting the town three-four times. Besides, out of personal interest, this clerk had gone up to Laheri on this side and Aheri on that side. On the strength of that, he asked, 'Well, I'll tell you something, whatever I understood of it. The people in the Bastar area of Chhattisgarh seem to be on the side of the Maoist Party, but if, after interacting with the people at Gadchiroli, a poet feels that the people's support seems to be waning there, should he then state it? The party has its own analysis, but can the poet have his own different analysis or not?'

'First of all, we don't believe that the people at Gadchiroli are not ready for revolution. We too go on fact-finding missions and talk to the people there.'

'But why do we not see the same intensity of struggle here as we see in Bastar? Maybe the people are tired, or there could be other reasons, but is it not the job of the poet to express this understanding?'

Bhaskar intervened, 'It depends on who you are talking to, and this is a kind of bourgeois attitude. The party belongs to the people, and it is the people themselves who mould the party. So, when the poet communicates with people outside the party, you have to check who he communicates with.'

The clerk didn't say anything here. He had believed that because the poet had borrowed the people's language, as a return gesture he should make an effort to understand what the people are saying. It's not that he should agree with them. Because people, and that means he too, would have lent the language to somebody or the other. So in this entire complex business of lending, isn't the honest use of language a commitment of substantial importance? That is not to say that he should say only what the people want. He will speak about the people yes, but it is through language that he will realize that he himself is also the people, and therefore what he has to say will be genuine too, this is what the clerk felt, one guesses. What he has to say comes later in an independent chapter. So if the reader finds some inadequacies here, they will be removed there. The entire conversation remained incomplete here. The youngster didn't say anything after Bhaskar had spoken. He couldn't say anything, perhaps. Bhaskar and the Delhi poet were together. A little more of some formal conversation, and Bhaskar and Mr Behl moved on.

Bhaskar thought that this young person doesn't look at the happenings as a process. He even talked about it with the youngster later. He advised the young man to examine whether the poet's questions emerge from the established order, or from the efforts at the creation of a new order. What investigation the young clerk conducted, how he conducted it, and to what extent, we will get to read later. Now that the topic of poetry has sprung up, it will be a good idea to use it to enter Bhaskar's past.

The past begins with a poem:

I tried to reach the bank

Astride the wave
The boat was moving forward
But the waves looked at me and laughed, teased me:
'Are you mad?
We are the flowing ones
We have thousands of eyes
How can you ever cross us?'
I withdrew
Today
The oars are not in my hands
I am in their hands

When the Telugu poet Cherabanda Raju had written this in a despondent state, Bhaskar had not yet turned despondent. When the Naxalite movement faded out, Cherabanda Raju expressed his regret through poems during those times. He was a poet who had lived with the movement, and he passed away in 1978. Bhaskar then went underground but not out of any despondency. A poet may get into despondency and write his poetry, but a professional revolutionary cannot start any revolution in that state. Besides, a poet may capture in his poem a feeling of the moment, but the moment passes as it comes. Tomorrow, for the poet, is another day and another feeling. The process continues. It's not as if an entire process can be captured in a poem. Hope, despair, all such things keep moving in and out of a process. Capturing the feelings of an entire process would be quite a different thing, one would imagine. It is difficult to guarantee their encapsulation in a single poem.

So, Bhaskar had gone underground with the hope of a better tomorrow. And from there onwards he laboured hard to realize that hope. The boat of revolution moved forward because he and others like him went on paddling and paddling. The seven groups of seven each that crossed over from Andhra Pradesh to Bastar around 1982, Bhaskar was not among them. He was sent later to the villages in central India. Right from teaching to providing medication, Bhaskar was everything rolled into one.

The beginning had been made much earlier, really. It had all started in the shack under the neem tree opposite the Banda Canteen of Osmania University, Hyderabad. Exactly when? The moon slept every day behind the neem tree, dear, but when did the rays of the revolutionary sun reach there? When George Reddy got murdered? Or even before that? Before that, yes. Even if not right before everything, but George Reddy had finished his Master's in Physics and had started on his PhD. Also established a left-oriented students' organization in the university alongside.

These things happened around the year 1970. Leftward winds were blowing across the entire country. And George laid the foundation of the Progressive Democratic Students' Union (PDSU) in Osmania University. There were rifts, and the Radical Students' Union came later. This was around the time when slogans like *Hamaara naam*, *tumhaara naam*, *sabka naam Vietnam* (Our name, your name, everybody's name Vietnam) and *Aamaar baari*, *tomaar baari*, *shobar bari Nakshalbari* (My home, your home, everybody's home Naxalbari) reverberated in the air. George had a very important role in making this air move around Osmania University. But does the air really have one single wind? Saying that the wind was blowing along the left lane would be a very general way of describing the situation. A sentence of this kind has to be written only to inform that the left-lane wind was perceptible. But in point of fact, the wind was blowing in the right lane, too. The Akhil Bharatiya Vidyarthi Parishad (ABVP) had its branch too in

Osmania University. Hence, a tug of war between the PDSU and the ABVP was inevitable. There would be elections of the students' representatives as a backdrop. Whether the moon was sleeping behind the neem tree or not, whether the sun's rays brought a saffron dawn or a red dawn, there was tremendous conflict among the students. George sent the roots of leftist ideology deep into the soil of the campus. From holding symposia on armed rebellion in India to making efforts to establish direct contact with underground Marxist–Leninist comrades, George was involved in everything. The consequence of these efforts and the students' elections was that George was murdered in April 1972.

In three months' time, Charu Babu too died in the Kolkata jail. Some say the police did him in. We had said that the wind was blowing in the leftward lane, so we may as well continue and say that this wind started losing its force, and it may be a decently acceptable sentence. But it wouldn't be altogether true. There were these boys like Bhaskar, in their twenties, with plenty of wind in their sails. Even if George was dead, he had left behind many followers. Hence the stand-off between the ABVP and the PDSU remained, and the left-lane wind kept moving.

It was around this time, 1974 perhaps, that Bhaskar had swung his knife at someone. The person was an ABVP guy. A weapon works in strange ways. There can be a good four-five of them growling at you, strong in body, strong in number. And you, just two. But what matters here is guts. You need guts. If you have guts, you feel the urge for a knife. And then you also get a sense of how much to allow the other person to close in upon you. Not easy, these things. However much that tough boy roared as he closed in on Bhaskar, when the blade entered his stomach and he saw the blood spurt out of it, his arse ripped into shreds. The tension lasts for just a small moment, the time it takes for the knife to twirl inside the stomach. Once inside, all issues get resolved. What to do and what not to do, this confusion vanishes too. The other boys with the tough one had no recourse but to flee. They had never imagined that a knife would be whipped out suddenly. They hadn't thought that there was so much heat in the atmosphere as to call for a knife. They had just wanted to surround him and rough him up a bit. But when he whipped out the knife, the ones in front lost their head and beat it. Bhaskar went and hid inside the hostel. His right hand had received a spattering of blood, with some sprinkling on his shirt too. But his hand was not soaked in blood.

In terms of convictions, Bhaskar had already moved close to the Marxist–Leninist groups, but he hadn't come in direct contact with the party. But people around you automatically get to smell it. And, of course, Bhaskar was already very close to the PDSU. He would forget his engineering and come sit at the Banda Canteen. The neem tree. The atmosphere was charged then. The charge then began dissipating slowly. There were scuffles within the CPI (ML) too. Between the party that had existed earlier and another separate group. From the very beginning, the opinion of T. Naga Reddy had been different here in Telangana. There in West Bengal, first Kanhaiyya Chatterjee and after him Charu Mujumdar passed away. The aura, then, that these personalities had once created had disappeared altogether. And then came factions and splits, till the factions became so many that there's no point wasting time counting them.

A person that Bhaskar met quite late in his career – Comrade Sureshchandra Das. It was during the time immediately after the uprising of the Naxalbari farmers under the leadership of

Kanu Sanyal and Jangal Santhal that a meeting was called in Kolkata, that Comrade Das had attended. This meeting was just a little before George Reddy had come into full form at Osmania University. When the meeting happened, Bhaskar was barely fifteen or sixteen; so he was not there. And that was why, when he had grown older and made the acquaintance of Sureshchandra, he would love to hear him tell stories from that meet. Sureshchandra had come out of the movement and opened up a book shop in Kolkata. But he could never forget the historic times he had lived through; hence, when he got into the flow of the narration, there was no way that the topic of the meeting would not spring up.

Charu Babu was a thin, small, bespectacled man. When the meeting took place, his Eight Documents had already been in circulation. In a quiet but firm tone, he persuaded the assembly that the coming decade of the seventies would be a decade of revolution, and the responsibility of participating in the revolution would be theirs. Cigarette smoke drifted around in the room, much as the people did. The people drifted in and out through a narrow alley and a small door; while the smoke escaped through two narrow windows, which were later opened fully. There was not much else in the room. There was a wooden table with some books and a radio. The Peking radio station had hailed the Naxalbari uprising just the other day: 'Spring Thunder over India'. Young city boys were instructed at this meeting to head towards the villages. There had been much talk about emphasizing Charu Babu's strategy of picking out every single class enemy and shooting them as a means of inspiring the people. The strategy was discussed at the Kolkata meet. The consequences of adopting this strategy had become visible in a big way at many places. With such quick and ready delivery of justice, the atmosphere in some villages of West Bengal had begun to engender the belief that people would rise and support them. Charu Babu, till then, was a district level leader looking after the party work in Darjeeling. His participation at the state level was limited to the extent of some internal work now and then. But these fast-changing developments had suddenly brought him on the national map. Also discussed in the meeting were the Naxalbari uprising and the urgent need for the establishment of a separate party to give shape to future developments. There was a mountain of chappals outside the room. After the meeting, the chappal-clad feet left in different directions, Marxist–Leninist and Maoist flames in their hearts, eager to deliver revolution in the villages. Charu Babu himself visited Warangal and Adilabad in Andhra Pradesh during that period. Personality cults were in the air. Small units started getting established in colleges in support of the Naxal movement. Comrades in Andhra, who had been active since much earlier, felt reinforced. The recent uprising against the landlords at Srikakulam had been blazing anyway. Naxalbari gave the movement a further fillip. Translations of Charu Babu's articles were published in the *Liberation*. When Charu Babu had visited Adilabad, Bhaskar was of poster-pasting age; but he never had the opportunity to meet him in person. The substance of Charu Babu's writings, however, reached him in Telugu translations. It reached other places too.

Bhaskar described those times much later in a book he wrote for the party (*Thirty Years of the Naxalbari Struggle*): 'Thousands of youngsters from colleges across Punjab, Bihar, Uttar Pradesh, Tamil Nadu, Kerala, Delhi and Mumbai had got attracted towards Maoism and the political alternative thrown up by Naxalbari. Idealistic students who had despaired of the corruption of parliamentary politics, the helplessness of the people and the value-destroying opportunism had found a purpose in life. Naxalbari represented a new future based upon justice, truth, equality, humanity, and it offered self-esteem to the oppressed and the dispossessed, all of which were lacking in the present society. These youngsters had set out with missionary zeal to destroy the perpetrators of injustice and inhumanity, to crush the hooded cobras and scorpions that sat at the door of power, to eliminate the demons of exploitation. They carried hopes of establishing a heaven on earth. They dreamt the same dreams that their leader Charu Mujumdar, whom they affectionately called CM, had dreamt. Nobody would go hungry; nobody would exploit another; there would be no discrimination on the basis of caste, religion and gender; a new human would take birth, possessing qualities such as unselfishness, modesty and cooperation in place of greed, selfishness, arrogance and the competitive spirit; precedence would be given to caring for others instead of caring for oneself – such were the dreams of a bright future. Under the guidance of experienced leaders, these young people were equipped to bring about Naxalbari-like struggles across different parts of the country, so that their dreams could turn into reality.'

George Reddy was one such youth. When he was alive, students from the government-run Film and Television Institute of India (FTII) from faraway Pune had arrived at Osmania University for making a documentary. Even if it is a mere documentary, it needs a script to make a film, doesn't it? Osmania University presented in miniature the script that was unfolding across the globe, and the students made a film on that crisis, they say. How could it be considered complete without a bite from George? What did George say?

Dressed in an olive-green shirt in the style of Che

Guevara, sporting a thin moustache, George looked into the camera and said, 'Our society is termite-ridden. These termites have spread across every aspect of life, which includes our university. We are left with no alternative today. We raised the cry of protest, our protest fell on deaf ears; we took out protest marches, our marches were broken up by the police; there was some spontaneous violence from our side, our violence was met by ruthless violence. There is no other way left for us now except to come together and respond to violence with violence.' George Reddy, MSc Physics (Gold Medal)

Since we are on the topic, let's move four odd decades ahead for a little while. As the name of the FTII has sprung up, courtesy George, there's a story connected to it that's worth relating. But there's a small request to the readers: they should not get away from the context of the seventies. There was this left-lane wind blowing in the seventies, we've already noted. As we have air in the atmosphere, institutions have their air too; you would surely have noticed. So, there was this air at the institute called the FTII right from those days. It's there even as Bhaskar is roaming around the Amravati University. The nice thing about air is that one doesn't need to make any conscious effort to inhale it. Inhalation and exhalation goes on as a part of the law of nature right from the time of birth. If you deliberately want to stop breathing the air in, then, of course, you have to make a conscious effort. Or if you want to register something about it, you would require some effort, but otherwise, in any case we live with air all the time. So, because we are on the topic, and also because we've met guys like Virang-Ayan earlier, and now that we are at the FTII anyway, no harm at all in getting another story in. Request, once again – as we do so, please remember that we were basically talking about George Reddy, because we'll again be going forty years behind. As of now, forty years having passed since George Reddy's murder and the documentary on Osmania University with the FTII logo pasted on the screen and deposited in the archives somewhere, and students continue to come here. In an institute so full of air, there is always the possibility of the students carrying some air or the other in their heads. Science would know what air contains. What happens when two atoms of oxygen meet, or what changes occurred in the air because of the smoke we saw coming out of Virang's motorbike, or what is the connection between the mango tree there not flowering and air? We don't know any of this. But air is dry somewhere and moist somewhere, cold somewhere and hot somewhere, we say these kinds of things when we are talking. We fill air in balloons too, you know that, don't you? That's air too.

To pay tribute to a Columbian writer who has died, a small festival of South American movies is being held here in a small cinema hall. Some fourteen-fifteen movies are going to be screened over the week. What was the film today? Wait a minute, we'll ask someone. There's Virang standing under the mango tree, but there's no point asking him. It was an interesting film, is all that he'll say. Looks like Ayan is standing there too. Perhaps we can ask him. But he's in a group now, so not him. If he were alone, maybe he could have said something. That girl in the pink jeans, we could ask her, but she too is headed towards the mango tree. She has a boy with her who's studying in this institute. Forget her. Now, who's this thin, bespectacled girl? She's talking very loudly with another girl, and seems to be walking out. Let her go. With all the noise around, can't hear what she is saying. Let's see if we can ask some non-filmy person. Can you zoom the camera in a bit? Ah yes, found one. This young boy with a moustache, a light brown shirt and blue jeans, a backpack, he's heading out too, direct, but the important thing is that when he reaches home, he writes something in a notebook he carries in that backpack about the movie he has seen that day. Writes whatever he has understood of the story of the movie, doesn't write anything very outstanding. You have all kinds of fancy expectations from that boy, have you? Come on, man, don't give yourself such airs. He doesn't have all that kind of reading and all. Films too he hasn't seen as many as you have. Look, he's nothing compared to you, okay? So, what do we do then? There's no harm in getting to know what he thought of the film today, is there? If knowledge is attained by standing under the mango tree, well, so be it. But hang on, anyway. One minute. Just listen. What did you say? You don't read anything, don't see anything; that's okay, no problem. But listen, just a minute. Hold on a bit. We don't have to go take any exams-vixams, do we? Don't get so tensed up. Listen, please. Okay. The name of the film is *Postcards from Leningrad*. So, this boy went home and this is what he entered in his notebook:

> *Postcards from Leningrad* is a story from Venezuela set in the year 1966. The armed revolution of Fidel Castro, Che Guevara and their colleagues happened in 1959; after that the efforts towards armed revolution in South American countries to overthrow the bourgeois states… some successful, some unsuccessful. The story contains references to the idealism of the revolutionaries, it keeps emerging from the memories of a little girl and her cousin; the parents travel over hills and valleys to bring about an armed revolution, the letters from them, the images from the dreams of the little children, sometimes factual,

sometimes mythical, this is how the story moves forward, and what is left in the end is memories – 'they came, they had won the three villages around us'. 'They were all young, and they were winning all the time.' Looking towards Soviet Russia as their ideal, children who had created a dream world about their parents, and armed revolutionaries nursing the dreams of a Utopia – the letters from Leningrad are a symbol of all these. Sometimes the dreams of little children, sometimes the reality of the bloodshed, the film takes the story forward in this manner. Where are their parents? The children have been told: Leningrad. For the children, their parents live in a kind of dreamland, Leningrad. And for their parents, the dream-like land is perhaps Russia, hence letters from Leningrad.

Let's let the notebook stay in his backpack. We've read what he wrote in it after reaching home. Let's go back to the time when the movie got over, and see what's been going on under the mango tree.

'We don't have this kind of work,' said someone.

'We don't have this kind of work,' said someone.

'We don't have this kind of work,' said someone.

'We don't have this kind of work,' said Virang.

'In that sense, it was not magical realism, but the film was interesting,' said Ayan.

'In that sense, it was not magical realism, but the film was interesting,' said someone.

'In that sense, it was not magical realism, but the film was interesting,' said someone.

'In that sense, it was not magical realism, but the film was interesting,' said Virang.

There was another person of Ayan's age, who wrote copy for advertisements; there was the girl in the pink jeans, who was doing her PhD in Political Science, and another person, and a number of other persons.

'But the director has juggled rather well between reality and dreams,' said Ayan.

'But the director has juggled rather well between reality and dreams,' the advertising guy said.

'But the director has juggled rather well between reality and dreams,' the political science girl said.

'But the director has juggled rather well between reality and dreams,' Virang said.

The discussion continued in a similar vein. Judging by the mango tree's report, the discussion wasn't particularly interesting or novel. All said and done, the tree is quite bored now. If the flowers bloom, good; if they don't, it'll be just so much of sorrowful life. It's been around for so many years now. So many would mean at least since the time the institute started. So, let's see, about five decades have gone by. The film market would have increased quite a bit during these decades.

❖

Notwithstanding what was predicted in Charu Babu's documents, the seventies didn't turn out to be the decade of liberation. Many sittings occurred after the sitting that sits so firmly in Sureshchandra Das's memory. Contrary to expectations, instead of growing stronger with the Naxalism inspiration, the CPI (ML) kept disintegrating into factions over this disagreement or that. Then Charu Babu passed away in 1972. George Reddy was killed the same year. Many different factions came into existence in West Bengal, as also in Andhra Pradesh. And later, in Bihar. The need for mass organizations, how to utilize the parliamentary route, what an armed conflict should be, any such issue was enough. Or the argument on leadership, this was the most discussed issue.

Even if one said that the Marxist–Leninist ideology and the Maoist ideology were the same, factions kept squabbling over the implementation of the ideology. What should be the proper line of action emerging from the basic ideology – propaganda wars flared up on this issue. One may see this happening anywhere. There is not enough space here to discuss the propaganda; even so, it is worth mentioning that ideology went on getting judged by action, and squabbles went on happening. Does ideology determine action, or does action determine ideology? But life itself is a paradox. Or a contradiction. It's there in everything, in every process; keeps appearing in newer and newer forms, and keeps resolving itself. Engels has said that where contradiction stops, life stops and death enters. And then, death exists because life does and life exists because death does. Mao has commented on this contradiction. It is out of such contradictions that conflicts develop. Such thoughts and other thoughts expounded by so many others. All these must have inspired many oarsmen like Bhaskar who kept paddling away during the middle period of the movement.

But are thought and action determined by propaganda? Does this kind of question emerge from the existing circumstances? An effort to find an answer to this question was made by the clerk who had met Bhaskar. Readers will read about that in a later chapter. Meanwhile, let us limit our discussion to this chapter... so, factionalism continued in the Naxalite movement, and...

And then, the left-lane wind kept losing momentum. But, although they were not obviously visible, things went on happening. As in many other places, work carried on in over a hundred villages in Karimnagar and Adilabad. Around that time, Kondapalli Seetharamaiah noticed the energy and zest in Bhaskar and called him over for an audience. His CPI (ML) group was quite powerful here, which was why Bhaskar was delighted to have been called. The sitting happened in the small house of a worker. There was a steel cot under a small square window. That is where Bhaskar sat with the owner of the house. Seetharamaiah sat in a wooden easy chair in front. Seetharamaiah's brow carried a mark of branding by turmeric. The branding must have happened as a part of some custom in his childhood, but it was a mark that a person who met him would remember forever. An ordinary looking person, but he had a big name. He spoke to Bhaskar about being officially inducted into the party. He also told him about the areas in which the party's work had moved ahead. It was comforting for him to learn that Bhaskar had already readied himself ideologically to join the party. There was no dearth of people wishing to associate themselves with the party out of enthusiasm. But a comrade like Bhaskar, who was already familiar with the party's ideology and had worked along party lines in some way or the other, would be a great asset. That was when Bhaskar officially joined the party. About two years after Bhaskar went underground, Seetharamaiah's party was christened CPI-ML-People's War Group (PWG). This PWG then joined hands with the Maoist Communist Centre, which was more active in the Bihar–Bengal area, in 2004 to form the Communist Party of India-Maoist. For another three years till he was arrested, Bhaskar was busy with party work.

In the interim, a number of people drifted away from the movement. Went the parliamentary way. So many different parties came into being: CPI-ML-Liberation, CPI-ML-New Democracy, CPI-ML-Janashakti, CPI-ML-Naxalbari, so many, and in so many places. So many of them remained in name, work vanished. A number of groups got into open work. Some of them just had the leader and his household members to run the party, no workers. Bhaskar, however, stayed with the PWG. That, anyway, was the strong group. After having done some initial years in Adilabad, he was in Vidarbha for some time. Here he met Samidha, a product of St Xavier's, Mumbai. She had come over to Nagpur in the early eighties to teach in a college. There was an entire group that had come over from Mumbai to places like Nagpur and Chandrapur in Vidarbha, and she was among them. Some had decided on becoming lawyers, some would become teachers. The atmosphere of the seventies had dissipated, but it hadn't disappeared. In response to the call of moving to the villages, people had moved to what they thought were villages. While the urban people were busy with all this, there were improvements that went on arriving in the strategy of groups like the PWG working in the villages of Andhra Pradesh. Earlier, an activist would go singly to open up a conversation with the people. It was then noticed that obstructions would be created by the local landlord, so two persons began accompanying the activist as bodyguards. Little by little it became a squad of seven. It was during this period that Peddi Shankar, a member of one such group, got killed in police firing when he crossed the river Pranhita into a village called Moinbinpetta in the Sironcha subdivision of what is today Gadchiroli district. In 1980. Although the original Naxalbari atmosphere had cooled off, a few cinders had still remained. There would have been no reason otherwise for Peddi Shankar's name to travel to St Xavier's, Mumbai. His killing became the first police encounter killing of a Naxalite in Maharashtra. Samidha had thus visited Gadchiroli as a member of a fact-finding team to inquire into this killing.

Peddi Shankar's mother was a farm labourer, and his father was a mine worker. Shankar had passed Std XII while working as a motor cleaner. That was when he had become a member of the Radical Students' Union. Then he started working in the mines. He continued to work for the movement in some form or the other till that day when he crossed into Gadchiroli. Gone.

As the movement dissipated further in the eighties, many people returned home. Those who could afford to do so went to foreign countries. Some, however, went deep into the movement and got into the jungles. Or went underground. Others continued to do some work or the other right where they were. It was during those times that Bhaskar met Samidha at a meeting. While he was a professional revolutionary, Samidha became a professional academician. She taught for a long time in Vidarbha, after which she started teaching in a social science institute in Mumbai, as we have seen. Things were quite placid during this period, one would have to say. There were some sensational events that occurred during this placid period, though. For example, the incident of Bhaskar's group cutting up a landlord in a village in Adilabad. It was in connection with this case that Bhaskar had been serving a jail term before being freed and coming to Nagpur. There's just one case pending in a Bihar court, a small one. The impact of the Adilabad episode, however, was big.

The landlords there lived in fortresses guarded by their own armed men. Proper feudal grandeur. People ours, their wives ours. People ours, their labour ours. People ours, their reputation ours. People ours, rule over the people ours – this was the feudal arrangement there as at many other places. The PWG had been working for a long time at one of these places on bringing the people together, and Bhaskar too had been a part of this effort. The entire exercise had peaked with the mounting of an assault on the fortress. The landlord had been a member of the state legislative assembly for three terms. The villages in that area were distributed among these four brothers, one of whom was this landlord. The entire water of a dam that had been built there passed through their lands before meeting the river Godavari. The property they owned was so huge that when it rained, the benefit was mainly theirs. Even so, they channellized the water of the dam to their own lands and that was bound to create difficulties for the others. But the issue was not of water alone. Everybody's services were dedicated to the master. There was this custom of imposing fines. Women, too, were required to be supplied sometimes. They, of course, controlled all land dealings. They maintained an army to impose their wishes. The PWG comrades worked very hard to get the people to stand up against this tyranny. Their efforts led to a campaign to demand the return of all the fines the landlords had collected in the previous ten years. The results were different in different places. In the village of the Bhaskar group, the atmosphere was explosive. The landlord wasn't quite ready to settle the matter through discussions. That led to the assault on the fortress. Getting into the details of who killed whom doesn't make any sense. But an important point to note is that having stabbed one person earlier and having cut up two others later, Bhaskar had had some practice. Another important point is that he was mentally ready for it all. And it was important to ready the people to take such an enterprise to its conclusion. The people's support was huge. It was because of this support that the mission was accomplished. And it helped the Naxalites gain great esteem in that Telangana belt. The case went on for many years before Bhaskar was finally convicted. It was after serving the sentence that he came to Nagpur four months ago. The torture he was subjected to in police custody before being sent to prison was quite unexpected. He was fifty-eight when he was arrested, and he had believed that the chances of his being tortured were low. But these kinds of things cannot be altogether unexpected in the case of professional revolutionaries. So, yes, Bhaskar was tortured. These are not things that one talks about. Both the torturer and the tortured reach such depths of inhumanity that it is very difficult to talk from that position. During those days Bhaskar felt as if his testicles had literally travelled up to his head. Every outer organ of his body, every crevice and orifice – he wished he had never had them. His awareness of each of his organs sent him into fits of terror. He suffered it all, anyway, during his days of custody. There was not much that the police could get out of him. Bhaskar was ready for that. What the police got were his books and a few documents. The handwritten manuscript of the book on globalization that he had been writing for the party vanished. Bhaskar had also been involved in the preparation of a curriculum for teaching children in the areas of Bastar under the control of the party. He had already submitted some of the earlier work on this project to the central committee. The recent work was among the documents that the police seized. But these were not really big losses. Very importantly, he had not disclosed links with anybody, and that was a great source of satisfaction for him. Once the sentence was pronounced upon him, there was no question of further torture. It was only during custody that he had had to suffer. Later he was sent to a Telangana prison, where he was treated quite well. He met a lot of old acquaintances during this period.

Actually, before going to prison, he had spent some time

working in a dalit locality in Nagpur, some time in Mumbai and some time in Bengal–Bihar. After using him in the rural areas in his early days, the party had engaged him in city work, mainly administrative work for twelve to fifteen years. He did some writing for the book *Thirty Years of the Naxalbari Struggle*. Alongside, he got an English booklet published from Kolkata on the development work undertaken in the area under party control in Dandakaranya. He wrote an English book for the party titled *Post-modernism: Challenges before Revolutionary Politics*. He was also required to deliver lectures in various places for readying new comrades for the movement. The constant travels and the long time he spent in Maharashtra made him lose contact with Telangana for a long while. The contact was renewed to some extent during his period of incarceration.

Bhaskar's arrest had figured prominently in the Hyderabad newspapers. He had been arrested in Kolkata. The news of a central committee member of the Maoist Party was bound to be big news. Bhaskar himself, however, had been surprised. He was brought to Hyderabad from Kolkata. He was released on bail earlier. But he was rearrested a couple of weeks later while still in Hyderabad. The next five years or so went in jail. During this period he had to be shifted to hospital a couple of times, and that again had made big news. The police had actually wanted to rearrest him as soon as the court had ordered his release on bail, but such a huge crowd of journalists had assembled that they had backed off. They had gone back and prepared fresh papers before taking him in the second time. A journalist had interviewed him during his brief bail interim. The fact was that Bhaskar had not wanted to attract media attention in such a hurry. But this journalist hailed from one of the villages where Bhaskar had worked.

He recognized Bhaskar. He remembered that Bhaskar would bring medicines for the villagers. The boy came to meet him in prison, but Bhaskar turned him down, although he found it difficult to do so. The journalist contacted him again when he was released. He couldn't refuse him a second time, so he met him. The journalist was in his mid-thirties, which would mean that he was barely twelve when Bhaskar had visited his village. Bhaskar was a hero in his village, and that is why the journalist remembered him. He had carried food cooked by his wife a few times while Bhaskar was in jail. The interview finished soon. It went like this:

Q. What do you think is the current state of the movement?

A. Since the time the People's War Group (PWG) entered Dandakaranya in the 1980s to establish a guerrilla zone, it has been steadily gaining public support. In 2004, the PWG merged with the Maoist Communist Centre to form the CPI-Maoist, and it has managed to liberate land spreading from Dandakaranya to Bengal – a landmass equal to Bangladesh in size – from the ruling class. Efforts are in progress to secure the participation of the urban labour class and the class suffering from caste discrimination in this struggle of the adivasis under the leadership of the Maoist Party. Some other revolutionary groups are expected to join this front in the near future for embarking on the path of a new democratic revolution.

Q. But it is said that by hiding behind the façade of discussions, the Andhra Pradesh government has externed the movement from the state. Also, with the killing of a number of senior leaders in encounters and the imprisonment of some of them, has a leadership vacuum been created?

A. The revolutionary road is never easy. There will always be ups and downs. If the final goal is the creation of a communist society, there will be victories and defeats before the goal is attained. Even after the great revolutions in Russia and China, we have seen the beginning of counter-processes within three or four decades, but even after these defeats, the day of victory will dawn. Our enemy is extremely powerful, but with the application of Marxism–Leninism and Maoist thought to suit the times, the experience of class conflict, and the lessons gained from local circumstances, our victory is certain.

Q. What would you tell our readers about the liberated areas? Without any news emerging from those areas, would you say that the party will break away from the people?

A. The party has undertaken development programmes on a massive scale in the last twelve years. Under the guidance of the Janatana Sarkar (People's Government), regional and provincial revolutionary committees are building a new, just society. From communal farming to the construction of small dams, from education to health facilities, the party has understood the needs of the people and is working on various fronts. The party has given first preference to the equal distribution of land. Because of the intercession of the party, the labour rates for gathering tendu leaves have increased three to four times. Speaking of education, it is for the first time in the history of Dandakaranya that, through the efforts of the party, education is being imparted through the Koya language. The party has given priority to strengthening the Gond and Madiya cultures. Mobile schools are being run in places where the winds of education had never reached. The party has raised public awareness on water-borne diseases and persuaded people to boil drinking water. As a result, the death rate due to contaminated water has come down by half. As for the empowerment of women, we can take the example of 40% of our People's Liberation Guerrilla Army being women. All this information is provided from time to time to the papers for dissemination. But the media have sold themselves out to the corporates, and they work as the propaganda machinery of the imperialistic powers.

Q. What is the direction that the movement proposes to take in the future?

A. Talking from the national perspective, 70% of the population works for less than twenty rupees per day. Twenty-five percent of the country's population consists of dalits and adivasis. Sixty percent of the population is employed in agriculture, but the contribution of agriculture to the gross domestic product is just 18%. Against this background, the strategy of the government is to put the agricultural profession, and consequently all the land, in the lap of the corporates. The present semi-feudal, semi-capitalist government is working as a tout for the international imperialistic powers. Besides, incidents of caste atrocities haven't stopped since the transfer of power in 1947. As a Maoist party, our role will be to give precedence to the equal distribution of land and communal farming. It's out of this that the party will be able to create a combined front of the exploited groups, and finally, the new democratic revolution will succeed in bringing power into the hands of the proletarian class. It's with the sacrifice of more than ten thousand comrades over the past forty years that the foundation of this party has been laid.

The interview was over. After he was arrested again, the main part of Bhaskar's incarceration began. He wasn't given too much trouble there. If one leaves aside the early days of police custody, he didn't have any problem. When he complained about having problems with squatting, he was provided with a commode. This, he guessed, was because he was in Telangana. Besides, he was also able to indulge his hobby of gardening. He hadn't been able to find time for it for so many years. He used to grow vegetables in his backyard as a child. There wasn't enough land for him to grow vegetables for the market, but he produced enough for his mother's kitchen. That was all he had been able to do for his mother. He couldn't do anything else later. To his father, he couldn't even give vegetables. The father, of course, did eat the vegetables he had given to his mother, which she had cooked and along with others his father too had eaten. Well, that much at least. But beyond that, nothing. His father died ten odd years ago in Kolkata. He lived there with Bhaskar's younger brother. His mother is alive, though she is confined to bed. She is being looked after well because Bhaskar's younger brother earns a decent salary. He must go and visit her one of these days.

Samidha had been telling him to come straight to Mumbai after his release. But he informed her that since they still had the flat in Amravati, he would stay there for some time before coming over. He needed a little time to adjust. It's now been four months or nearabout. He had been out for just a week between his release and rearrest; but after finishing his main jail term, he hadn't stayed behind in Hyderabad. He had come straight to Amravati. And actually, he would have left straight from Amravati for Mumbai, but then the boy who had interviewed him came to Amravati exclusively to give him an invitation. It was an invitation for the wedding of the boy's brother. He had come to Nagpur for some work, and Amravati from Nagpur doesn't take much time. The wedding was not the only reason for Bhaskar to go to Hyderabad. A very old friend's collection of Telugu poems was due to be published in the week following the wedding. The friend had sent him an invitation for the event on e-mail, then got his mobile number and invited him all over again on the phone. This was bound to happen. It was important, too, to participate in these things. The friend was from very early times too. This friend had stayed with the movement for about four years and then taken up a job. They had stayed in contact for some time and would meet very occasionally, as had happened with all the others. So Bhaskar now plans to meet them all together and go from there straight to Mumbai. He will let Samidha know, most likely; she may book his flight and send the ticket by e-mail. Meanwhile, Bhaskar has already dispatched his books and a few sundry things over to Mumbai. He will need to make another round sometime later to gather the remaining stuff, but he will need Samidha then. Whatever he could collect by himself, he did. Gave away four-five books to the bank clerk. If they could help him understand things better, then good. As he handed over the books, he also remarked, 'Your main problem arises on account of the way you look at death. The issue of weapons is not all that important either. You will find more weapons with one of these Uttar Pradesh feudal lords than the Maoist Party has. And a party like the Sena in Mumbai, the economic capital of the country, that openly talks of cutting up people of other religions is called democratic. It actually goes and kills someone on the issue of house rent, and yet thousands assemble at the death of the leader of such a party. Newspapers come out with full-page photographs. Paeans are sung for him on the TV. With all this happening, you decide who has how much space.' The clerk made no response to this. He gave Bhaskar a framed photograph of an egret he had shot with his mobile. A buffalo is sitting very gloomily as always, and the egret is sitting very peacefully on it, and the greenish water can be seen indistinctly behind. He'd got this picture put into a four-by-six horizontal frame to give to Bhaskar.

Bhaskar got everything in order and went to Nagpur, and from there he boarded the Nagpur–Secunderabad train that had been introduced recently and reached Hyderabad comfortably. He would be roaming free over there after a very long time. There was just a slight risk, of course, of being apprehended again. The last time when he had been released and then arrested again, he hadn't expected it; otherwise he wouldn't have stayed on in Hyderabad. He was walking down the street towards his vehicle when, as he was crossing another vehicle, two men had come from behind and shoved him into the rear seat of the vehicle; one of them had got into the front seat, and they had deposited him at the station. He wasn't tortured after that, but he had to remain in prison for five years. The probability of this happening again was almost non-existent, but there was always a bit of risk.

The journalist had arranged to have him picked up from the station. He had also made arrangements for him to stay with a dalit leader of his acquaintance, Shyamalu by name. Shyamalu had worked for all kinds of parties and was also involved in the construction business. He was quite an affluent person. He owned a palatial three-storey bungalow. He had made grand arrangements for Bhaskar on the third floor. Shyamalu had no connection with the Maoist Party. He was earlier with the Telangana Sangharsh Samiti. In those days he had established a forum for disseminating the thoughts of Ambedkar in Telugu. Telangana then became a separate state; so his present political agenda is known only to him. Shyamalu doesn't subscribe to the Maoist way. What the public wants should be the line to take. The people had fought against the landlords, but now, when there are no landlords left, who do you fight against? Waste of time, waste of life. Sometimes they blow the right people, but if there is an error, who will be responsible? The more the mistakes, the greater is the number of lives lost. How long can this go on? Society moves in a certain direction, just as water flows in a particular direction; what happens when you go against it? This is how Shyamalu thought.

Nevertheless, shouldn't a person have respect for someone who has devoted his life in the service of the people? Shyamulu would any time have invited Bhaskar home with great respect. It's only been about a couple of years since he has made this bungalow. All the others in this area are Reddys, so it hadn't been easy for him to construct his bungalow. Nobody says anything openly, but there are all kinds of things said behind his back. And the vocal ones can sell dust, but the silent ones can't even sell gold. This law is eternal. The mere buying of a piece of land is such a hassle. Shyamalu's parents had been farm labourers. He stayed with them in their hut and did his matriculation on the strength of their labour. Then he added his labour and his political work to their labour and made a lot of money in the construction business. He is around fifty years of age. Bloody hell! The Reddys give money, but I too give money; so, what the shit do they mean by not giving me land? Riled up at this, Shyamalu stirred himself enough to buy himself land in that area. He went beyond that and built such a bungalow there that the neighbouring Reddys, while watering the plants in their galleries, would break into a sweat in the thick of winter. This is the only non-Reddy house in the entire area. It had become a prestige issue, but Shyamalu resolved it peacefully. Which also allowed him to make this beautiful house. Despite being a palace-sized structure, he built it in such a way that one is not overwhelmed by it. There are about ten rooms. The ground floor has an office and accommodation for occasional guests. The first floor has a kitchen, a dining room and a big TV room. Shyamalu and family live on the second floor. The third floor has two master bedrooms for guests. It was a bedroom on this floor that he had readied for Bhaskar. Bhaskar had been quite touched by Shyamalu's gesture. But he had gone through similar situations before, so there was nothing new about it.

He was going to meet his old friends. Since he had just arrived, he hadn't thought of meeting them today. The journalist's brother's wedding was a couple of days later, on Monday. And the publication of his friend's collection of poetry was the following week, on Tuesday. Bhaskar had left his programme open, ready to meet whoever came along. Shyamalu had made grand arrangements here. Uttappa or idli or dosa for breakfast, whatever the guest wanted in whatever quantity; chicken and tamarind rice, the ultimate treat; the insistence was unrelenting. Pachi pulusu, Bhaskar was tasting this dish after an age and he was thrilled; top class, absolutely.

Later, when people came to meet him, so many of his memories would come to the fore – old, old memories. It would be the same people who had met him during that short time when he had been out of jail earlier. He would be able to meet them at complete ease now. There still is a bit of risk, yes, but certainly not where he is staying at present. But out there on the road, it would not help to be loafing around too brazenly. Hence, it would be best to stretch out and relax. A friend named Krishna is going to come over in his own car in the afternoon. As a matter of fact, Bhaskar would have wanted to avoid this, too. But Krishna had insisted on dropping by on his way to some place. Well, he would finish that meeting and then two days of rest. He wondered which car Krishna was likely to use. He had so many. This friend who would go poster-pasting with Bhaskar had later joined his father's hotel business. Then he had invested in god knows how many other businesses. Many people had made huge profits out of the granite extracted from the Karimnagar mines. He was one of them. In 2008, tons of granite was exported to China during the Beijing Olympics. Other than that there is always a demand for granite for the construction of temples – not just in India, but also in America and Europe. Now that Telangana has become a state, shouldn't its economic status begin to improve? A lot of news keeps emerging with regard to that, so more cubic metres are going to go cascading and Krishna is going to make more profit. Bhaskar was not aware of Krishna's progress. But he learnt of it on meeting him. Bhaskar had no intention of meeting anyone today. He had just arrived, so he didn't feel up to roaming around Hyderabad. He did intend to visit the Osmania University campus and a few bookshops and the like in due course. A friend had a bookshop; he would meet this friend. Another was suffering from cancer, he got to know on reaching here; he should meet him, too. He has all these plans, but he will start tomorrow or the day after that. Now this Krishna had insisted on visiting him, so he met him but didn't go out anywhere. He had tea with him at Shyamalu's bungalow. He then told Krishna that he would meet him again at leisure as he was here for another ten days. That made Krishna happy. He is about the same age as Bhaskar, but looks older. He had brought some delicious biscuits for Bhaskar. Freshly baked, from a shop near Charminar. Wow, that added another dimension to evening tea.

❖

After Krishna had left, Bhaskar decided to go to his room on the upper floor and stretch out. That Shyamalu has a grand house nobody should have any problem accepting. Don't know where Shyamalu got his granite from, but he's made a truly impressive house. He's made this stylish spiral staircase. Watch TV? Shyamalu asked. Bhaskar said he'd do it later in the evening; he'd like to stretch out now. Shyamalu is a perfectly relaxed guy. Matter of fact, Bhaskar and he have no old connection as such. But people show respect sometimes. Bhaskar had experienced this in jail and in those days in between. But when it suddenly happens again, something does move inside, doesn't it? And age also matters. Whatever one may say, he's crossed sixty, so this little bit of deference is going to happen, isn't it? He went round and round and up those circular stairs to the third floor and took his evening pills. There is a big terrace attached to the room, so he went there for a five-minute stroll. It's a very big terrace. There's another cork-screw iron staircase leading to the water tank. Bhaskar took a small round there. Yonder was the sky spreading out everywhere. This locality is a little outside the city, and the houses are of smaller size. Besides, with Shyamalu having made a tall house, there are no houses as tall as his in the vicinity. So, one can see a long distance. There's still time for the sun to set. The redness of the evening has just about begun to spread. Pigeons fly everywhere, so they're flying here. Bhaskar took his small round and came to his room. The toilet-bathroom is attached to the bedroom. Neat and clean. He went to ease himself. He had been feeling the pressure since tea. He then splashed water on his face and came into the room. In a full-sized mirror, Bhaskar saw his full image. Half-sleeved kurta and track-pants. Shyamalu had placed that day's *The Hindu* and a magazine named *Aksharalu* in his room. Shyamalu, here, of course, means one of his men. Bhaskar had been told to call for this man if he felt the need for anything. But he didn't want anything now. Bhaskar picked up *Aksharalu* and stretched out on the bed. It's a lovely room. A big double bed. Bhaskar is stretched out peacefully on it. The issue had poems and stories. Now that he's come here, he should gather his Telugu poems and earlier-published stories and bring them over. It's good to have them published in a single collection some time. These kinds of thoughts are cooing away like the evening pigeons in Bhaskar's head. It's in this state that Bhaskar is drifting off to sleep. Well, let him. Let him sleep a bit. He's been travelling since yesterday, a good ten-twelve hours. Then he had this chat with the journalist in the morning. Then Krishna had walked in while he was having his post lunch chat with Shyamalu. Then the sitting with Krishna, and now this little stretching out, and then the dinner. Well, he's old too, after all, and he's gone to sleep. Good. Let Bhaskar sleep in peace now. What's going on with the pigeons outside? Cooing. What's the sun being doing? Turning reddish. Let it happen, then, peacefully.

Sayali

Sayali does not want to be a Bhaskar. Well, actually, she does not deliberately want to be anything. Had never wanted it. But the political movement with which she got associated, it's because of this attachment that she has become something, that's certain. But what is certain is difficult to unravel.

Sayali is really the name of a flower. These flowers are like jaayee and juyee. Difficult to identify at one glance. It would be identifiable to experts, but if we casually see garlands on the road, we might think of them as juyee, but they could well be sayali. These flowers grow on lovely vines. It's likely that a vine existed in the courtyard of Sayali's house, but it is impossible to determine whether she got named that because of the vine. Besides, you can find these vines in the courtyards of plenty of other people. It can also be an out and out coincidence that there was this vine in her house, and she got named Sayali too. This flower is a little less fragrant than jaayee-juyee, they say. But if you look at the families of flowers, it is certain that sayali belongs to the same family as jaayee-juyee. Its fragrance spreads nicely. If you have a woman or a child selling sayali garlands, weaving through the smoke-emitting vehicles that stop at the traffic signal, you can smell these flowers so strong right through all that smoke.

Actually, it's not as if the family of Sayali – who is not

a flower – has been directly connected with any movement. Well, her grandfather had been a worker in a mill in Mumbai; so, whatever he might have seen then and maybe recorded his participation, just that. But Sayali, who has never met him, got to know from her family that even that little participation brought about a change in him. Dr Babasaheb Ambedkar's name and work had been reaching him from various sources. After he had returned from Mumbai on the completion of his service, he had tried to create some kind of an organization in the village. But the reaction of the upper castes was so strong that it was very likely the cause of the heart attack he suffered, they say. Sayali's father, however, got himself a good education and retired as a government engineer.

Sayali has this distant cousin by the name of Shridhar. He is connected with some movement or the other in some way or the other. But she and he are not all that much in contact now. There wasn't much connection earlier either because they are distantly related. But they had got to know each other rather well at one point. Sayali has a partner by the name of Ajay. Ajay and Shridhar became friends, so Sayali too got to know him better, that's all. Later, Ajay and a few others were accused of being connected with the Maoist Party and of having undergone some training in the jungles. They were arrested on account of this. Ajay is still in jail. Sayali didn't have to go to jail. There's no case against her in any court. Some people get released, some don't. There's news on some, there isn't on some others. There was just a small news item on Ajay and the two others with him. The episode didn't blow up. Good too. That may lead to his early release. Another complication that does arise is that some episodes get so much talked about that release becomes a long-drawn-out process. On the other hand, some episodes get so less talked about that the arrested people never get released. Ajay's case stands somewhere in the middle. Consequently, the circumstances are not such as to fetch immediate results, nor is the whole thing likely to last beyond a year. The probability of his being released in a few months exists. Sayali is out, but a number of her connections are as good as broken. A number of her friends got wary of her since this episode, and some started to avoid meeting her. This has helped Sayali understand people better. However, she doesn't hold anything against anybody.

People behave according to their individual circumstances, she thinks. And she is always busy making estimates of people and their circumstances. It's a full-time job with her. One of the things that draws her to the political ideology that she subscribes to at present is that it affords her the opportunity to indulge in this activity.

There is an example of this from the time she was in the jungle for those seven-eight months. She had made the acquaintance of an unmarried young adivasi couple. Because of the language problem, it had just not been possible to talk much with them. But they could understand simple Hindi. The boy was about twenty or twenty-two. The amount of work he did completely overwhelmed Sayali. Right from filling up water to doing sentry duty, he was never seen out of breath or sitting. Continuous work, without any sign of tiring. Such was the boy, and his partner was that comrade girl. After having come out of the jungle, Sayali got to know from someone that the two had eloped. They'd wanted to get married. They could also have been hoping for children of their own. They could have said all this to their immediate leaders, thought Sayali, and opted out of the movement. But they didn't do any such thing and just eloped. Out of love. When the boy was working, Sayali had never sensed that he would run away with the girl. Matter of fact, what the boy would do further on, Sayali had no idea. Nobody could have anticipated this from the boy's behaviour or from any expression of feelings. He had never let anything show. Very likely, he himself would not have known what he should do next. But whatever he had decided, he had decided from deep inside, that's for sure. What he had decided, he had done. But it was unlikely that anybody could have guessed. Obviously, Sayali also couldn't guess it. That is why she was amazed.

Although her partner is in jail, her capacity for enjoying life hasn't reduced. She's always had this capacity. It could be the result of the freedom her father had given her from the very beginning. But now he has stopped speaking to her because of the police case, although he doesn't know much about the work she does in the party. Now she does not stay at home, she lives in a rented room. Her joy, however, remains undiminished.

There used to be this government advertisement on the TV: *The sun has risen in the east, light has spread*. It was for the National Literacy Mission. Sayali was probably in the second grade then. She used to love this song: *Poorab se surya ooga, phaila ujiyaala – Jaagi har disha disha, jaaga jag saara* (The sun has risen in the East, it has spread its light / Every direction has awakened, the entire world is awake). By and large, she liked the jingles of the government advertisements of those times. *Miley sur mera tumhaara, toh sur baney hamaara* (When your notes mingle with my notes, the music is ours) was one. And another: *Bajey sargam har taraf se, goonje ban kar desh raag* (When music emanates from all directions, it reverberates as raga Desh). *Saverey saverey yaaron se mil, ban-than ke nikle hum, rokney se na rukey hum, marzi se chalein hum, baadal se garjein hum, saavan se barsein hum, sooraj se chamkein hum, school chale hum* (Early in the morning, in the company of friends, we set off all decked up. We cannot be stopped, we do what we want, we thunder like the clouds, we pour like the rains, we shine like the sun, we are off to school). When this National Literacy Mission jingle was aired, Sayali was in Std XII. The purpose of these advertisements was perhaps to make people aware about education. The surya in these jingles turned into suraj over ten years of Sayali's life. The Sayali who used to love these jingles slowly began to be different, different from her people at home.

For the three undergraduate years, she was associated with a number of organizations. While in college, she had taken the initiative and started working for a socialist organization. Sayali becoming different simply means that she didn't want the institution of the family to be what it was. She didn't want to get married, she wanted to have a live-in relationship; and towards the end of the three years, her opinions on the institution called government also began to change. The end of that period was the beginning of her work with an organization with leftist ideology. In the camps of this organization, in the resulting interaction with people, in the lectures she heard during those years, in the processions, Sayali went on receiving plentiful nourishment. Sayali became different, meaning that the girl who once loved those government advertisement jingles began to dislike the government itself. As a matter of fact, she wanted it changed. As a matter of more fact, she wanted it overthrown. As a matter of yet more fact, she also began getting convinced that there is need for an armed revolution for overthrowing this government. Nobody in her entire family had ever thought such thoughts. None of her friends, none of her close ones had ever thought such thoughts. This was how Sayali had become different. This, of course, does not mean that there are no people at all who don't have such thoughts. There are plenty of such people, and Sayali's association with such circles increased.

This is now Sayali's circle. This circle supported Sayali. Why should one say that it has supported her? One reason for saying this is that she is now twenty-eight, but even so, she can live alone in this frightening city. She doesn't call for money from home, and she doesn't have a job either. She did her Master's in Marathi after her graduation. Then she spent the next three-four years in the movement. Well, actually, during this period she took admission in Law. But the next twelve to eighteen months she had to go underground. And because of the movement, she doesn't do any regular job. But the movement supports her financially. There are always sympathizers, and two such people from Mumbai provide her with seven or eight thousand rupees per month as a full-timer. Hence one may say that she gets support in return for the support she offers to the movement. This mutually supportive journey goes on. But the movement is superior to an individual, this Sayali knows, as everybody else knows. The conviction grew stronger since her trip to the jungle. The way the comrades survive, move around, live, eat, she doesn't have the spine to do that day after day after day, this she has admitted to herself. So, people may have limitations, and she may one day get out of the movement because of her limitations, perhaps. But that doesn't make the movement any smaller; if anything, the shortcoming is always in the individual, she has learnt from her jungle experiences. The awareness that she herself has a few inadequacies has stayed with her as a continuous, conscious stream in her head.

Appears reasonable too. Her awareness has arrived after

having had to walk a good twenty kilometres or so at a stretch, managing with barely two hours of sleep, doing sentry duty, staying forever on the alert, and so on. So, if you look at it that way, she doesn't any more carry in her head all those romantic notions of being a revolutionary. She won't refer to herself as a revolutionary right now. She has seen for herself people staying nameless, identity-less, and fighting on. This has strengthened her faith in the movement and weakened her faith in her own self a little bit. So, her own inadequacies may cause her to opt out of the movement; she will certainly not look for inadequacies in the movement, she has decided.

There are a number of reasons for Sayali thinking along these lines. A number of events are responsible too. For instance, when Sayali went into the jungles, she had around her several comrades with urban and semi-urban backgrounds coming from various places. Quite a few of them had no idea of what a real jungle is. Around the time they joined, an important leader of the movement was knocked out by the police in an encounter. Some of these city dwellers came up with the suggestion that they should observe a day of fast as a mark of protest against the police killing of the central committee member Azad. This kind of thought could never have occurred to the local comrades working in the jungles or the leaders stationed there. But these comrades who had just joined were coming from a different set of circumstances, and their thoughts could well have been a product of those circumstances. The circumstances in the jungle are different. Here, it is necessary to think of one's own body first. Whether it's drinking water or carrying water in a plastic bag for defecating, the thought of the body always comes first, unconsciously. Hence, the satisfaction of staying without food and water and fasting through a day would be considered a laughable idea under such circumstances, and that's how it turned out to be. But the comrades from outside needed to be explained: the death of our leader is painful to you as much as to us, to everyone; but there is no point in demonstrating our protest by not drinking and not eating; in fact, this kind of a protest here is suicidal, and so on. How much a person learns out of such experiences one doesn't know, but Sayali certainly learnt. Call it her natural facility to learn things by herself or call it what you want. From this incident onwards she began making greater efforts to understand things by herself.

Then there is this other very moving incident. There was an adivasi boy of about nineteen. This boy was one of the bodyguards of the leader in charge of the area through which Sayali had entered the jungle. Then, you know, this happened, quite a surprising thing, really. This boy went to the leader and asked, 'Dada, will our name be written in history?' It wasn't an easy question. And Sayali had never imagined that this otherwise silent boy would come up with such a question. She got to know because she was somewhere around there when this question was asked. Perhaps – history, inspirational history, Russian history, the history of Marx, Lenin, the revolutionary movement of China – it was perhaps his proximity with such subjects that had prompted the boy to ask this question, she thought. The leader, after all, was a leader, not someone who would get flustered by such a question thrown at him. He tried to satisfy the boy by telling him things like how books are brought out these days on any comrade attaining martyrdom, and so on. No evidence can be gathered now on whether the boy was satisfied with the answer or not. The boy spoke so little that there is no likelihood of his having left evidence with somebody of his satisfaction with the answer. And now, of course, there is no way of learning about his satisfaction because the boy himself was martyred within eight months of the conversation. There was no possibility of a separate news item about his martyrdom. Even if such a news item could have been published, it would have carried neither his real name nor his real history. He would have been merely one of many killed, and the news item would have given the reader no idea of his sorrowful eyes. The item wouldn't have reported his having asked a certain question either. What does a news item have to do with such questions? Sayali got to hear of the news from someone in the movement. And she became all the more aware of her limitations. The boy's question was not irrelevant. Even if one doesn't fight for the glory of one's name, the boy had felt what he had felt and had posed the question in his innocent way. But how exactly does one look at the question that compelled a silent person like that boy to speak out?

Sayali tried to broach this subject with her leader there. Probably the leader himself has covered this subject in his various conversations. It's like this, when comrade leaders have come in from cities like Mumbai and Delhi and joined the movement after sacrificing all the comforts of an affluent home, their sacrifice gets talked about. When such leaders are arrested, the perspective from which they are seen carries a great deal of respect for their sacrifice. But if it is a person of the lower classes who has lived a life of struggle, and learnt through these struggles and got into the movement, and has begun to struggle for the existence of the movement more than for his own existence, the perspective from which he is seen doesn't carry the same kind of respect for his sacrifice. So, isn't the sacrifice of the have-nots sacrifice enough? It was the kind of question that would figure in the conversations of the leader and of his other comrades, and the comrades who had come from the affluent sections of society. Sacrifice is sacrifice. How will it do if sacrifice is categorized too? If the martyred leader belonged to Mumbai and had studied in a reputed college, a lecture series gets started in his or her name. But that boy…what was his name? Sayali herself doesn't remember his name. So, what happened to him? Okay, forget the name, but keep alive at least the memory? Somebody may erect a memorial stone for the boy some time, somewhere, and that's some satisfaction. Very deep the boy had penetrated into Sayali. Sayali completely acknowledged the legitimacy of that question.

The question deserves introspection, she believes. The entire movement, of course, cannot be branded as suspect. Hope exists because this movement exists. Otherwise, look at where all the other movements have gone, feels Sayali. That is why she doesn't subscribe to Shridhar's notion that all has turned dark. However distant, he is still her cousin. She had been upset for some time on noticing that he had started keeping distance from her and Ajay. But finally, she should understand. He has a family. Or, probably, he has different thoughts, and that may be the reason he has stopped communicating with Ajay-Sayali. True, he had always known where their thoughts lay; in fact, he has stopped communicating out of fear of police inquiries, but so what?

Well, that is how most people react to such thinking. These views seem quite attractive at a distance or for a good conversation. But when it comes to acting on these views, it becomes difficult. Well that could well be true of all other views or beliefs. Sayali gets sucked into such thoughts now and then. But she likes thinking, so you can't say that she gets stressed. Sayali liked the communist ideology and got ready to work in accordance with that ideology. She began learning of the groupings and variations in her study group sessions. And it was through these sessions that she got the opportunity to get closer to the present Maoist Party. She even attended one of the sessions addressed by Bhaskar. When there is so much to learn around, Sayali hates the idea of imposing her own thoughts on others. Since her return from the jungles, she has become particularly non-confrontational. If you are working in the city, it is important to take the people along with you. There's a different system at work in the jungles. Since she can't work there, she keeps thinking about how she can work here. A good part of her day is spent in these thoughts.

One can take what happened the other day as an example. A big procession was brought out to protest against the inability of the police to hunt down the culprits responsible for the murder of Dr Narendra Dabholkar, founder and president of the Committee for Eradication of Superstition in Maharashtra. A number of programmes were organized in this context. Sayali attended these, naturally. One of the slogans raised by the processionists was 'Doctor, we are ashamed, your killers still live!' For a while, Sayali felt like laughing. An entire year of investigation had revealed nothing; but the assemblage of such a large crowd would also not achieve anything perhaps. There are two or three big shops on the main road that sell rings and amulets and gem stones on the pretext of telling your future. Why doesn't even one of these processionists fling a stone at these shops? How will taking out such processions help? If they are ashamed that the killers still live, they want the killers dead, right? The slogan suggests, perhaps, that the people want the killers to be hanged. Otherwise, instead of raising slogans about catching the killers and procuring justice, why did it occur to them to make slogans about being ashamed of the killers still living?

Why do the makers of these slogans then refuse to agree with the Maoist movement? These very same people would much rather sit debating on the issues of violence and non-violence. There was a veritable procession of such thoughts that marched up and down Sayali's brain.

People ultimately shy away, and that's the truth. They may agree to kill a killer, but they can't agree when people respond to violence with violence in order to overthrow a regime. Their circumstances are different, what else can one say? Sayali walked on, trying to understand people and make sense of their attitudes. Shridhar was in the procession too. She spoke to him. He is quite a simple person. Although his attention is now focused mainly on bringing up his son, he does write occasional articles. He gave Sayali an issue of their magazine. It contained an article by him: 'The Fight for the Annihilation of Caste and the Weapons of the Intellectuals'.

There was a time when people like Shridhar would enrage her greatly. They keep changing their stances according to convenience, she would feel. But taking circumstances into consideration, she doesn't get angry any more. There are lots of things she doesn't agree with, but she simply lets them go. One should understand people and their circumstances. 'We should love all!' She believes she has begun to understand that it's very easy to say this but very difficult to put into practice. Therefore, she shouldn't be so upset with Shridhar either.

The way it happened with Shridhar was that once, long ago – that is, before becoming a full-timer for the BSP – he was associated with an organization called the Non-Brahminical Awakening Forum. He had actually been very keen to do some really worthwhile work for this forum, but what he was made to do was editorial work for their mouthpiece. He was reasonably interested in this work, too, but he should have been given decent wages at least, shouldn't he? How long could he pull on with two thousand rupees and bed-and-breakfast? It was a husband-and-wife organization. 'We'll fix you up in *Loksatta*.' 'We'll get you a job in *Lokmat*.' The assurances kept coming all the time. They were very well connected with big newspapers, and they kept Shridhar deluded all the time. He could see the leadership of the organization raking in benefits from these connections, so the contacts very definitely existed. But Shridhar never gained any spill-over benefit from these contacts. Forget benefits, he couldn't so much as make the most basic ends meet. He finally chucked the organization and got into the BSP. There too he began to notice the limitations under which organizations work. Then, of course, there was the antagonism that existed between this organization and that. Go here, and the people there get upset; go there, and the people here climb all over you. He had to think of marriage too, and there were also the family pulls and pressures. Finally, he got his BEd. degree and began looking for a job. Once he found a job as a teacher, he stabilized. But the mind continued to remain unstable. 'Circumstances,' says Sayali, 'circumstances.'

'Circumstances must be changed,' says Sayali.

It's one thing to merely say that circumstances should change, but quite another to do something consistently about it. Most movements talk the language of changing circumstances, but just talking doesn't actually make it happen. In the Naxalite movement, however, Sayali believes, good efforts are being made towards it. Other movements do work on some subsidiary questions, and we should make an effort at understanding them, all that is fine. But when it comes to preparing a battle plan after taking note of the entire gamut of circumstances, the Naxalite movement is truly path breaking, she thinks. She began thinking along these lines after attending the classes of Bhaskar and others, getting into discussions with the other comrades and observing them in action. But even so, she began feeling that whatever she had been learning in those early days about the activities in the jungle, that learning was only from a distance. She was acquiring her understanding of the party from observing the leaders in the city. She wanted a deeper understanding than that, if only for her own satisfaction. This was the reasoning that she gave to herself. It was because of this that she had gone into the jungle. A few comrades arrived from different places, and Sayali was one of them. She had with her some comrades she had known quite closely. Her bonds with the movement strengthened after she had worked in the jungle for about seven months. About the other movements and their leaders, she had formed good and bad opinions at a personal level. But considering the whole work together, the Maoist Party has its own definite structure. It has liberated a portion of land almost as big as Bangladesh; its presence has apparently brought work to a halt in the Bastar mines in Chhattisgarh. Even in Gadchiroli district, the party has intervened at Surjagadh and finished off three-four company officers, thereby delaying mining operations there. The party has a definite goal, and a definite work plan for achieving it; its understanding of the circumstances is solid. Sayali appreciated this. There will always be ups and downs in a movement. But for the last forty years the movement has plodded on; in fact, it is expanding. The liberated zone may not be much in relation to the size of the entire country, but it is there, and that's no small achievement. Even in the matter of caste, the Maoist Party is a great deal more alert than the other left formations, she felt. This may not have been true earlier, but now, certainly, it has begun to give importance to this issue. Taking all these things together, along with how other organizations' movements are being run, Sayali was quite satisfied with the decision she had taken. She has received a great deal of support from the organization too. The education she has received from her jungle experiences is never going to drift away from her. The jungle experiences were incomparable: those trees, that endless walking, all those tough, resilient adivasi comrades, a disciplined movement, the unceasing discussions, the reading, all those majestic teaks, those lake-side campings, the need to be always on the alert.

There is this story on alertness that is worth telling. Sayali had been instructed about the need to be alert, but no amount of instructions ever readies you for the actual exercise. You think you have understood it all, but there is a great deal left to understand. She realized that soon after reaching there. It happened this way: she needed to defecate. The adivasi comrades would carry water in discarded plastic bags and relieve themselves in a pit dug in a secluded part of the jungle. The city comrades had been instructed to always take a local comrade with them for the job. They were told to strictly observe this rule at least while they were new to the jungle. But one day, she was in too much of a hurry to remember the instructions. In any case, she believed she would not take long, so she took some water in a bag and set off for a spot a little in the deep. Perhaps, she shouldn't have gone so deep and down such an incline. It was just that the bushes looked denser there. Within fifteen seconds she heard a rustling sound behind her and she flipped. Perspiration broke out on her brow. She didn't jump up, though, just sat holding her breath. She slowly counted ten in her head and then turned her head around cautiously towards the sound. There it was, a giant of a bear within a distance of a few feet. She let out a loud shriek, shot up like a spring and scrambled up the incline. Don't know what happened to the bear, but it didn't move ahead. Something might have moved inside the bear after Sayali's shriek or it may have remained unmoved by the shriek, nevertheless, it went back. Bears are generally not known to turn around and go away. It could have attacked Sayali and opened up her skull. A gun-toting adivasi comrade came running at the sound of the scream. Sayali saw her while ascending. She noticed the bear walking away at a distance. Sayali could now feel her heaving chest. With an impassive face, the adivasi comrade complained, 'What's this, comrade? You should tell us when you go.' Sayali merely smiled weakly.

What do the adivasi comrades think of their city comrades? Both are working in the same stream, although at different locations. They are our friends. Comrades. But for all that, they are not keen to close distances in a hurry. That's understandable. You can't develop instant closeness with a city dweller who finds the difficulties of jungle living heavy. How then, against a far more difficult background in 1982, did those seven teams of seven each manage to draw so close to the locals of Bastar? And from there on, how did the party create bonds with the natives of such a large tract of land? Starting from using the Gondi language to highlighting the inspiring events in adivasi history, the party did phenomenal work! Getting connected to a people means getting connected to their circumstances. Her jungle experience made Sayali realize how small her own contribution was in comparison to the contribution made by so many of these people. She also realized the importance of shouldering her responsibility, however small it may be.

There was plenty for her to do in the jungles: making butts

for guns, writing texts for pamphlets, listening to the news on the radio and writing down the important points in a notice format every day, standing on sentry duty, getting involved in the cooking, and keeping up with the reading. There's much talk about finding a balance between theory and practice; how this balance is found, she understood better in the jungles. She found answers to some of her questions without even trying. In this context, one can talk about a small book that she read. The title of the book was *How to Become a True Communist*. The author was some member of the Chinese Communist Party, an early associate of Mao. He later had to face action during the Cultural Revolution. A few years later, a re-assessment was made, and all charges against him were withdrawn. Many questions generally arise with regard to the party, the role of the party, and the activities of the party. These questions are raised mainly by the outsider, but as a comrade you are required to undertake the responsibility of responding to these questions some time or the other. You have to confront them. There are times when we have our own questions. Sayali found a number of answers in this book. One has to persistently try to move closer to the communist ideals. Also, one should not paint the entire party black because of members who cannot move closer to these ideals, or those who do not try to do so. On the contrary, efforts should be made to make such comrades aware of the need to convert themselves. If need be, internal action could be instituted against them. These were the issues that Sayali found in the book.

Sayali read this book while she was in the jungles. And then she came out. The copy of the book, however, is still inside. It rests in a pit, along with some other books and a few other effects, neatly wrapped in a piece of plastic. She had liked some of the points in the book very much. She hadn't marked every point that she liked, but she had put a small dash against some of them. She had wanted to jot them down at some later time. But because of the hurry in which they had to leave, she hadn't been able to copy all of them. She had been able to note down some on a piece of paper. If ever an occasion arose for her to conduct a class somewhere, she could use these reference points. The points she noted down are given below. Besides, the pit in which the book currently rests, made the book available for the purpose of this novel for about twenty minutes or so. The pit was critically useful in helping recognize the dashes that Sayali had made in the book. The tree of the novel has also been planted in a pit. The pit of the novel sent a recommendation to the pit where the book was buried, and that is how the points marked by Sayali came to be known. The six points jotted down by Sayali and the four points that she had marked, but could not jot down are given below:

- We communists are the vanguards of revolution in modern history. The responsibility of changing the society and the world lies on us, and we are the main power that is going to bring about this change… We communists shape ourselves by fighting against reactionary forces in every aspect of life and by cultivating ourselves.
- For bringing about a change in oneself, and for becoming a better revolutionary through self-cultivating and developing oneself, it is absolutely necessary for the communist never to stay away from revolutionary programmes, and to take an active part in them. Alongside, while staying involved in such activities, it is imperative for us to keep striving and teaching ourselves and forever continuing to study. Progress will not be possible without such efforts.

- Confucius says, 'At fifteen, I was bent on study; at twenty, I began thinking independently; at forty, doubts ceased; at fifty, I understood the laws of Heaven; at sixty, my ears obeyed me and I could hear the voice of truth; now, at seventy, I can act according to my inner will, and never swerve from right.' This philosopher of feudal times tells us here of the process through which he shaped himself. He says here that we are not born as saints.
- There are many good members of the party who have arrived from the working class, and have no deep knowledge of the principles of Marxism–Leninism. If they are asked in an examination to give quotations from the Marxist–Leninist books, they will not be able to do as well as some others. But if these party members are told about these principles in a language that they can understand, they are generally seen to take a more passionate interest in these principles than members who come from the intellectual class. They also show a better understanding of these principles. For example, some party members find it difficult to understand the part in *Das Kapital* which discusses the concept of surplus value, but members belonging to the working class don't find it difficult at all. How the capitalists calculate labour and working hours, how they exploit and subjugate the workers in their lust for profit, this the workers know well through the production process and through their struggles against the capitalists. That is why, generally, members from the working class understand Marx's theory of surplus value in greater depth than do members of other classes.
- What is the meaning of ideological self-cultivation? Its basic meaning, in my opinion is: every party member fighting against non-proletarian ideologies with the help

of proletarian ideologies; using the communist worldview; defeating the individualism inside them by accepting the primacy of the interests of the proletarian class, the people and the party.

- The goals of communism are so great and so difficult to achieve that some social reformers even now doubt whether these goals are attainable at all. These people refuse to believe that the human race can develop itself and transform itself into a communist being of the highest class under the leadership of the proletariat and the party, or that all the obstacles that arise in the process of bringing about a revolution may be defeated. For one, they cannot anticipate the nature of the obstacles; and then, when the obstacles crop up, they fall into disappointment and despair. A number of members begin to vacillate and abandon the party. We communists have to inculcate in ourselves a courageous viewpoint and a revolutionary determination. For the realization of the goals of communism, every party member is required to work with joy and with seriousness. This is the greatest and the most difficult goal to achieve in all of human history.
- Comrade Mao Tse-tung has said, 'At no time and in no circumstances should a communist place his personal interests first; he should subordinate them to the interests of the nation and of the masses. Hence, selfishness, slackness, corruption, seeking the limelight, and so on, are most contemptible, while selflessness, working with all one's energy, whole-hearted devotion to public duty, and quiet hard work will command respect.'
- Whatever problem arises at whichever time, party members must always give first priority to the overall interest of the party and place their own personal affairs and interest in

the second place. The principle that the party is supreme should influence every thought and every action of every party member. As per this principle, all party members, in their thoughts and actions, should consider party interest as their own interest. Whenever there seems to be a conflict between party interest and self-interest, self-interest should be sacrificed without the slightest hesitation or vacillation. The unhesitating readiness to sacrifice self-interest, and if the occasion demands, sacrifice of one's life for the sake of the party, the proletariat, the country, and the liberation of all humanity, this is called 'party spirit', 'party consciousness', or 'organization consciousness'. This is the supreme manifestation of communist ethics, of the principled nature of the proletarian party, and of the purest form of proletarian consciousness.

– For us communists, there is nothing more meaningless and unjustifiable than sacrificing the good of all for the benefit of any individual or a handful of people. The most valuable and just thing is sacrificing one's all for the sake of the party, for the proletariat, for the nation and for the liberation of all humanity, for the development of the society, and for the supreme interest of the vast majority of the people. It is a fact that countless members of the communist party have unhesitatingly embraced death. It is natural for most communists to sacrifice their lives, if the need arises, for the sake of their goal and for justice. This feeling has arrived not out of any revolutionary insanity or the desire for publicity, but from a scientific understanding of social development and a deep political consciousness. The class-ridden society has no morality that can compare with this high communist morality. The concept of universal morality that goes beyond class is humbug. On the contrary, it is a morality that forwards the interest of a handful of exploiters. The concept of this kind of morality is always idealistic. We communists alone create our morality based on historical materialism, and we use it for the protection of the interests of the proletariat and to wage a war of liberation for all of humanity.

– Our comrades should understand that a member, whether a leader or a hero, can look after only a part of the work of the communist movement, can undertake only a part of the responsibility. The combined effort of lakhs of people is required for a very long period of time for realizing the communist ideal. It is not work that can be handled by any single individual. Even great people like Marx, Engels, Lenin and Stalin could manage to do only a small part of the work necessary for realizing the communist ideal. We, ordinary communists, too are doing our share of the work for the communist ideal, undertaking a part of the responsibility. Quite naturally, when compared with Marx, Engels, Lenin or Stalin, our share is considerably less. Whether it is big or small, it is a share of the work for this noble ideal, and therefore, we can say that if we do the work that has fallen upon us, we have done our duty.

Sayali liked the example of Confucius. She liked the idea of cultivating oneself. But he says he went on cultivating himself till the age of seventy, and then did what his heart felt like doing. We won't be able to do anything if we follow his example. Who can start a revolution at seventy? All the strength to fight would be depleted by then. So, does it mean that a person does nothing during his/her youth? And being able to live according to one's desire, how long does one wait for it? So much better, therefore, to go on cultivating oneself, that should be plenty.

Sayali loves reading this kind of stuff. Stuff that she can put to use in her everyday life. Stuff that she can mull over. Otherwise...

Some time back she had gone to listen to a speech. The professor was talking something heavy about brahminical and non-brahminical traditions, giving all kinds of references across thousands of years of Indian history. But what one was to do with all that information, Sayali couldn't fathom till the very end. The professor's lecture was based upon something that Comrade Sharad Patil had said, and that was the reason why she had gone. When she had first heard about Patil, she had been astounded at how the man could have put in so much of study: Vedas-Sanskrit-Ramayana-Mahabharat-Sita-farming! What a head the man had! Otherwise, she had no connection with him. There were some acquaintances of hers who had met him. But she herself had never had the occasion to listen to his lectures. However, she had heard so much about him that she had tried to read his book *Daas-Shudraanchi Gulamgiri* (Das–Shudra Slavery), but she had found the reading too heavy, and had dropped it after just a few pages. There would be study camps organized on his writings, and those she would attend. In fact, there was going to be a camp organized by him in the city, but then he passed away and the programme got cancelled. Sayali would otherwise have got the opportunity to listen to him live. Actually, she had heard Shridhar talk about his writings once. Shridhar had said that the class-struggle aspect of Marxism could not be applied in toto to Indian conditions because the caste-system in India is quite unique. Unique means one of its kind, he had told her when asked. But she had already known about many of the things he was talking about. In the study-group sessions or in interactions with other comrades, this point would be discussed. The party had taken cognisance of it too. So... there were no class divisions in India before the British arrived, Shridhar was saying. Sharad Patil had done noteworthy work in the area of what Gramsci had called the problem of cultural hegemony, Shridhar had said, she remembers distinctly, among a lot of other things. She knew about the Italian thinker Antonio Gramsci and so on. In her study sessions she had got to know that Gramsci believed that the exploited classes should be represented by the organic intellectuals who had emerged from their own milieu, etc. And then, Shridhar had suddenly gone and lost himself in the clouds, the kinds of things he was talking about! She hadn't learnt anything from him that would be useful to her thoughts. Later, some people had organized a meeting to pay tributes to Sharad Patil, for which she had gone. But even there, there was nobody who had talked much about his writings. A large number of them had narrated anecdotes about his nature; some had tried to show how close they had been to him; some had even made a little fun of him. There were others, as always, who had wanted to display their own superior knowledge and had spoken in a belittling manner. But nothing they said could throw light on his thoughts. However, from that meeting and from whatever she had heard from others earlier, Sayali had learnt enough to respect the man. All this had nothing whatsoever to do with the party, of course. It's just that the topic emerged from the book she had read in the jungles. For the rest, Sharad Patil had walked out of the Communist Party of India-Marxist in 1978 and established the 'Satyashodhak Communist Party' in Dhule based upon Marxism–Phule–Ambedkarism. And then he mainly got to be talked about for the work he had done relating to Indian history. That was how Sayali had heard of him too. But after her visit to the jungles, she didn't much care for all this raking up of thousands of years of history. She had got to know a little bit about it, and that would be enough.

And when you actually get into the middle of a jungle that is engaged in a war, there is no question of worrying about what teak or saag was known as a thousand years ago – teak, saagwan or shaak or sal or saal or whatever. Teak is one kind of tree, straight, that's it. It has quite a litter of leaves under it. They grow straight up, these trees. It's because of this attitude, really, that Sayali would have learnt a great deal. Learnt means, not about trees. She just went on introspecting and learning. As for trees, there, in the jungle, whether they are teak or sal, they looked the same to her. There were plenty of both kinds there. In fact, they all looked like teak to her, tall trees with broad leaves. So, it wasn't about trees that she learnt, but she did learn other things.

See, with her, it's like this. She learns whatever she can learn to converse easily with whoever she is talking with. Like, if the party line is faulty, if you understand it straight, then you can get on with criticism and self-criticism. Now, she believes that the party is taking proper cognisance of the caste issue. There has been this accusation against the left parties of ignoring the caste question, but the sole exception to this has been the Communist Party of India (Maoist). Hence, she believes that it is a party that constitutes a real political alternative. After being in the jungle, her understanding got strengthened. Her faith also increased. Her faith in the party and in the basic Marxist-Leninist ideology increased.

So, she did read that book. Actually, she loves reading books. She can put them into effect while talking to herself; she could also use them when talking to her fellow comrades in the jungle. Now, here in the city, if she wants to get into conversation with someone, she feels nice to have read some ground-level books. For example, she had met Smita once. Then…

❖

Tears that flow down the eyes. That was one single thing that brought about a meeting between her and Smita. Sayali's mobile rang as she was on the road. Since she knew that she would be talking for a little while, she had gone and sat on the iron bench next to the sugarcane juice stall on the footpath. There's a small temple there too, and fifty steps away is the local bus stand. She could hear the low sobbing from behind even as she was talking. However, the conversation went on for ten minutes after which she turned round. Smooth-skinned, hair done up neatly, dressed in a salwaar-suit, this girl sat with her backpack on her lap, crying with her head buried in it.

Sayali went and put her hand on her shoulder. The girl lifted her face and wiped her tears with a handkerchief. Sayali gave her a soft smile. The girl looked up but didn't smile back.

'What happened?' Sayali asked. If she was a college-going girl, she was perhaps in Std XI or XII. If she was coming back from a class, she could well be in Std IX or X.

'Nothing,' said the girl.

'What's your name?'

'Smita.'

'Want some cane juice?'

'N…no.'

'Have some. You've done quite some crying.' Sayali placed her hand on the girl's shoulder again and ordered two ten-rupee glasses of cane juice.

'Why were you crying?'

Smita was not going to let a stranger draw close so easily. For the year that she had been moving around the town, she had gained quite a bit of confidence, true, and except for an occasional bad experience, by and large people here behave well, she knew. But people instinctively learn not to trust strangers at the very first meeting. Smita had learnt it too.

'You go to college?'

'Yes, madam.'

'Which one?'

'HV Nikam College.'

'Which class? Where are you from?'

'I'll go to XII now. Gadchiroli.'

Sayali knows Gadchiroli quite well, the town as well as the way to the jungle further ahead. Although it is a small town, it's not half as bad as it has been made out to be. Sayali, of course, hadn't stayed there for any length of time, but she had liked Gadchiroli. A bit like an overgrown village. With a Gadchiroli girl sitting next to her, she slipped into the Gadchiroli mood without letting the girl know about it.

'Why were you crying, then?'

The girl had stopped crying, but she remained quiet. Sayali then asked, 'Which stream?'

'Science.'

'How do you like the college?'

'It's nice, madam.'

The answers were so brief that Sayali gave the girl a little information about herself to encourage her. She was doing law, hails from a village in this district, and a few other trivia. She told her that she had visited Gadchiroli on some NSS work. Smita had no time to get into things like the NSS and all. For Sayali too, relative to the movement she was in, NSS was chicken-feed, so, really, she wasn't much into NSS either, but she had used it as a gambit to throw Gadchiroli into the conversation. And it worked. Smita cooled down and began to talk. The cane juice would have done its bit too.

'In beginning, you know, I cannot understand English, it was big problem, and I feel very bad. Then I came and sit here and cry.'

'So, how are you with English now?'

'I now understand complete, no, madam. And my sir he give me a book, and I work full time on the book. So now I have no problem. Even now also I do lot of practice.' It was obvious that Smita had started getting the hang of English. And for understanding the other subjects too, it was important for her English to be strong.

'In beginning, you know, I think Marathi important. But now, I know, English very, means very very important. They give learning tips on e-mail also, no? I read that even. I read English newspaper even.' Then, suddenly, out of the blue, Smita said, 'May I ask something, madam?'

'Of course, and no "madam", please.'

Sayali does not need to do something special to get someone talking. Maybe it's an art she has, maybe it's a part of her nature, or maybe something else, but Smita opened up to her. Smita fished out a notebook from her backpack, opened up to a page and pointing at some lines, she asked, 'How I get perfect meaning of this word "exploit", madam?'

Sayali took the notebook from her and saw the following:

exploit – an act of bravery (in Marathi)

exploit – to use, to take unfair advantage of (in Marathi)

exploit – to put to use. Ex: We are a rich country in terms of resources. Unless we exploit them creatively, we cannot keep the dream of superpower alive.

'I cannot understand meaning even small bit,' said Smita.

Now, what does one say to this? See if you are okay with coincidence. Or you may want to call it an accident. Or if you feel like it, you may say that people get the words that somehow connect with their roots. But when Smita lands this exact word to worry about, how do you explain this?

Sayali didn't know the first meaning of the word, but she knew the other two, which she explained to the girl, 'The word is used for both the meanings. If you want to use something, you use the word "exploit", or if someone is squeezing someone else to get some unfair advantage, you again use "exploit". But the first given meaning, a brave act, I too didn't know that. Where did you get this sentence?'

'It came in the paper, then, na! The Prime Minister made speech. It was that news.'

'There it means using the natural resources. And… okay, listen. This cane juice stall here. If there's a boy working here, and if he is made to work far more than he is paid for, then it is the second meaning, taking unfair advantage of someone. Where did you get the first meaning?'

'Which one?'

'Act of bravery.'

'Saw in dictionary. Same I wrote here.'

Sayali had never come across this use of the word. She said, 'Look up the dictionary again. Why don't you ask your sir?'

'Sir gone on leave, na. One week gone.'

'All right.' Sayali returned her notebook. 'Where do you live?'

'We have hostel, na. Seven kilometres from this side. I come by bus.'

'How do you like it here now?'

Smita didn't tell her everything, but she said, 'In beginning lot of tainshun. But now I like it. I come from Gadchiroli naa, so everybody ask, you Naxalite? Lot of peopal ask that in beginning. So, that bore me. But lot of peopal help me also. I also have lot of friends, so now I don't get bore.'

Sayali sat and listened. From the way she talked, Smita appeared to be a confident person, so she couldn't have been crying only on account of English. And if she keeps trying the way she is, her English will improve. Smita asked Sayali whether she was on Facebook. Sayali told her that she would send her a request. This, of course, she didn't do, and she didn't give her mobile number either. No point in taking risks. This contact could be riskier for Smita than for Sayali.

It wasn't as if Smita would open her heart at this first meeting. And Sayali too didn't want to put her under the pressure of having to talk. But it would be nice if she could get some hint on what Smita thought about the movement. So, Sayali tried to ask about it. Smita responded, 'Naxalites maybe did good thing in starting. But now it don't feel right. What I think, madam, that peopal have problem. The police give problem, yes, but now I go to home only one time in every year. Otherwise, na, madam. Naxalites come and tell me to join party. I don't like this. So I don't go home more than one time. They want new new people in party, na.' Smita didn't talk much more on the subject. Whatever she said, Sayali heard out. Smita has eyes dark as coal, and there is no fear in them. It would be difficult to believe that the girl who is talking now is the same girl who was crying a while earlier. She had clammed her lips tight when she was crying. Now, as she talks, her sparkling teeth look so pretty.

As they were talking, Smita's mobile rang. It was her friend. She informed her when she would return to the hostel and cut the call. She had started feeling so much lighter at heart talking with Sayali. Otherwise, there aren't many occasions for lightening her heart. Once in a while she sees Hollywood movies on her room partner's mobile, that's big entertainment. The technology there is so fantastic, na. So, Smita loves watching those movies. Otherwise, she hasn't gone to the theatre to watch a movie or anything since the time she has arrived. She had tried once to get into a mall to see something, but the security person had blocked her way. But that's another issue. Smita and Sayali would have sat chatting together for about forty-five minutes. Sayali felt nice too. She likes sitting and chatting with people.

While in the jungles, Sayali had read a novel called Raago dealing with a girl about Smita's age. It was a novel, written by a male comrade called Saadhana. She had read the Hindi translation of the original Telugu novel. Raago:

She was as pretty as the untouched mahua flowers fallen off the tree early in the morning.

Far away, deep inside Gadchiroli, a small village named Juvvi. The village was surrounded by jungle on all sides. The jungle is not as dense now as it used to be during the times of their ancestors, but it is quite dense, all the same, and it holds within its insides this village called Juvvi. There is no proper road leading up to or leading out of the village. In fact, till a few years back, there was nothing more than a couple of jungle tracks in and out of the village. These two jungle tracks connected the villagers to the rest of the world. One track led to a village called Nagulwai, and it had turned quite powdery with consistent use. The other track skirted along a spring to the village. The priest of the village Kattejhari ten kilometres away was quite famous in the villages of those parts. There was track enough for a bullock cart to carry a dying person up to the priest's village. That track would go on further to connect with a rough road that went up to Allapalli via Bhamragadh. That rough road then goes further and loses itself into the tar road that connects Chandrapur to Sironcha. Little by little, the people of Juvvi had got accustomed to go up to the tar road. Initially, the people there wouldn't stir out of their village; they would take a companion if they had to go to the market.

A number of things keep changing here, some remain the same. Some of the rough roads remained as they were, some improved. The road going towards Juvvi improved some bit, but nothing else did. Raago belonged to this place, then. The people at home wanted her to marry a boy she did not want to marry, so she ran away from home and took shelter in the house of the person she wanted to marry. This man, however, was already married, but Raago still had hopes. However, the man could not find the strength to stand up for her, and she left his house and went into the forest. As she wandered in the forest, she ran into one of the Maoist squads and joined them. Girijakka there understood her plight, and so did the commander of the squad. Little by little, she got acquainted with the other comrades too. When you are walking through dense, dark, black jungles, these acquaintances are bound to happen anyway. So dark that if you are moving in a single file, you don't see who is walking in front of you. In this darkness you need the faith that the person walking in front is on the right track. That faith arrived as Raago stayed on with the squad. A gun too arrived in her hand. Starting from sentry duty onwards, she began learning things. As they moved from village to village, there would be actual confrontations with the police, but Raago would not back off. Such, then, is her story. Towards the end of the story, she is sent as a deputy to another squad. This new responsibility too she accepts with a joyful red salute. Raago means a parrot, trapped in a cage. As

Sayali read the novel, she felt the urge to get the parrot out of the cage, to liberate her.

Sayali had met many girls like Raago when she was inside. She hadn't had the opportunity to get into a chat with most of them. If she had gone on to spend the rest of her life there, maybe there would have been chats; but what conversations could one get into in barely four to six months? She too had once tried the round, red badge with the letters PGA – People's Guerrilla Army – imprinted upon it on her shirt front. It carried a logo of a sickle, a chopper and a Kalashnikov intertwined to form a pattern. Not everybody had this badge. Somebody had stuck it to the chest as if for preserving. A good distraction, anyway. There is of course all this jungle on all sides to call our own. One doesn't even fear death. But that's not the state of a comrade who has come from outside. The pull of the jungle gets grounded in a few days. The ground is rough, stony, littered with leaves and vines. Yet, it's important that the feet are firmly planted on the ground; for walking, for sitting, for sleeping – feet always on the ground. What the actual war of revolution in the jungles taught her, Sayali would never have learnt outside. She has never suffered the pain that the people here suffer. But after observing this pain, she began to understand a little bit about what attaching oneself to the masses means. She also understood that the work is a great deal more difficult than what she had expected it to be. Work in the city is quite different, but here, living is painful and dying is painful too.

But this experience only increased her faith in the party, as it did with Raago. The party structure spreads right from Raago to somewhere there in Delhi. It's this structure that keeps hopes alive, she's quite sure. She's been to Delhi too once. A workshop dealing with law had been arranged there, and she had been instructed to attend. There were to be some lectures on human rights, and there would be special focus on the provisions therein that could be put to use for state prisoners. She was in Delhi for about a fortnight. The workshop was somewhere in Chanakyapuri, and her staying arrangements were at the Jawaharlal Nehru University (JNU) hostel. She had great fun there. The students there had no idea about inner details of her visit to the forest and all that, but since there was a matching of thoughts, she could join their group to participate in the discussions. The spot where these students gathered together had a wall behind it made of red bricks. The bricks give it a very distinctive look. Some of those students were in the human rights workshop too. Sayali got to understand what exactly the students here felt. For example, some of them had open sexual relations. Some there believed that if there is free sex, then first the family and later private property will automatically melt away too. Sayali merely laughed at this notion. A friend of hers from the movement, a comrade named Kamini is studying there. She's doing her PhD in Political Science. Also does plays. They have a big group there. She had also staged a single-character play called Jenny. All this Sayali got to know from talking to her. Her parents have been party sympathizers of long standing. Delhi people. Her father writes a column for an English weekly. They also have their own publishing house that brings out English books. Her mother runs an NGO. They have their own house in Delhi. Sayali went around Delhi a little bit with Kamini: Red Fort, India Gate, Jantar Mantar, and such other places. India Gate looks so beautiful when it turns dark; the flood lights on those big arches look so beautiful. A woman was selling... you know, those tiny cube things with English letters on them... that you can string together to make a bracelet of your name? Well, she was selling that. Sayali got one done with her name. It's not as if one has to go to Delhi for it, you get it everywhere these days. But she just happened to see it and felt like getting one done, so she went and did it. There is always somebody or the other sitting on a fast at Jantar Mantar. When Sayali went there, there was this person named Suryavanshi from Latur sitting there. For months now he has been coming and sitting there every day. He has some land issue. Overgrown beard, Gandhi cap on head, and dressed in a loose kurta and pajama, he had pasted a poster on the compound wall that read: *When you ask for justice, they want bribes. They sell injustice in the name of justice.* The poster was signed off with his name and the name of his town. When Sayali saw the name of the town, she felt like enquiring and went over to him. He immediately pulled out a bundle of papers from his bag and began giving her all the details. He told her about who had killed whom and went on elaborating on the theme. Sayali, however, had no time to stand listening to him. Kamini laughed and pulled her away from there. This was an everyday affair there. There were some others too sitting with their own posters.

Sayali liked some of the many discussions that took place at JNU, but her overall opinion was that they were really not well informed enough about the ground-level realities of the issues they discussed. She had an understanding of a lot of the topics that were discussed. They would keep discussing even the so called '-isms' of some thinker of a self-proclaimed Maoist group in America. This '-ism', that '-ism', this '-ite', that '-ite', this thought, that thought. There would be passionate discussions, big articles would be written. How caste questions can be seen from the viewpoint of class, the character of the present ruling class, adivasi history, subaltern politics, many such subjects would come up for discussion. There is no dearth of subjects, is there? They had a website named 'Radical Red'. When a senior person was arrested on the charge of being a member of the politburo of the Maoist Party, the students had campaigned for his release, claiming that there was not enough evidence against him to warrant an arrest. Then there was this issue that had flared up at the Maruti Suzuki factory at Manesar in Haryana next door. The workers had mounted a big campaign over the issue of contractual workers, and a manager had been killed as a result. Hundreds of workers had been put in jail. Members of the group had written ten articles discussing the damage caused by trade unionism in India, how revolution was losing its direction, and so on. No dearth of subjects, is there? Those articles were later compiled into a book. Kamini had written a review of the book in the *Economic and Political Weekly*.

These students too were applying so much of thought and showing such commitment to the movement. That wasn't a small thing, thought Sayali. She thought that if they were made aware of the ground realities, they would come down to the ground. It's a good thing, isn't it, that they have the facilities to do intellectual work, and they use these to do some thinking on the movement. Finally, if the movement inside the jungles does not have this kind of outside base, then the movement will snap away from the rest of society all the more easily. That is why it is important that these people keep their discussions going, she was convinced. This was also the time when she had her first taste of wine. The tour also brought about an increase in her Facebook friends. Not much else, otherwise. For the rest, Delhi is the capital of India, all things considered.

So, this is how it is about Sayali. It was because of the

movement that her ambit suddenly expanded from Palli to Dilli. She got to know so many people; some friendships drifted away, but a number of new ones arrived. Even if we were to take the example of these Delhi students, there are so many people. She got to know a number of young journalists from Delhi and Mumbai who were attracted towards the dalit movement, Left movement, and such like. But after all this, she feels lonely sometimes. Why should it be so? Well, there could be plenty of reasons. One big reason, she has realized lately, is that Ajay is still in jail. She can't forget the times she has spent with him. And, these days, he too has been sending her sentimental poems through his letters, so she's begun missing him a little more. The lawyers were saying the other day that he should be out on bail next month, so waiting that long is no problem, really. If the event had flared up in the newspapers, things wouldn't have been so easy. Of course, this month can well extend to another two or three months, but the case is weak, the lawyers say, because the police do not have sufficient evidence. Sayali has had so much of experience with Ajay that this prolonged separation has intensified her need for him. It's obvious from the letters that his need for her is of the same intensity. It's evident from the revolutionary greetings and stuff he keeps sending her through letters-poems.

Here's a letter that she received last week:

Dear Sayali,

This vehement concern for the people
And this distanced companionship of ours
Why did this outrage happen?
Why did this cinder bloom?
These questions have now turned hollow

Since the songs of revolution sprang from your lips.
Revolutionary greetings for the new year.

Yours,

Ajay

1 January 2015

There have been many such letters in the past few months. Amidst all this, Sayali has to prepare for her law course. But that goes along. College studies happen along. The teachers in her college have given her much support. Since she'd gone underground for some time, two consecutive years of her course had got lost; but on returning, she had been allowed to resume from where she had left off. This is no small favour. If she has to work in the city, this course is bound to be of use.

Although we have said that the fun in Sayali's life hasn't reduced in spite of Ajay not being there, there are times when she feels low, naturally. Not as low as Smita does, let's say, but even so. She remembers his biceps, his back, his smiling face, and plenty else. When he comes out, they will have to find him a job. He's done his MA in English, so he won't study any further, but if he has to work in the city, some independent source of money will have to be organized.

Looking at the state of the urban work of the movement, Sayali wonders when a revolution will happen in India. With the situation being so bad, why is a revolution not happening? At the same time, whenever she is in conversation with a new comrade, she always advises the person to think about earning a living. Matter of fact, this doesn't quite match with the advice that comes from the party. What is the point in telling a comrade who is just joining to look for job opportunities too? But she still feels that if the person wants to step out of the movement at any time, there should be something in hand, right? It's different for those who already have something in hand. But it shouldn't happen that comrades coming from truly impoverished backgrounds should have nothing to fall back upon; some care needs to be taken in this regard. Because all kinds of other obstacles can crop up – and increase the confusion. An instance of this kind had happened a few months back. There is this comrade who belongs to the Matang community, and he decided to marry another comrade who belongs to the Mahar community. Their affair had been going on for two years. But if her family had been told the name of the boy's community, they would certainly have shot down the proposal. They could have got married without telling anyone, but the boy had no resources for a decent earning. So, when the girl informed the people at home everything about the boy but his community, they shot it down anyway. By sheer coincidence, or whatever, it was through Sayali's assistance that in about three months' time, the boy got a job as a helper, so the preparations for marriage have begun. The girl's family still doesn't know about the boy's community. Why explode another bomb right now? The two have decided to reveal things bit by bit.

Sayali and Ajay had not felt the need yet for getting into a documented, legalized marriage. But now, when he comes out and the need arises, they will have to go through it. They too would have run into caste difficulties. Ajay is a Maratha-Kunbi. But as it has happened, since the time he has gone to jail, his people have begun seeing a daughter-in-law in Sayali. Besides, with the background that he now has, what chance has he of getting a good match? In comparison, what is currently going on is good enough, is how his family members have worked it out. It's not as if Sayali is not aware of all these calculations. In any case, there is time enough for all that. What's the time now?

It is half hour past midnight. Quite late.

Sayali, why are you up so late, aren't you sleepy?

'I'm thinking.'

What are you thinking about?

'Just generally.'

Yes, but what generally?

'There are many thoughts that pass through the head. I'm thinking of buying a pair of jeans, so I'm wondering what jeans to buy. When exactly is Ajay going to get bail? Then I'll have to give up this room, and we'll have to look for a new one. Where all can Human Rights be used? What exact role will I be playing in all this?'

But it's quite late now, please go to sleep.

'Yes, okay. But where's my mobile?' She begins looking for her mobile. The other two girls in the room are fast asleep. The lights are off, but Sayali is awake in the dark. Her hair had been left loose. She gives it a twist and clasps it in a clip. She has never worn a string of flowers in her hair, not sayali flowers, not any other. She simply doesn't like wearing flowers in her hair. After putting her hair in a clip she visits the toilet. Her mobile... ah, there, it is under the pillow. It's turned very cold. Her sweater lies on the chair there, moss green. It's quite pretty. Sayali puts on her sweater and goes to sleep. Let her sleep. It's quite late in the night, let her sleep. Half past twelve. The screen on her mobile shows that the next day has arrived. So be it. Let her sleep now. Good night.

Lattakka

How you write my story now, huh? Ha ha ha ha! I wunly know Gondi, you wunly know Marathi, my Hindi not good, your Hindi not good also. So, how we do? I wunly tell you, and you wunly, mmm…

I from that village, my man also from that village. My name Lattakka. I see this jeep, this building fust time. There in village? When sound of jeep come there, na, that time police come. So, police. Police come. Jeep come mean police come. It like this now.

Look, govmen say, make road. For development. But why we let road come in our village? Not let. Jeep will come on road. Jeep mean police. So you want to make road for police, how this will do, Dada? Now you tell, this will do? To my brother, this police, mmm…this big…rope, so…

They hang my brother by this big rope, put him backside of jeep on ground and run jeep fast. So, some time tree, some time big…mmm…stone, so like this they kill my brother. He die there like this. So, why we want road come, huh?

Now, seven year I keep in jail, why? My man also keep in jail. So many peepal keep in jail, why?

I now here, live here. Yes. My man work like guard in that building, like sikoorty guard.

We not return back to village now.

Peepal ask, why you help dada peepal. See, they help to us,

so for that reason we help to them. Who help to us in good time, what we do with them? Who help us in bad time, we can do help to them, na? If you do help to us in bad time, I can take you as brother, na? Who help us in good time, we cannot remember also.

Dada peepal come to our village. I see them from chil' time. Then going with them. Eating. They eating with us. Then telling. Didi peepal telling, you woman peepal also stand by side of man. Man peepal go out and talk other woman, why you no talk to other man? Why like this? Didi peepal say like this. Then every peepal think. Then we will support them.

Then Dada peepal tell us pick up gun. So we can have to pick up, na? If front person have gun, so we also can have gun. If Dada peepal give us gun, how it is bad? No anything bad in this. Now, if amboos happen, so then kill some police peepal.

Who will fire bullet fust, he will live; who will no fire, he will die, it happen like this way.

Ten peepal sitting in jeep, they go up one singal time with one bum. Peepal should to be together. Then they go up together. In jeep will always happen like this. Now look, for to stay living you can have to stay together, and peepal die also together.

Today also to die, tomorrow also to die. We all die, but our chillun at least live then, so we can have to die for our chillun. Dada, you write.

[*Note: Lattakka's Hindi perhaps cannot find voice in English translation. Her Hindi could somehow become part of the Marathi novel, but not the English version. The author assumed that most of those who read Marathi can more or less understand Lattakka's Hindi, but one cannot assume this in the case of most of those who prefer English for whatever reason. However, the effort here has been to bend English so that it can carry the sense of Lattaka's original Hindi expression. - Author*]

A pit of sorrow beyond all imagination
Ninety feet deep
On the confluence of three rivers
There are red ants there
As you find them in Konkan too
Here too at the other end of Maharashtra
There on the confluence of the long and wide flowing rivers
That pit in the river
Deep beyond measure

Lattakka's grief is deeper than this pit. Words cannot plumb that depth, you may say. Or you may say, this was how Lattakka's story had to be written. It is just this size, and just this. There are tears in Lattakka's eyes, always. Dried up. And here sits the author, writing, drying the ink on paper. There are red ants in the author's village. They have a distinctive way of making their nests. They keep tucking leaves, one into another, and make a nest the size of a palm. There are red ants here too. You can make chutney out of these ants, nice and sour.

The author's village is at one end of Maharashtra. On the sea shore. The rivers in the author's village would be mere rivulets compared to such big rivers at this other end of the geographical region. Rivers so wide. Lattakka's sorrow couldn't turn into ink. There are some things about which, instead of writing, it is better to accept defeat. Lattakka's sorrow won, the author lost, you may say. Or you may say, the author has conceded his cultural death, and as a memorial of this death, he has not written Lattakka's story. A stone has been erected somewhere; in remembrance of this death on account of Lattakka's unwritten story. So, what's the name of this stone? Let's say, it's Kalbanda.

So, this stone – Kalbanda – said, 'Who named this river the Pranhita, the giver of life? Must have done so by looking at the water. Water means life. There are so many details in geography on vanished rivers; why, then, are there no details on secret rivers? Why are there no details on these secret rivers either in geography or in history, or any place else? One such secret river has been flowing from very early times, perhaps; its name is the Prangheta, the taker of life. It flows with blood. But how much of blood can you convert into water? Enough to fill up an entire river? That's why, in Lattakka's eyes too there's a redness. But the colour of water in her eyes is more, which means that the river in her eyes flows quite a bit.' It's good the stone does not know any language. If it did, it would say a lot more of this. Could you bear it?

Rani

The boy is in the police and the posting is in a Gadchiroli village, so there will be problem of security, I knew this. I mean, pappa also said this, and sir also said this. But it is riskier than what I had thought. Have to sit inside the house day after day. There's not much tension, that way, but you get bored sitting at home all day, na? It's now seven months since this has been going on with me.

I did BA, then did BEd too. So then I should go out and do some job, anything wrong in thinking this? But no. Sir says, shouldn't get into a job in such a hurry. Well, maybe he's right. If wife goes to work, who will look after the children? We don't have kids now, but we will have them someday, na?

Now, how do I say it...but let me say it. The road from here to Chandrapur, hell cannot have a road worse than this. If you look at the distance, it is barely a hundred and twenty-five kilometres. But the time it takes by a vehicle is three hours. Oh, mother...you just don't know whether you are travelling on a road or on what. But the big city near this village is Chandrapur. You go to Gadchiroli, and it takes the same time. But what would you do going there? No theatre there, no nothing. That way, theatre is of no use. What we wanted was a hospital. We would go to Chandrapur for checking. Routine checking happens, na? I was pregnant. Look, this was six months ago.

As a husband, sir is nice. No problem regarding that. But this job itself is bad. Police job. He is a police inspector. We got married on 30 January. I came over three months after that. The police deployment here is very strict. The village is full of Bengali people. Earlier I was very surprised. The very first day I reached, sir brought home Bengali sweets. Surprise! I loved it. Sir said, your name is Rani, queen, and I shall keep you like a queen. He really does keep me in great comfort. There's a Bengali chap who comes and does the cooking. A woman comes to do the dishes and clothes. So I have no household work at all. Top class food all ready to eat. I just get awfully bored. Our quarter is in the police station premises. I am used to living in quarters right from childhood. My pappa's posting was in Hatkanangale, and we lived in quarters there too. Same here. The officers' quarters and the quarters of other workers were different there in Hatkanangale. Here too, the officers have different quarters, and all those SRP and others have their quarters on the side there. There are some girls among them, but I haven't ever spoken to them, you know. It's not as if there's any bar on officers' wives meeting the other women, but that's the system they've got into, you may say. It was the same at Hatkanangale, but there you had the quarters of the City Council authorities, so there were plenty of officers, and so their wives would always find people to talk to. There are just two other officers here, both unmarried yet. One of them has got engaged, sir said yesterday; but by the time his wife comes, we will get transferred. In the next three-four months, he said, the transfer order will come. Biding time here till then, it's boring stuff.

After our marriage we had gone on a tour of Kerala. I spent some time at my parents' place after coming back. Then sir brought me over here. Then I got to know that I was carrying, so then we would go for checking to Chandrapur. The road to Chandrapur was so bad that don't even ask. Continuous jolts. Never seen so many and such huge potholes in my life. Nature here is good, though. I like it. But where do you get the chance to step out? Even here, that wall on the right side of the camp there, I haven't even been there for the past three months now. They are making a small temple there. I haven't gone there either. Even to the weekly market out there I've gone exactly twice. But that day sir told me not to go because it is risky. He's right, too. Something happens to your life, and there'll be news on the TV, pointlessly. There's the TV, though, as time-pass. There's a dish on top, so you can see all the serials. And I love music, so I keep the channel on all the time. I watch *Mrs Annapurna* for an hour in the afternoon. The kitchen is with me on Sunday. Then I cook fish or chicken or some such stuff. Some of my time goes in checking out Facebook and WhatsApp. I sit for a little while at the door in the evening. You can see one of the camp walls a hundred feet away, the sentry's place there is always unoccupied. At all other posts, there's always a gun-toting sentry constantly looking out. Here in front, though, there is no one. It's all dense there with vines. There's a big peepul tree on the other side of the wall. The women who come and do the dishes and clothes sit there on the steps during their spare time. Once sir and I sat there near the vines all night, watching the deer. Felt like we were in a dream. It was a starry night, and a lot of deer had assembled behind there on the meadows. It was so romantic. Nature here is so grand, and that's some entertainment. Another three-four months here, anyway.

The other night, it had got to be quite late and sir hadn't come home for dinner, so I had strolled over to the police station. It was after ages that I'd gone there, I tell you. And it's not more than a hundred steps from our house. Never have the occasion. Even that day, I phoned up sir some four-five times; he just didn't pick up. Then he picked up and said he would call back, but he didn't. So I thought I'd go and see what's going on. There was this man, sitting on his haunches. There was a woman sitting on the iron cot by the side, and a school-going girl next to her. There's a colleague of sir, who belted him and made him get up. Looked good in health, this man, only he was quite short. His hair was all messed up and dusty. He stood there with his palms joined together. Sir's voice could be heard, 'She's your daughter's age, isn't she, you bastard?' I didn't venture much farther. Then I saw sir walk over to where the man was and he stamped upon the man's toes with his boots and said, 'Where did you do it? Tell us.' There's this other sub-inspector who said, 'Asked him so many times, refuses to tell.' I couldn't understand much. That woman was not his wife, I could guess, because she appeared taller than him and didn't look like she would be his wife. Then sir instructed that other sub-inspector and he hit the man on the calves with his baton. He then shouted 'aaa aaa' and scratched his calves. Sir then slapped him on the temple. Sir has charge of the entire station. I could hear the sound of the slap right up to here. But that man just stood there rubbing his cheek and narrowing his eyes. Sir asked the other sub-inspector, 'He has admitted to doing it, no?' The other officer said yes. 'We'll take a round there tomorrow,' sir said, and looked towards me. I was in a dark spot, and there's a tubelight in the station, so sir wouldn't have seen me earlier. He then noticed me and smiled and signalled me to wait for five minutes. So I hung on a little while. Sir then asked that woman, 'What's the girl's age?' The other officer said, 'Sixteen, she says. There would be some document somewhere.' The woman couldn't understand much, very likely. I too didn't much get what was going on. Then the officer again hit that man on the leg and stamped his toes with his boot, and the man again started screaming 'aaa aaa'. He would suddenly sit down in the middle. Then I saw sir getting busy reading something, so I came back.

It was an hour after that that sir came home. Told him it was so late. He said, 'It was a 367–376 case. Have to be very careful. It's okay if a 302 case stretches, but 376 and you start getting calls from the top immediately. Once you start remand, then it stays till the case is submitted.' What do I understand of all this? I had never asked him ever. But now that the topic had come up, I asked, 'What are they? Sections or something?' And he said, 'Yes, 302 is murder. It's okay if such cases are delayed. But rape... There was this rape incident in Delhi, remember? All this has come since then.' I remembered that a college-going girl had been gang raped in a bus. So many news items had come then. It was horrible, really. Sir said, 'Since then, eighteen new clauses have been added to 376, so one has to be very exact while applying the section.' I asked if that man had committed rape. He said, 'You saw that girl there? She and her mother? He forced himself upon that girl. He is related to their family. He admits to have raped the girl twice at the same place but refuses to say where.'

Dinner got very late that night. And then something strange happened. Two days later sir said, 'That girl and that man had a consensual relationship. It had been going on for a year. But the girl is a minor, so the case becomes complicated.' Oh mother! What kinds of things keep going on? The PSI and a constable went with sir to the site of the event. Then he talked to the girl. Then again to the man. The girl had come to him on her own, the man said. Don't know what will happen next. The girl was not even sixteen; she was just fourteen, though she didn't look that young. When I had seen her earlier, it hadn't even looked as if she had been raped. Now this new information doesn't appear true either. Forget it.

So occasionally, yes, you get to see a few things. But for the rest, it is a big bore. The other day, you know, there was news of a bomb explosion in a village there in the same taluka as this, under the control of sir. There was some work going on for a small bridge. Oh god, what a mess it was there. The Naxalites had done it, that's all sir said. These days now, all policemen have to go for night patrolling once, compulsory. Then I have to stay all alone at home that night. There's the TV and then I spend some time on the internet. But in final, it gets to be very boring sitting – sitting alone at home. It's nice that he's a nice man. But I've begun to feel very frightened now. It's always risky, living here.

Nobody to talk to either. I love talking. When I meet friends, the way the time flies in chattering, one just doesn't notice. You know...I...look, it's always like this with me. Simply forgot to tell what I had begun telling. I get so easily diverted. We would go for the pregnancy test to Chandrapur, and the roads were so bad, na? Full of potholes everywhere. You keep getting jolts in the car. I was three months into my pregnancy...and I lost it. Lost the baby. All health checkings done on time, my health too perfect, and sir used to take such care too. Even I had become so careful. Then how could it happen? Know what the doctor said? This, our road. It was because of the travel on this road, the jolts I received. Injured my womb. No way I can tell you how miserable I felt. All those other pains and all, I never minded it. Women get used to it, no? But then, with something getting created inside, and then suddenly dropping out, it's bad. I keep trying to divert my mind now, but it's impossible, na? What would my baby have looked like? However many songs I hear, I can't find peace of mind. We'd also decided to name our child with 'R' as the first letter. Both our names begin with 'R'. But the child never came to us. Gone. I couldn't stop crying that day. Sir tried to pacify me. If all had gone normal, I would have delivered my baby, would have been carrying it in my arms right now. I would have... no point, let it go. I can only feel bad talking about it. Sir said, 'We'll take another chance after the transfer.' Quite right too. What's the point in bringing a life in here? Better off without it. Another three-four months for the transfer. See the time through and...

A story

A friend of the author lives in Bhusawal. Her name is Saavali. There was no reason for her to figure in this novel. But there was something that happened, so she is mentioned here. She works there as a lecturer in Political Science, and recently she got married to a lecturer of English named Saumya who lives in the same place as her. Saumya is basically a Bengali, but he speaks Marathi. It was around the time that their marriage was being settled that I had been to those parts, and that was when we had met. There is no reason to record the history of our friendship here, but whatever she got to know about me in that history, on the strength of that she handed over a few documents to me. I write, and that might have been important in her estimate. Among the papers she had given me, three contained a poem each, which I had read and returned to her. Some other papers had Marathi translations of some of Saadat Hasan Manto's shorter stories.

I asked her where she got the papers from.

She said that there was a trunk lying under an iron cot in the inner room of the house where she lived. She was doing some dusting one day, and she pulled out the trunk and found stuff in it, and also these yellowed pages.

She works at Jalgaon and lives in a rented house in Bhusawal. Why so, I asked her. She said that the landlords have shifted permanently to America, and they have been thinking of selling this house, and she and Saumya are interested in buying it.

Good. It's an old house but a nice house, no argument there. What's there to argue about? But these stories of Manto, could one of the earlier occupants of the house have translated them? I asked Saavali.

She said she had no idea. She had asked the landlord, and he was sure it wasn't one of them. So many tenants would have come and gone. But there was this person, people say, who stayed for barely eleven months. He was working as a clerk in a bank, they say. He had a lot of books, the neighbours had told her. He could be the person. There's this senior lady, a couple of houses beyond, for whose son this man had written stories in a notebook. The kid was in Std II. That led her to believe that he would have been the person who had written all those pages. Who wants to hunt around any further?

The three poems she had shown me had loneliness as their subject, connecting the loneliness with the tagar tree next to the house, about getting mixed up in the sun, about the loneliness and pits and pain, and so on. I asked her what else there was in the trunk.

She said that there was a bit of turmeric tied up in a piece of paper. Some papers carried the names of some plants and some other stuff. It was really no concern of theirs. Did I want anything out of that?

I left the poems with her, but took along the Manto translations. I should have got the poems too, but I had a feeling that she was interested in them deep inside. To be honest, I had also felt that the poems should remain there.

Saavali and Saumya got married later, as had been decided. I didn't go for the wedding. They got married at the registrar's office, and for some reason I couldn't make it for the occasion. I mailed them my best wishes later. I get so sentimental sometimes that I can hardly speak. Now, these two, they stay so far away from their homes, and in a relatively smaller town. Saavali comes from Mumbai. She was saying once that she had sort of drifted away from her people at home. But once she went away on her job, I lost track of how she was getting along. But later I got to know about their marriage, and I felt nice. And it's quite easy to understand her interest in the house. I had paid her a casual visit, long enough to have a meal there. I had had a very unusual feeling for the house then, I remember. It was out of this feeling I had felt that the poems should stay in that house. As if... the poems belong to the house, and the house belongs to the poems. The tagar tree out there, that house, and in it the poems, they fitted so well.

One of the Manto stories that I had picked up from her house stood up and demanded to be included as a part of this novel. I told her, look lady, for one, the Marathi words inside you, I don't even know which writer has written them. For another, you have come out of the pen of an author who belonged to another language. So, how can I get you in without asking him?

The story, however, refused to sit down. Now, where in the world does one go around searching for Manto? One would have to go into the clouds.

The story then started tossing her words up and said something. What she was saying quite plainly was that the words in the story were so few that there wouldn't be any problem incorporating her in my story.

It's quite true that I had picked up the stories then and brought them along because I was interested in them. But if a story starts intruding into your head in this fashion, how does one write one's own story? Like, here we are assembling our own story one word after another, and if this story keeps butting in, how will it do? But that's exactly what began happening. Finally I made some space for her. I was compelled to put in here that short story of Saadat Hasan Manto, which was translated into Marathi on yellowing paper by some lonely individual. The responsibility does not rest on me, but it is a part of the novel.

There is no need for me to say anything about Manto. He is a celebrated writer. His birth centenary was celebrated last year, and there were lots of articles on him published in national and international media, so his words have reached those people who control these media.

I give below, word for word, the English translation of the story translated into Marathi on a page by a lonely individual in that beautiful house.

COMMUNISM

Saadat Hasan Manto

He had put all his household effects into a truck and was heading towards another town. Some people blocked his way. One of them cast an eye on the stuff inside the truck and said, 'Look guys, how smartly this chap is carrying all this stuff all for himself.'

The owner of the goods said, 'Sir, all this stuff is mine.'

Some of them laughed and said, 'We know all that.'

One of them shouted, 'Let's plunder the truck. He's a rich man, goes around thieving in a truck.'

Quilt

He is thirty years of age. We have known each other since the days when vada–pav was sold for three rupees on the carts outside the Radhakrishna and Shriram theatres in Ratnagiri. The dish now sells for between twelve and fifteen rupees. We could afford just one vada–pav between the two of us, but we were such good friends that sometimes he would eat the vada and I would eat the pav, with all the chutney sticking to it; and at other times I would eat the vada and he the pav. There were other times, of course, when we would share both the items fifty-fifty. Such was our friendship. Talking of food, at 'Rasraj' in front, there you could get bhel for five rupees, and that too we would split fifty-fifty. There wasn't much that went into the bhel: some churmura, that is puffed rice, some fine sev, some green-pepper chutney and tamarind water. As we grew, the prices of these food-stuffs grew too. So did the value of money. It was just these contacts during our school/college-going days. Then, the need for money went on increasing. I began doing odd jobs in the writing line, and he started taking banking exams. His graduation marks were so low that he couldn't have sat for the officer-grade exams. So he became a clerk. He wasn't interested in the position anyway; he wanted the job for the money. The advantage of working in a bank was that the money was much better than the work involved, and there were other facilities.

It is not the intention of this chapter to give full details of his life, so no point going that way. But there are some things that are worth telling. Once he had graduated, you know, he took admission for a master's, first in Political Science, then in Marathi, History and a few other subjects in the University of Pune. I have information that he spent at least three months in each of these programmes. In none of them, however, did he stay an entire semester. But during this period he found some excuse or the other to go visit other Maharashtra universities: the North Maharashtra University at Jalgaon and the Shivaji University at Kolhapur. Not for doing any course, but on the pretext of visiting some friend's village or some such thing. And he began to believe that the campuses of all universities are terrific. Later, when he had passed the bank exams, he decided that he should be sent to a branch in one of these university campuses. Sit admiring the university buildings, the trees there, the breeze, the air, soak it all in, time should pass quite nicely. He knew, of course, that his would be a transferable job, so he wouldn't necessarily be sent to a place of his choice, but try he would, he had decided. As a result of this effort, he is currently posted in the branch at the Amravati University campus. Another thing, he's married, okay? Got married a couple of years back. Wife works at something like a company that works for mutual funds, so they are getting along nicely.

There was a reason for thinking about him in the context of telling the story. For one, our tastes are exactly alike. Our thoughts are also similar in many areas. So, it's natural to think of him. And the reason why I remembered him was that he is in the habit of making jottings, which have been of use for this chapter. I guess it was in the holidays after the Std X exams that he got into this habit. Whenever he read something, he would make jottings on it at leisure. He would copy down an occasional paragraph in his notebook, or a sentence, sometimes with his own opinion on it. Or if he suddenly thought of anything unusual, it would go into his notebook. He has always been a bigger reader than me. Also, he has been reading from earlier, since school. There was this mention of Hitler in the history books, and he was quite impressed. The history book also mentioned Hitler's autobiography *Mein Kampf*. He then got himself membership of the City Library. Twenty-five bucks a month is nothing much really. He then searched out and read the Marathi translation of *Mein Kampf*. Then a few more books on Hitler, and about the Second World War. That was when he had made jottings, and that's when it most likely began. Hitler taught Germany to fly like an eagle: was the sentence he read in all those books, and he was mightily impressed by Hitler. The earlier books he had read had also eulogized Hitler, how some of the blunders of his associates were blamed upon him, how the victorious powers – the Americans and the other Allied nations – had gone on a mission to malign the defeated foe, all of these actual sentences from the books he had dutifully entered. It was later that he ran into a Marathi translation of some book about the gas chambers. Oh shit! He had not realized these things even from his Std X history book. It was one thing to mention in passing that millions were killed, but quite another to read a few books that sounded as if one of the dead were talking. He felt so much like going back to his notes and scoring out all the stuff he had noted earlier, but does it ever happen? Does one really go back and score out earlier writings? One just wants to move forward. So, by the time he reached Std XII, his Std X thoughts had changed. But as he went on recording the changes that he was undergoing, his habit of making jottings became firmly established.

Little by little, all these jottings, and sometimes his own opinion accompanying them formed a write-up which can be called a very long note. Some of the points from his jottings were part of these notes. He also realized later that if he got to know something related to a particular text a few months or even a few years later, he should go back to the text and do it all over again. So he began doing that too. He normally wouldn't bother about sending these articles for publication anywhere, but after all that, a couple of his texts did get published as articles in a weekly. But once they were published, he didn't have any facility to publish another new article making a back-reference to the earlier written ones. So, he started a blog and started writing there. He could also put his jottings in there. There was the added facility of adding new information to an earlier text and publishing it all over again. It would remain linked to the earlier text too.

This effort of his was like journeying through a topic as a reader, and slowly weaving a text. My hunch is that he would incorporate the highs and lows of his own feelings, and also include what he felt on that topic on account of the ambient circumstances. He would, of course, record whatever appealed to him, but he was doing it, nevertheless. Reading the notes that accompany the jottings feels like reading a story sometimes. That's because he puts into it whatever he is feeling at that moment. Like in the jottings related to Hitler, I have also read a jotting that talks about a girl he liked in Std X without naming her, and talks only about how beautiful she looked in a particular dress. Later, in many of his jottings he would talk about some woman or the other. If all that was influencing him in some way or the other, so be it. What's wrong with it? Like in one of the jottings used here he has written, 'An attractive woman of about thirty-five or forty comes for a walk here dressed in a salwaar-suit. Very beautiful lady. Triangular faced, wheat-complexioned, quite tall. Does not smile.' Sometimes I suspect he merely spins out some of them; and it's not as if he puts all of them in his final text, but he does put them in the blog. Well, anyway, because of all this, it feels like you are reading a story, at least to me. He, however, considers all this slogging the same as slogging for a novel; in fact, he sometimes says that if he continues writing in this manner, it may finish off as a novel. Can't say much about that. Just that I found his habit of jotting down things interesting, and then he keeps on weaving imaginary stuff into it too. Can't elaborate much on that now, but this much I can say. You would have seen a quilt made of patches; it is made by patching together big and small pieces of cloth; it can happen that one or two of the patches are really big pieces too. Well, all these big and small patches are sewn together to make a quilt. When the whole thing is ready, it is called a quilt, and not the patches, okay? There can also be people who pre-select pieces according to a plan and patch them all together to make it look like a quilt, but that's not a true quilt then. A quilt should basically be a product that puts together pieces that would otherwise have been wasted, right? And whatever pattern has to emerge emerges by itself. It's the companionship of the pieces that is important; where else will the warmth come from? So is the companionship of the notes with the jottings. The thread with which he stitches together the pieces, that thread is important, I should think. The jottings are the big and small sized swatches, and the notes are the matching cloth that runs underneath, and together they form the quilt. If there is no thread running through it, how will it all stay together? It's brought together by a nice, sturdy needle. The thread has to be a little stout too. You see all the myriad colours, but you don't see the thread; but it's there, all the same. The value of it you realize when it turns nippy, and you want the quilt to pull over yourself. So, what's required here is collecting whatever pieces of cloth you get. The thread you have, the needle you have too. You have to supply it with warmth. The quilt is just perfect for the kind of cold you get in Amravati.

Let me add just one other thing for the information of the readers. This novel had taken me drifting once to Gadchiroli, and there I had spent a long time just sitting next to a lake. Meals were forgotten too. Quite like a crackpot, I spoke to anybody I came across; I observed things and did whatever I wanted. That was where he too met me once, suddenly. In the town. A little tired, I was sitting on a cement bench in the compound of the Municipal Council, taking in the sun. And he popped up, standing there right in front of me. There was some garbage lying some distance away, and beyond the garbage you could see a line of bungalows running deep into a lane. He said he saw me from there. Some relative of his wife lives there in one of those bungalows, and he had come visiting them. He had been to some other places too, he said. I was certainly happy to run into him like this. Looked like he was happy too, running into me. We were meeting after a very long time and that too at such a faraway place. He had now come to stay at Amravati, he said; he talked about his job. We went and had nice, syrupy tea on the other side of the road, the Konkani kind. Then, when we talked of our wanderings, there turned out to be quite a similarity between the subject of the novel and the subject he was interested in at that time. Coincidence, you would call it? Call it what you think proper, but the subject of the novel got to be dug a bit deeper. He said he had made some jottings and written a note on this subject too. Could be the hangover of having split our vada-pavs in our younger days, and those bhels too, so here we were, splitting a subject and eating it together; this time, however, it was not fifty-fifty. His share of it was much less. He had come over for the weekend, so he went away the very next day. I then wandered about here and there and went to Amravati too. He opened up his laptop and got proper printouts made of his jottings and a note and gave them over to me. I read them all.

He would post some of his jottings on Facebook occasionally. People would then give their comments on it, and it would happen sometimes that he would get a new perspective. Lately, however, he hasn't been posting many jottings. That way, he is not the kind who is afraid of the outside world, like I am. His opinion of Facebook too is not as good as it used to be earlier, but I suppose he continues to dabble in it now and then, perhaps. Although there is quite a match between many of his likes and dislikes and thoughts and mine, there is a lot of difference between us. For example, novels are a habit with both of us, but I write novels and he merely thinks of writing one, and keeps on making jottings in preparation. He often wears jeans and T-shirts, and I don't much care for them. He shaves every day, I don't. He uses the internet on his mobile, I don't.

Another example: he is also fond of writing letters to the editor. When he sees his systematic, well-organized responses appear in the newspapers, he feels very satisfied. This is quite in line with his jotting habit, I would imagine. Sometimes it so happens that he is engrossed in a thought and a parallel idea is expressed in an editorial, and he finds that the editorial has not dealt with the subject in sufficient depth. Even the editor himself or the rest of the journalists would not take the newspapers articles as seriously as he does, so he dashes off a letter. If it appears in print, he is delighted. Good. But if it doesn't, he shares the newspaper article's link on Facebook and posts the text of his letter along with it. Chasing an editorial in this manner, expressing his opinion on it, expressing his anger too, this he does with the utmost seriousness. Where this anger of his has come from, I have no idea, but one does get an idea of it from reading the notes given here. I didn't have anger of this kind, and this is one more of the differences between us.

So, then, I told him that this was how my novel went, a kind of collage, in a sense, and I asked him whether I could add one of his notes to the collage. I had always been sure that he would agree to it, and he did too. Accordingly, he handed over a few papers to me containing a note and some of the entries he had made earlier. Whatever entries appeared on Facebook have been marked (F), an F in brackets, and the rest of the entries are given straight. For the sake of maintaining uniformity and continuity among the Facebook entries that he had made from time to time, and so that they may not appear disjointed when read at one go, he has modified a sentence here or there, and added or deleted a word or two. What you read from here on is his text, that's his quilt.

JOTTINGS

The number of birds I have seen in the Amravati University campus, I haven't seen such numbers anywhere else. Saw them, got interested and hunted out their names. Kingfisher, bulbul, lapwing, egret, jungle babbler, woodpecker, magpie,

Indian cormorant, sunbird, green bee-eater, any number of such birds keep flitting across the campus in the morning. Since the time they began holding my attention, I have begun arriving a little early to office, and my observation in the last six-seven months is this: the birds that fly in a swarm make the louder noise, and the ones that fly solo let out a call only occasionally; for the rest they are silent, like the sad cormorant that comes and sits on a tree next to the little lake inside the campus.

❖

Read the French novelist Milan Kundera's *The Art of the Novel*. I've read two of his novels, which was why I bought this book. Besides, also, his statement right in the beginning that he is not a theory person and the book is simply a practitioner's confession. I am not a theory person either. Theories are important, of course, but so many charlatans have now got into dishing out theories that the word 'theory' has now become almost a dirty word. But then there are charlatans everywhere! There is deception both in theory and practice. My concern is with practice, which was why I bought the book.

This is what Kundera writes about the novel: 'Man desires a world where good and evil can be clearly distinguished, for he has an innate and irrepressible desire to judge before he understands. Religions and ideologies are founded on this desire. They can cope with the novel only by translating its language of relativity and ambiguity into their own apodictic and dogmatic discourse.' This view is acceptable to an extent.

The entire book is in the context of Europe, so there's no reason to complain about it. In fact, this limitation has been openly stated in the book. But at one place, this eighty-year-old writer says, 'In the richness of its forms, the dizzyingly concentrated intensity of its evolution, and its social role, the

European novel has no equal in any other civilization.' I felt sad to see him making such a generalized statement when all his references are limited only to Europe.

Here is a writer who is so aware of the political and other forms of power. But when he talks about the novel, why does he not show an awareness of the mutual relationship between European culture and the present power equations in the world? He would then have been constrained to acknowledge his ignorance of the other cultures. I don't think Kundera made the above statement merely out of love of the environment in which he grew up. But having read on Facebook our Marathi people speaking in the same vein as Kundera, I can see the hollowness of this assertion of Kundera. One needs to find one's own vein, that's all.

Another interesting thing: Kundera at one place talks about the fusion that takes place between reality and dream in the novel. The American novelist Jack Kerouac had also had something to say on the subject. Open to the rest of the world despite being an American novelist, Kerouac has said in his novel *Doctor Sax*, 'Reality and dream get intermixed in this mad universe.' It's so right. (Actually, in the original novel this sentence has the word 'memory' in the place of 'reality'. But I don't really know how my memory saved the word 'reality' there. Every time I remember this sentence, it comes out incorrectly. I wrote what I remembered, but immediately I realized that this particular word in my memory is misplaced. Memories and reality and dreams seem to have gotten intermixed.)

So, Kundera, okay, I forgive you. And since you don't know Marathi, you will not be able to read this (now, this English translation might help), and in any case you are so old that it isn't fair getting into an argument with you. Even if you do not have the ability to accept me, I accept you. Okay. I accept you without malice. With friendship, let's say. Also, your statement, 'The sole raison d'être of a novel is to discover what only the novel can discover' – this statement can be the basis of our friendship because this has also been my belief. (Not many people will agree that it has been my belief even before reading Kundera, but what can we do if they don't agree? This is exactly what can be done in a novel. Basically, this statement has been made by somebody else, says the book. Kundera has just repeated it.) (F)

❖

Once again saw today a number of blue, grey, dark blue, dark grey, saffron and red strips in the sky. Although something appears to us for the first time, it must have happened many times before us.

❖

Mutually contradictory thoughts on a single subject come to mind these days. One thought wins, the contradiction disappears, and then another contradictory point crops up, and the contradiction continues, and goes on till again one thought wins. Again, then, one survives and another gets ready to contradict this one. If this results in the writing turning self-contradictory, then I sometimes think why write at all? But then somebody says, it's not just contradictions, it's dialectics. (F)

❖

If one doesn't ponder over the prevailing *vichaar* (thoughts),
then it is easy to turn into a tool for *prachaar* (propaganda)
Aachaar (action) nobody wants –
They'd rather turn *laachaar* (helpless)
Than abandon *vichaar*.
With such people

Existing in the world,
What's so bad then about
The hole of writership?
Whatever destined, then is
P
R
E
F
E
R
A
B
L
E

❖

Where does the arrogance of power come from? Does the desire for power exist in our very existence? Again, this proper waxing and waning of the arrogance of power can be seen in any system, that's quite another thing – right from the family system to the democratic system. As a citizen, I understood this. As a human being, I pondered:

– When a person encounters a weak person, why does this person get into the role of a dominator?
– When a person encounters a weak person, why does this person get into the role of a compassionate person?
– When a person encounters a weak person, why does this person first get into the role of a compassionate person, and later into the role of a dominator?
– When a person encounters a weak person, why doesn't this person continue to be what he/she earlier was?

(Though all this appears a little too black and white, thought I should jot it down because the idea was to see whether some shade of grey could be spotted between the questions. The questions, therefore, have become four instead of two. If one has to remain what one is, then what one intrinsically is will need to be something really great. Otherwise, it will be like staying blank, empty, and that's not expected here either.) (F)

❖

We continue to remain ourselves. We cannot become the other person and the other person can't become us. It's the same with sorrow. Our sorrow is ours and the other person's is theirs. There's just one remedy for this: the novel.

❖

If there ever is a commonality, what is it in, then?

❖

I am not a political scientist, nor a linguist, nor a historian. I am not a psychologist; I am not an economist either. I am not an archaeologist, I am not a philosopher, and I am not even wise. But since I am, I could be a human being in all probability. Hence it is only possible for me to write a story about him. And like all the others mentioned above, I am a human being at the barest minimum.

And like the ant, the teak tree, that two thousand kilo horned rhinoceros suffering solitary confinement for ages in the zoo for the benefit of the entertainment-obsessed Mumbai crowds, that cormorant on the tree, or that egret, I am a living organism like all of these.

And like this table, this chair, this room, this paper, this stone, I also am.

❖

In principle, hadn't wanted to be anything
Hadn't wanted to be unprincipled;
Of the tunnel of survival
Of steady sinking year after year

Of the wars of isms and weapons
Confined
Just a hole, long, very long

❖

The ladies hired to keep the university premises clean work under a single contractor. Each of them gets eighteen hundred rupees a month, and an identical amount goes into the contractor's pocket. What does the contractor do to earn this money? Occasionally gets a broom and whatever else the women may need, and keeps an eye on them. Some people in a certain department of the university had been observing this and started paying two of the women in their department directly. So, the contractor was deprived of his share. He was upset, but the women started getting double the amount they had been getting before. They say that the contractor accosted one of the women and she has just stopped talking to him. 'What else could I do, sir? How can I talk to him?'

❖

One of these two women was saying the other day: the head of her household, that is, her husband was in the SRPF (State Reserve Police Force). Her neighbours too were the SRPF kind. The wife of one of them was the daughter of a Naxalite. So beautiful, one could just keep looking at her! Didn't look like a Naxalite at all, her father. Would come over sometimes to visit her, na. She had some kind of cancer, tube cancer or whatever it's called. Lived next door, this woman. She had a small daughter, two years or so. So, this woman died, and . . . such a young, beautiful girl. So, this woman went along with a few of her neighbours to Gadchiroli for the funeral. Stayed the whole night at the police station. Then the girl's widower husband married the girl's sister. The girl's father, the Naxalite, was killed. There was a bomb that had exploded there, na, so the police had opened fire. This was the story told by this woman, who looked melancholic like a cow. This woman lives here in Amravati, miles and miles away from the bomb that had exploded.

❖

How these birds fly! Great! Some people come for a walk. Some drive right up to the lake on the other side, take a round and go back in their cars. Some just walk around aimlessly. And these birds, how they fly! Great! There is no chance of my becoming a bird. I wish there was.

❖

Amravati is many times bigger than Ratnagiri. The public library in Ratnagiri was established in 1828. By my information, it should be the first public library in Maharashtra. (It's also written on the board there: The first library for the public at large.) The Amravati public library got established in 1867. What abiding towns, these! The pani-puri at Ratnagiri is called gupchup here; delicious, sweet-sour-hot crunchies these. Ratnagiri is a nice town; Amravati is a nice town too.

❖

Had been to Maltekdi the other day. There's a dargah there, about twenty feet by twenty feet, painted white, with stripes of green thrown in. Fifty feet away is this huge equestrian statue of Shivaji Maharaj, done in dark brown. The statue was installed in 1979. And quite lately, as late as 2014, the height of the pedestal for the statue has been increased. When I went visiting, the work on the pedestal was still in progress, wrapped up in gunny cloth. The statue is now taller than the dargah. So, the dargah people will have to think of doing something about it, you know. (F)

❖

The sight of these birds here put me in mind of Anil Barve's novella called *Horpal*. It is the story of birds that live in jungles. These wild birds are used for research purposes, and then put in an aviary where they eventually die when a fire breaks out due to administrative negligence.

❖

These jottings that I make and the notes that I draw on them, I hope that one day I'll be able to think up a few characters out of them and do a proper novel on it. It doesn't really matter if it doesn't happen that way. My notes will be a coherent novel enough for me, every note a character.

❖

Any time a thought occurs to me, I've got into this obsession of trying to find out if somebody has mentioned something along the same line. It's a difficult search, this. Look not for the lineage of a sage, nor for the source of a river, they say. Well, it's something like that. Okay, forget the source, but an effort is being made, at least, to measure the depth of a river. Purely a habit. The limitations of these attempts are also known. I am now tired of all these efforts at depth-measuring, so I've decided I should sit down and begin writing a story. It will be new at least for me, novel. Our novel, you know. (F)

❖

In the process of looking for lineages and sources, I came across Durga Bhagwat's book, *Kadamba*. The book says: 'Kadamba' is a Sanskrit word. One of its meanings is 'group'. It's not for no reason that the word means 'group'. It's derived from the shape of the flower. The flower is like a ball, saffron or yellow in colour. But it is not like other flowers. It consists of hundreds of miniscule, long-stemmed flowers that are bunched together. The densely packed pollen is encircled by delicate greenish yellow fibres. Independent, yet together. This togetherness, this bundling up of various parts into one, is the distinctive mark of the kadamba flower.

Also learnt from this book that the intoxicating drink made from the kadamba flower or fruit is called 'kadambari', which also means 'novel' in Marathi.

A natural grouping: kadamba.

And the alcoholic drink made out of this grouping: kadambari.

This is indeed terrific. This meaning of the word 'kadambari' (novel) fits so well. It sends your mind spinning. A hangover! A collective hangover for a lifetime.

At another place, the book says: 'In the book of the *Charak Samhita*, chapter 25, it is given that liquors, wines, meads and other intoxicating drinks are prepared from eighty-four trees. But kadambari, the intoxicant prepared from kadamba, finds no mention there. The *Arthashastra* of Kautilya also mentions the recipes of plenty of drinks but makes no mention of kadambari. It is strange then, that a drink that was so popular during the Puranic times should have disappeared altogether from the Ayurvedic book as well as *Arthashastra*.'

But what's novel there? Yes, everything about kadambari is novel, ha ha ha! It's a liquor that doesn't fit within the confines of a shastra and cannot even be stuffed into the barrel of a gun.

This kadamba tree is called neev in Konkan, says the book. Actually, I have eaten this kadamba fruit very, very long ago. It's sour-sweet, kind of. I had never guessed, of course, that it would have a heavy name like kadamba. It was there in the backyard, so the fruit would be popped into the mouth every time one went past the tree. Must have been fermenting inside the system since then, who knows? Somebody brought that tree down later. Well, the wood would have been useful to somebody, then. (F)

❖

Another thing I have heard. There was this person named Banabhatt who lived fourteen centuries ago. He wrote a book in Sanskrit called *Kadambari*. Did a little hunting and finally located a book called *Kadambari Saar*, a condensation of the original book. This is a very old book too, also in Sanskrit. It was translated into Marathi some time very long ago. At least I got to know that one of the female characters in the book is called Kadambari. Well.

❖

Amravati: Seems to have a rich history. The original town had a fortification. The fortified area still exists. It's in the inner part of the city, somewhere in the centre, with a market inside the walled area too. The walls have crumbled at a few places. There are five huge gates. Wide open now, so much so that closing them now is impossible, what with the earth having gathered at the base of both panels and jamming them. The huge rivets all over the two panels of the gate – that would together have looked outwards at the world when the gates were closed – now stand looking silently at each other. Trying to dig into the history of such a town as this would mean penetrating through many such dilapidated gates of many such dilapidated walls.

❖

Read a book called *Chintanika* translated by Sane Guruji. It is the diary entries of European philosopher Amiel. I had read Sane Guruji's *Shyamchi Aai* in my last days at college; hadn't wanted to rue later that I hadn't read it. Probably I didn't read it when I should have read it, but it bored me. I read a few of his other stories too later, but, again, I didn't care for them. What Sane Guruji was trying to achieve, perhaps, was different from telling stories. But I liked *Chintanika*; I found it honest. There was no trying to ride any fake looking moral horse there. On the contrary, it looked like it was marking out the limitations of these moral stances. This book comforted me as its style supported my endeavour of writing notes.

You can get any of Sane Guruji's books for fifty rupees in the market these days. The copyright expires sixty years after the author's death. It has been three years since the sixtieth year of Guruji's death was crossed. His books were reintroduced anew into the market. Now, this fifty-rupee pricing looks like a dangerous case, actually. Some books are as long as four hundred and fifty pages. And in fifty rupees – that's a luxury. With some enquiry, though, I got to know that the publisher is related to a big publisher and is busy punting around to convert the big fellow's black money into white. So, fun all the way. I too brought my *Chintanika* for fifty rupees. I don't consider Sane Guruji's stories anything great, true, but if Sane Guruji himself is seen as a story along with his writing, would the fiction side of him also get seen with sympathy, perhaps? Yes. (F)

❖

I've been hearing the sound of this bird called coucal for a long time. It comes in reverberating hoots from somewhere: hoop, hoop, hoop. Measured from the tip of the beak to the tip of the tail, it is about a foot long, yet I couldn't spot it instantly. Since coming here, I have been seeing it pop up somewhere or the other. It's a loner. You may see a pair pottering around occasionally, but never a flock. And it never sits at the top of a tree. You see it for a flash, and then it gets lost in the leaves. Goes grubbing around for something in the vegetation. Brown body, black tail, black head, eyes like red beads. Despite its big size, despite its black-and-brown body, it conceals itself so effectively in the green leaves that it is difficult to spot. Playing hide-and-seek with the world, how deep inside does it go, and where? How long will stay hidden so? Anyway!

❖

In the market called the world, all birds are not alike. Are the customers alike either in this market? I doubt it. As I sit and observe from my counter at the bank, I see so much that the words just sink in deeper and deeper. Now, here was this lady who arrived at the next counter one day. She was quite dark and very short – her face reached up to the counter, just about. Result, the staff sitting inside could not easily spot her across the counter. So, the person immediately behind her, obviously hugely taller than her, pushed his pay-in-slip over her head. The lady would surely have resented it, but the water in her eyes stayed tranquil. The tall person finished his transaction and left. The next person behind the tall person, however, helped the lady pass her pay-slip to the counter clerk. The water in the eyes of the lady stayed tranquil this time also. I, sitting at the next counter, could see this entire episode happening; that was the only difference between me and the person sitting on that counter.

❖

The Nobel Prize winning Colombian writer Gabriel García Márquez died in April this year at the age of eighty-seven. I have read only one of his novels, and bought another one because I was getting it cheap. And now, six or seven months after his death, his papers and documents and other things have got deposited in the library of Texas University in the USA. Got to know all this because I read it in today's news. I remember that Fidel Castro, Che Guevara and the rest of the group had taken over power in Cuba a little before 1960. But in the initial years, they were not ruling under the official banner of the Communist Party. It was only a good six years later that systems were put into place for the Communist Party to take charge. This I got to know from a Wikipedia entry. America blockaded Cuba and began squeezing it from various directions. The entry, recording aspects of the Cold War, also noted that it was sometime during these six years that the USSR had deployed ballistic missiles in Cuba. Márquez openly backed Cuba in this confrontation and was critical of the USA, resulting in his being banned entry into the United States, said the news report. It was only in 1995 that this ban was lifted. And now, after his death, all his documents go and settle in an American university. Would have cost them a bomb! It all looks so funny. The spokesperson for the university said, 'We are deeply interested in the creative process of the writer. Our effort will be to better understand how this writer created his great works of art.' Wow! Wonderful! The Colombian government then expressed disappointment at the Márquez papers being sent to the US. The Colombia spokesperson said, 'These documents having moved out of Colombia is extremely unfortunate.' Great too! Here's what an academic from Colombia said, 'At the minimum, it should have been put up for international auction. That would have given the Colombians the opportunity to bid for it too!' Super! One of Márquez's sons said, 'The Colombian government never showed any interest in them.' Well, then, the Colombian government representative again delved on all the efforts they had made. Here's another titbit: another of Márquez's sons lives in California. Another American expert recorded his opinion in a news item, 'In such cases, the economic aspects and the assurance of preserving these documents and making them available are more important than ideological aspects.'

What does this person mean when he says 'in such cases'? Wouldn't it have worked if he had said 'in all cases'? Well, anyway, this is how it happened. How can one know a dead person's opinion? He can't be brought back to life by magic in the real world, at least for now. You can do what you want in the novel.

Whom does one trust? The people in power? The universities? The thinkers? Wikipedia? Or the novel?

Among the effects that Márquez left behind are: two typewriters, five computers, about two thousand letters exchanged with Milan Kundera, Graham Greene and many others, photo albums, personal letters and the incomplete manuscript of a novel – said the news item. (F)

❖

Read the news item on Márquez and then came the news of the US lifting its sanctions on Cuba. In this regard, an editorial in the Marathi newspaper *Loksatta* said: 'Even if this can be viewed as a defeat for the US in a way, it cannot be considered as a victory for Cuba and (Fidel) Castro. Within four years of power coming into their hands, serious differences erupted between Castro and Che. This resulted in Che moving out of Cuba. He then went to Bolivia and was hanged in 1967 at an undisclosed place. Thirty years later, that is in 1997, his remains were brought over to Cuba and he was given a reburial with full state honours. All this happened before the eyes of the person who had sculpted this period – Castro. The US has re-established diplomatic relations with Cuba, and he has been a witness to this too. "There is no point in living when the flame that lighted the brightest moment of one's life has weakened," said Castro. However, he has to continue to live. In his view, capitalism is repugnant and the US is its personified form, but now he lives on to see his life-long principle crumbling. There are a large number of Cubans residing in the US today, and these expatriates do not consider it wise for Cuba to be in a state of conflict with the US. In this changing global scenario, the US has extended a hand of friendship, and Cuba has accepted its hand; this too Castro has had to witness. Poetic justice. His comrade-in-revolution Che Guevara had to be buried twice. With the US and Cuba becoming friends, the third chapter of Che's death has begun, with Castro again as witness. It is a big enough lesson for all who speak the language of revolution.'

Both sides seem to have worked hard for the sanctions to be lifted, we learn from the paper. The American President Barak Obama is mentioned in the article, but there is no mention at all of the Cuban President Raul Castro. Even the website of the *New York Times* is not as one-sided as the *Loksatta* editorial is. And the misinformation that Guevara was hanged. In an editorial. That too written in a manner that nobody would ever learn that he was actually shot dead. The entire article is written in this vein.

I have given the example of *Loksatta* because I have been reading this newspaper for a long time. The daily reading had created a natural bond with the newspaper; an emotional one, you might say. Lately I had been reading this newspaper on the internet; a local newspaper *Deshonnati* and this alongside, but the *Loksatta* website would be the first. But for some time now the newspaper has lost its attraction for me. I have also sent letters in this regard. Some have been printed, some haven't. It's not just that all my other reading has caused my faith in newspapers to dwindle; also, the kind of arrogance that is visible overall in their editorials and articles is difficult to stomach. One doesn't even feel like trusting the news. And the editorials appear to be just responses; there doesn't seem to be any effort at getting deep into a subject. There is a terrible similarity between Facebook and the editorial – in both the cases the position taken is that all investigations are over and we carry morality in our hip-pocket and can pass opinions with all the arrogance we possess. It's black and white all the distance. This shooting off with superficial morality, or pontificating without carrying any guilty awareness of being humans too is crushingly sickening. And it's not good at all to place trust on mere information. I am noting this example as representative of all the newspapers and because it's in my daily reading list.

Loksatta – *lok* and *satta*, or people and power – what is it? People's power or power upon people? We have both the language and the space for recording our opinions. Some people do not have the language and do not have the space for expressing their opinions; what about them? So, those who have the language and the space, what is it that they should say? The *Loksatta* kind of editorial gets to be written – I have begun to think – when the availability of space is taken as an opportunity to exercise power over people who have no space available. One also begins to realize, even if in a small measure, why a lot of people write in the same manner on Facebook too. It will be so nice, though, if the arrival of these new channels makes space available to everyone; but it doesn't really happen this way. There is this saying, isn't there, that the vocal ones can sell dust; the silent ones can't even sell gold.

And every single person doesn't get real space, which is unfortunate. If this state of affairs continues, those who do not get the opportunity to speak are not going to fight shy of stuffing dust into the mouths of those who speak. The colour of the dust? Could be red, could be dark red, or grey-black, or blackish brown, or reddish grey, or brownish black. It certainly won't be stark white or pitch black.

❖

The legislature, the executive, the judiciary and the media, these are the four pillars of power (in the India of today). One comes face to face with the fourth one every day. Is that why it generates more anger?

❖

Two rough paragraphs:

There was this youngster who would visit the gym every day and do a hundred push-ups at one go. When working on the biceps, he would add weights up to two hundred. Wouldn't exercise his legs, and as a result the calves were quite ordinary. The top, though, was fabulous. It's all right I suppose because once fine trousers are on, who wants to pull them down to see how muscular the legs are? The splendour of the torso is enough to give people cold feet. He would grunt loudly while doing his exercises, and that made the other boys exchange whispers in the corner. Since the gym was for both sexes, there were girls too, and they would turn red with embarrassment. The boy would go on full swing. He once caught one of those boys in the act of passing a snide remark about him, confronted him and landed a sharp one under the ear. The fellow was not of the same dimensions and so thought it best to fall in line. The boy then got back to his grunty pushs-ups. Later, this youngster joined as a worker in a political party.

Another youngster would visit a circle of intellectuals. He could read about five books in a week. Sometimes he would finish a book in a day, which would mean seven in a week. Difficult to identify his favourite subject because he would read on all kinds of subjects, or so he would say. There were other readers too in that circle, but his reading was visible

– from his face to the clothes he wore. The first article that he wrote was titled 'Bhampakaanchi Bhatti' (Furnace full of vacuous men). That article created an aura around him. Often, his titles would be really fancy, but there would be no substance inside. But the titles were good enough to floor people. Later he became the editor of a newspaper. (F)

❖

These rough paragraphs may help release anger, but they are not satisfying. Yet, this gymnastic kind of writing possesses a lift, there's a certain style to it – this is my vacuous opinion.

❖

There's no harm being posted at the branch in this university campus as long as there are birds here. But the bank is not likely to let me continue with this drama of working here for very long. The show is bound to get over sooner or later. It's okay, I guess; the birds are singing.

❖

Read a slim novel called *The Story of Being Useless*. The narrator-protagonist is a journalist. He's begun to get a sense of uselessness in comparison with what is happening in the world and in comparison with even the news of what is happening. But even in the tumult of all the occurrences, he feels supported by a tattered, cardboard collecting old man who would be considered useless in comparison with the main stream of the masses, and by a useless three-legged mongrel too. With these live examples around him, I think the protagonist of the novel realizes what a terrific thing it is to go along living with the uselessness. There was another thing I noticed regarding this novel. It could be because of his daily association with newspaper writing or perhaps out of an instinctive interest that he wants to search for writing-work that goes beyond this. That's why there are references in the novel to two writers: one who very clearly looks inwards (this should be Franz Kafka according to the details given in the novel), and the other who very clearly looks outwards (this should be Bhau Padhye, going by the description in the novel). Wonder why the writers haven't been mentioned by name; there wouldn't have been any harm in doing so. But all told, the author did appear to be pondering over the durability of words. Although this novel might not have much durability, it was okay. (F)

❖

Read a book of Che Guevara's selected writings. In a 1962 article, he says, 'Will imperialism continue to lose one position after another or will it, in its bestiality and as it threatened not long ago, launch a nuclear attack and burn the entire world in an atomic holocaust? We cannot say. We do assert, however, that we must follow the road of liberation even though it may cost millions of atomic war victims. In the struggle to death between two systems we cannot think of anything but the final victory of socialism or its relapse as a consequence of the nuclear victory of imperialist aggression.'

This article belongs to the period when there was a strong probability of a nuclear war between Russia-Cuba and the USA, but even so. And he may have said it in view of the history of 1,50,000 lives that had been wiped out at a stroke with the use of the atomic bomb barely twenty years ago, but even so. About the people of Cuba, he once said, 'Here is an electrifying example of a people prepared to suffer atomic immolation so that its ashes may serve as a foundation for new societies.' I read another book which compiled what Castro said about Che. After having said good things about Che in an interview, Castro also makes a reference to Che's reckless nature and says, 'Che seemed to be a man who sought death.'

Not much happens by merely reading about such things, but even so. How does it hurt recording what has been read? The recording may appear dry and dull, but even so. The actual circumstance is often scary, but even so. The book suggests that Che was a great deal more honest than the then Presidents of the USA. There were at least some things about which he would speak openly. It wouldn't be like the truth coming out a few decades later when the official documents were opened to public. It talks about faults too at some places. In some circumstances, since taking a risk was not possible, some people were killed without sure enough evidence against them; however, nobody was tortured, says the book. 'Our great virtue is that we have never engaged in torture or other similarly terrible behaviour, that some peoples have fallen into in many other countries in the course of defending correct principles. We established a principle energetically defended by Fidel: that no prisoner, even if they are to face execution, must be touched in any way. There may have been exceptions and I personally know of one, but we continue to uphold and defend that attitude. This is extremely important: anything and everything that happens makes news, including things we don't publish in the (Cuban) newspapers and things we ourselves don't even want to know about. We hear about them later on. When I get home my partner says, "So-and-so took asylum in an embassy," or, "A soldier shot up a bus." Everything becomes known. Everybody would find out about abuses and other bad things if there were any, no matter how secretly and far from the public eye they were carried out. The people know and evaluate all such things.'

On reading such positive appearing things, I instantly went to Google to search for the untoward things that happened in Cuba. Like Cuba + torture. A number of entries cropped up.

Some have even written books on their painful experiences in Cuban prisons. This information just popped up. I didn't know what to do with it. But I also got to know that the health facilities there are excellent; there are books on that too. It wasn't possible for me to examine all the details. After all, South America is so far away. But Che Guevara's picture you run into all the time, printed on people's T-shirts. I've met some T-shirted people who have told me that he was an old singer, and so on. There were others who possessed passing information on his rebellious, revolutionary activities. In fact, one of my relatives had gifted me a Che Guevara T-shirt too some four years back. It looks nice on a pair of jeans. I wanted to know about the man in the picture, so I had given a search. It gave me some primary information. Then there was some reading that I did. This was how I read Castro's book. I had then read this quote of Che on Wikipedia, about millions of people dying in the nuclear war. I had earlier wanted to merely jot down this quote as it was, but thinking that this alone shouldn't satisfy, I ordered the book. And that was when I realized the limitation of jotting down just that one quote. The image that is created by the entire book is very different from the one created by the quote. It's not as if I want to form an immediate opinion on all that happened so long ago. When it takes so much time to form opinions on immediate happenings, how much can one do for something so far away? (I've also heard people muttering behind my back that after all I am just an ordinary bank clerk who jots down trivia in Marathi. A couple of them have thrown my clerkship on my face on Facebook too, but I continue with making jottings.)

So, I tried to do some close reading to get to know the face that stared out of the T-shirt a little better. Then I tried to get a little closer still. But, ultimately, I can't just hop over to Cuba to see what really is going on there. There are limits to a person's vision. But it's also true that some new things emerge as you go digging deeper and deeper into something. For example, it feels different when you examine weapons from close quarters. If you have them close, have them close always, it's sure to feel different too. Che himself has written in this book, 'We would sometimes begin to feel more confident in the might of our weapons than in our ideals.'

❖

If the dream of bringing about a communist society has to be realized, every single person will have to live by the highest standard of honesty. And this business of morality is killing anyway. Making a simple-looking superficial layer constantly visible seems to be the concern of most institutions, right from the family to a political party. Well, be that as it may. The thoughts that I carry about every individual, there is nothing new to that. It is old stuff. But I don't think I have anything to add to it for the sake of it. I just think that the thought is worth thinking, so it should be done. Also, every word that I write is very old too, but each time I put them together, something new emerges out of them, perhaps.

❖

There is this website that has Marxist documents, and there I happened to come across this piece that Engels wrote in English, complaining about an English translation of *Das Kapital*. Engels says –

'To translate such a book as *Das Kapital*, a fair knowledge of literary German is not enough. Marx uses freely expressions of everyday life and idioms of provincial dialects; he coins new words, he takes his illustrations from every branch of science, his allusions from the literatures of a dozen languages; to understand him, a man must be a master of German indeed, spoken as well as written, and must know something of German life too.

'But there is something more required. Marx is one of the most vigorous and concise writers of the age. To render him adequately, a man must be a master not only of German but of English too. Mr Broadhouse, however, though evidently a man of respectable journalistic accomplishments, commands only that limited range of English used by and for conventional literary respectability. Here he moves with ease; but this sort of English is not a language into which *Das Kapital* can ever be translated. Powerful German requires powerful English to render it; the best resources of the language have to be drawn upon; new-coined German terms require the coining of corresponding new terms in English. But as soon as Mr Broadhouse is faced by such a difficulty, not only his resources fail him but also his courage. The slightest extension of his limited stock-in-trade, the slightest innovation upon the conventional English of everyday literature frightens him, and rather than risk such a heresy, he renders the difficult German word by a more or less indefinite term which does not grate upon his ear but obscures the meaning of the author; or, worse still, he translates it, as it recurs, by a whole series of different terms, forgetting that a technical term has to be rendered always by one and the same equivalent.'

There is a paragraph placed between the two paragraphs given above. In that paragraph Engels makes a reference to a news item to support his stance. There were four students rowing a boat in the straits of Dover. One of them got his oaring wrong, and something may have happened. The news item that covered this incident used the idiom 'caught a crab' to describe the oarsman's error. A crab, literally, is the name of a sea creature, but here it idiomatically means making a false stroke with the oar, says Wikipedia. But the correspondent of a German newspaper in England didn't get the meaning, so he reported a crab getting caught in the oar of the novice oarsman. This paragraph hasn't been recorded verbatim here because the basic points are covered in the other two paragraphs. There are a number of doubts that crop up here. How good was Engels' German and English? How good is my own English and Marathi? And how much, really, can a person get to know about somebody else's lifestyle? People who pick up other people's sentences as the main support for proving their own points would find Engels' paragraphs a useful weapon for flooring plenty of their opponents without thinking left-right. But this is not a good thing to do. A better thing to do is to set aside the fanciful mask that these paragraphs have put on and focus on the basic issue. You are not likely to win any contest on the use of masks as a strategy, but you will gain the satisfaction of having tried to reach the meaning. This is exactly what the paragraphs talk about.

❖

During this meandering around the campus, I have got to know a person who is in his sixties. He has strong leftward leanings, and I have good conversations with him. This meeting with him can be called a coincidence. He retired as a professor of Political Science, and is an open-minded person. I had spotted the golden oriole bird once and was looking at it when this man was on his round, and he got interested in what I was looking at and stopped. That was how we met. A good thing too. We once got discussing how each individual will have to raise his moral standards to a high level. At that, he said, 'This thought itself is of the typically bourgeois kind. If you sit explaining things to every individual, even three hundred years will be insufficient for bringing about a revolution. When circumstances change with power, changes begin to occur in individuals too. When you begin looking only at the individual trees, you lose sight of the forest, Lenin has said. And this way of looking at things traps you in the quagmire of class interest.'

But I hadn't wanted to talk about raising the moral standards of every individual as a means of preparing for revolution. If the kind of balance that is expected to be attained by a society is inculcated in every individual because of the change in circumstances, then this thing called morality will create terrible stress. And I cannot believe that this depends completely on a change in outer circumstances. Perhaps I think this way because I can see so much immorality in my own self. This is also the reason why I cannot talk about values or morals at the drop of a hat. There are others who can; they could be the morally elevated kind, maybe.

This sixty-plus friend of mine is very good at heart. Meaning, I can have friendly conversations with him. He did call my views bourgeois once, but generally he doesn't say this. He is understanding. There are plenty of people you meet here and there who flaunt their commitment to a movement. But this person doesn't do any such thing. People outside the movement are human too, hence he maintains a certain level. That is why it becomes possible for me to throw these questions at him.

❖

Read *Brothers Karamazov* by the nineteenth-century Russian author, Fyodor Dostoyevsky. 'Guilty before all people, on behalf of all and for all, for all human sins, the world's and each person's. And I, worse than all those in the world, guilty before all people, on behalf of all and for all, for all human sins' – this idea occurs in the book so often and is expressed by so many characters that it is amazing. There is plenty else in the book, but I found this theme particularly interesting.

When a person finds himself in the presence of someone weaker than him, why does he slip into either a dominant role or a compassionate role? When he runs into someone weaker, why doesn't he remain as he has always been? I had noted this down in an earlier jotting. Being what you have always been doesn't mean being indifferent, though some readers can arrive at that conclusion. Another aspect of my question is: why a person doesn't live with a permanent feeling of guilt. If he were to do so, he would have his feet planted firmly on the ground, whether the person before him was weaker or not.

Tukaram has said: I am a heap of sins and you are the best.

Could Tukaram have used Vithoba as a peg to hang his power on? I don't know much about Dostoyevsky's private life, but the winds of the Christian faith blow through every bit of this novel. Could he too have been using religion as a similar peg? If one speaks of the absence of pegs, then... should power be invested in the Communist Party? If the party functions with the Vithoba kind of integrity, good; but a party comprises human beings, not the stone icons of Vithoba. It would have been different if it had not been so.

Therefore, what's wrong with using language/words as pegs? That gives us a sense of guilt too.

❖

This constant feeling of guilt, it's all right as far as it goes. But does this sense of guilt create a mould for those various methods you see around of punishing oneself before god? Chyaayla! Don't know a bloody thing about this; no reading, nothing! Shit! So, then, carrying this feeling of guilt may not be the right thing either, while roaming the streets!

❖

Even so, there should be equality for everybody to indulge in social falsehood with equal strength; no one should object to that. But objections there always are. Is it just the birds, poor things, that do not get into this objection business? Wherever the footsteps of human progress start advancing, ringing, they just abandon that place and fly off elsewhere. The congregational chorus of the jungle babblers will just keep going farther and farther away. And the water that rests in the eyes of the cormorant will spill over and fill up the lake.

❖

Right from Facebook to the TV, this continuous litany of morality has begun to scare the shit out of me. Well, sometimes I too catch myself speaking the same language. And as I write here, I hit the diametrically opposite end, consider myself as completely amoral. And I don't want any of it. As a remedy, I've learnt to cook vegetables; I still can't roll out a decent chapaati, though. Once I can do that, the dread will subside somewhat, I think. Chapaati, the Indian bread. Bread, dread, rhymes nicely, doesn't it?

❖

The neem tree on which the cormorant sits, a big egret also sits there in the afternoons. I don't have much time to spend outdoors in the afternoons, but I came one Saturday afternoon to see this fellow with his gaze locked into the infinite sky, sitting absolutely still. Alone. I don't know how many types of egrets there are. This fellow is big in size, a faint grey stripe or so on the back, a small stripe on the face too, for the rest, sparkling white, staring into infinity without moving a muscle. His tranquillity is astounding. The cormorant looks a touch sad, but this egret is more tranquil than sad. But amazing...yes, these birds are such a help for us to stay grounded.

❖

One thing that has struck me after making all these jottings: I seemed to take everything on face value. It should not be so, and even this took me so much time to realize. At the most, words may help modify face value. The real value may not be within the scope of words to catch. Being able to frame questions, if I can do just this one work in these notes, it should be adequate enough for my abilities. Using language, what more can be done beyond this.

❖

Feeling nice, really. This is a face value statement too. Or, better still, it has begun to feel like how you feel while scrubbing dishes. Wow, this is good. The decision to name the Amravati University after Sant Gadge Baba carries good face value too.

❖

Drinking water is my need, and drinking a novel is my habit. Oh wow! Such a joy.

NOTE

What to do with Mr Glad?

Read Anil Barve's Marathi novel *Thank You Mr Glad*. Found it melodramatic, but it was fun reading it. Besides, the author appeared honest. *Rokhlelya Bandooka, Uthleli Janata* (*Pointed Guns, Revolting Masses*) is another of his books I have read. It contains a reportage of the early days of the Naxalite movement. Barve had roamed around the parts of Andhra Pradesh where the movement was in full swing and had published a long article in the Marathi weekly *Manoos*. This book is the outcome of that article. The writer clearly takes sides. The party-partiality is visible everywhere. When the book arrived, Barve was an 'under-trial prisoner' for eighteen months in the Pune Naxalite case. Being such a party-partial person, his ideological leaning is clearly visible in the article, that is, in his non-fiction writing. Actually, it is visible even in his fictional writing, that is, in *Thank You Mr Glad*, but something else has happened there. The kind of partiality Barve can afford in non-fiction writing, he cannot in a work of fiction. It appears that he has been compelled to confront certain complexities there, consciously or unconsciously. Virbhushan Patnaik is a Naxalite doctor on whom the death sentence has been pronounced. The name of his jailor is Mr Glad. There is also Glad's daughter Jenny. So, these are the characters of this interesting, 104-page novel. Virbhushan is the hero, outright. However, at one place, Barve writes:

> ...Whatever one may say, it is true that Mr Glad was a staunch loyalist of the State. He would have sacrificed his life for staying true to his salt. In the 1942 movement, Glad had hunted out reasons to emasculate the agitators who had fallen into his hands. But when the Union Jack was lowered and the tricolour was hoisted, Mr Glad had suppressed his sorrow, offered a cracking salute and given himself over to the service of the tricolour. The loyalty Mr Glad had shown for the white sahibs, he transferred to the brown sahibs.

Further down, Barve says:

> ...Glad's heart would start palpitating violently at seeing the Naxalite movement gaining strength. He began to seriously believe that there would be a genuine communist revolution in India. Well, even if the revolution had really occurred, it wouldn't have made much difference. If the tricolour had been lowered and the red flag had been

hoisted, he would have suppressed his sorrow, offered a cracking salute and got busy serving the red flag.

So, this is how it is. 'What to do with Mr Glad?' looks like a genuine question. Mr Glad snaps into attention for whichever flag rules. Barve may not have thought it necessary to record this point in his article, or his intentions there may have been different, or maybe there were no doubts in his heart at all at the time of writing his article. But had the doubts of the writer crept in the novel – a little bit? Maybe that's why the novel accepts that Mr Glad always exists. In spite of staying stapled to the communist revolution line, the novel accepts the possibility of Mr Glad staying on. This was not there in the article. This is the strength of fictional writing, of the novel.

Strength – it seems to be a dangerous word to use. What if one seeks power through strength? So then what other word to use? Ability? All right then, this is the ability of the novel. And it's good if the novel works according to its ability. Its speed may be slow, but that shouldn't matter. Why does one want speed, anyway? If there's enough work to fill up the time, that's good enough.

The main point of Barve's novel brings to mind George Orwell. In an essay, Orwell writes:

> Progress is not an illusion, it happens, but it is slow and invariably disappointing. There is always a new tyrant waiting to take over from the old – generally not quite so bad, but still a tyrant. Consequently, two viewpoints are always tenable. One: how can you improve human nature until you have changed the system? The other: what is the use of changing the system before you have improved human nature? They appeal to different individuals, and they probably show a tendency to alternate in point of time. The moralist and the revolutionary are constantly

undermining one another. Marx exploded a hundred tons of dynamite beneath the moralist position, and we are still living in the echo of that tremendous crash. But already, somewhere or the other, the sappers are at work and fresh dynamite is being tamped in place to blow Marx up to the moon. Then Marx, or somebody like him, will come back with yet more dynamite, and so the process continues, to an end we cannot yet foresee. The central problem – how to prevent power from being abused – remains unsolved.

Orwell's distinctive feature is that he does not consider it necessary every time to take sides in a complexity, but to present the complexity in the clearest terms. It's because of this quality of his that it becomes possible to get into a conversation with him. I also think that in this passion for speaking with clarity, he lets his train get off the tracks sometimes; it's like trying to protect one's image somehow. But that's another subject. Even here, the two disputing positions that he talks about, not that one has to accept his argument exactly as it is, one would agree with the main thrust.

By propping up communism with such an immense number of words, Karl Marx has created an entity that always manages to help people either in creating a dogma, or in making fun of someone, and in plenty of other things too. So many people have made a career out of tossing his words around or constructing gratuitous philosophies out of them. But if you look around generally, it appears that wherever a vacuum is created out of people's power struggle, there Marx's beard spreads out, throws roots. Even when a person dies, so much depends, perhaps, on how the world keeps him alive. That is, a person has his own flow too. While alive, he feels that he is giving direction to the flow, but he most certainly cannot say that once he is dead. Then other people take over to give direction to that flow. As the flow moves forward, some of the stuff moves on, while some gets left behind. Then each person can take his pick of any sentence and circulate it according to convenience. Here is an example: 'Marxism is a science.' Here's a quotation from Gandhi too, painted on a wall at the Sevagram Ashram at Wardha: 'It is not right to use fasting as a tool for threatening.'

Possessing the facility of turning sentences around is cleverness. Difficult to say whether the cleverness belongs to the writer or the reader. It's the cleverness of language, most likely. This cleverness is for preventing a person from acquiring power. But the animal that knows language is man, and among men there is always the fear that those whose language reaches a larger number of people become powerful.

In the context of the author's sceptical tendencies, we ourselves have stated in this note that (this may be the *ability* of the novel and) *it's good if the novel works according to its ability. The speed of the work may even be slow, but that shouldn't matter. Why is speed needed, anyway?* – Well, somebody might say, the option of slow speed may be all right for you because your circumstances are robust! And this alternative will also be perfectly acceptable for people in power; in fact, it will be particularly convenient for them. The argument may thus get stretched further. Orwell has talked about the slowness of progress, and so this objection can be applied to him too.

Till such time as the meaning of words does not become as exact as two plus two equals four, these differences will always come butting in. That was why I had placed a few jottings before the reader before beginning with this note. So, even while we talk about 'the speed of the novel', the meaning that lies at the heart of the novel should reach you with as much exactness as possible. Extreme care has been taken to ensure that a few sentences going this way and that do not alter the meaning.

We have talked about how some things flow well with the people, haven't we? So, what are the things of the Marathi writer Sane Guruji that have stayed in this flow? I alone cannot give an answer for the entire flow. One often hears of the recognition he earned as the author of *Shyaamchi Aai*. Here is a piece of his I read the other day:

> We do not recognize brotherhood. We do not understand the soul of religion. We recognize power and bow before the cane. Musalman brothers may draw water from your wells, they may sit with you at the house-front and you lovingly offer them paan–supaari (betel and areca nut). But a harijan (untouchable) is unacceptable to you. It's good you allow the Musalmans in, but you have not given them this privilege out of love. They ruled over this place for hundreds of years and acquired this privilege. You bowed before power.

Now, whether this house-front intimacy exists between the Muslims and the Hindus remains a question. But I myself have seen it happen as mentioned. The headman of our village was a Muslim. And the behaviour of Hindus with him and their behaviour among themselves were quite different, as noted by Sane Guruji. But how true it is at the general level, it is difficult to say. Anyway, getting back to the basic point. Sane Guruji had identified the man who bends before power. We have his mother who always bent before the power of the institution called the family. That, perhaps, was the reason why she was so loving. He wrote her story. But it is this very tragedy of bowing before power to which he has given the frilly ornamentation of love. Could he have suffered a shock when in actual practice power proved superior to love in the end? Was that why he killed himself with an overdose of sleeping pills?

So, then, this question: What to do with Mr Glad? It's

not a new question. It's been asked several times. It sounds the same. But one can hope to find an answer only if one asks a question. So, it's alright to keep asking this question. Words change, but the question remains. It sounds the same. But different dots are joined, and the same question pops up in different forms. There shouldn't be any problem asking at least this.

Moh*

Just moh and moh of moh.
The moment you down a quart
Fifteen bucks worth,
Then there's no stopping
Till it's three quarts down
We speak and roam around.
Then flies in the sky
An ashen
Layer everywhere
Trees are green
Shingles are red
But all get coated with
The ashen layer
Of moh.
    Power be screwed
Want to dunk all of life into it,
Focused,
Pupils steady.
A thing reveals itself only when touched,
Else keeps loitering and swaying
The sky
Full of massive letters.

---

* *Moh is a Marathi word for the mahua tree and also means temptation. Here, it is an alcoholic drink made from fermented flowers of the mahua tree.*

All numb
Yet moh and more of moh.
    Aayichi gaand to power
    Bugger all power
Hooch is any day better,
But that of moh alone.
Loving
Beautiful greenery all around
Bamboo wonderful green-gold
Sitting by it
Hitting the tankard hard
Yet staying erect.
Flying and flying,

Brooks and bourns
Rivers and gutters
Mountains, suckers
Motherfuckers;
All ours
To take along.
Massive letters strong.

Story.
As each comes to sight
You want to hold it in your hands,
Not out of any infatuation
But can't get the hang.
So, needs holding,
The story

If back, then back it goes
If forward, then forward lurches

Head heavy
Sleep sleep
Should come again and again
Drink up again and again
    Fuck the world
    Bugger all sophistication
As if losing a hold on one's own self
Feels real, feels really real
Creative
What is feels different
Downing each draught,
Rocking, swaying,
Sun sky aslant,
Just moh
Moh
Nothing else
Nothing
No dying
No killing
Just be there   swinging
    Tottering
    Till the day of death

(Some people
spilled some moh on the earth while distilling it.
A pen lay there, red with black cap.
The pen came alive for a couple of minutes
and tossed to the author the words recorded above.
The pen perished in the brazier
that held the pot from which the liquor came.
Near Laheri in Gadchiroli, 14 July 2014)

Egret

When a flock of egrets was flying from north to south somewhere on this side of the centre of a country called India, the sun, as always, was setting in the west.

A rough road, called a 'tarred road', goes past a lake. On the other side of the road are trees, forests. There were some cows grazing there. As they grazed, a few egrets tapped their beaks close to the hooves, looking for grubs. These too flew away like the flock mentioned earlier.

As the flocks were flying, one of the egrets trailed behind a little and, don't know why, came back to the lake and descended. A conversation got started. The egret knew everything, including why I was sitting beside the lake; also, why I was writing a novel. Though he knew everything, the egret was loath to start a conversation. It just came down and stood meditating on one leg in the lake. The water was as silent as the egret. I had been sitting by the lake only with the hope of getting the lake to tell me a story, but the lake wasn't ready to talk either. The water spread everywhere. With the lights fading, the water looked darkish. The trees that had looked green some while ago had turned dark too. The egret stood silent, with his head turned towards the sun dying out in the evening sky. The shadow he cast was aslant, and an exact egret was visible in the water upside down. This fellow was straight up, and the other was straight down. As the light disappeared, the one that had gone straight down disappeared. The shadow held on because the moon had moved in.

The egret too relaxed a little bit. As he had come down, he had informed me that he knew why I was sitting there and had then become silent. Now, however, when I said, 'You have any information you can give me?' he responded, 'I have no interest in talking to humans.'

'Why, brother?' I asked.

'Saalya, as if you don't know,' he said.

'What, brother?'

'Maligned us, you bastards, and now ask what's happened!'

I kept quiet. What else could I do, with the egret throwing abuses at me? Men too behave the same, so I let it pass. And I really didn't know the reason for the egret's anger. So I stayed silent for a little while.

It was he who started. 'You haven't read that Sanskrit aphorism about water–milk–wisdom, it appears.'

I then remembered it somewhat. Of course I don't really know Sanskrit, but I remembered the existence of some story related to water–milk–wisdom. In twenty seconds or so, I remembered a lot more. Couldn't remember the aphorism, but whatever little I remember of the story goes like this: The swan is white and the egret too is white, so how can you tell the difference? When you place a mixture of milk and water before the swan, it drinks the milk, leaving the water behind, and that's what distinguishes them from each other. It's quite obvious that the saying related to water–milk–wisdom has its origins in this story. It is regarded as an important quality among humans, being able to separate milk from water.

When I told him that I didn't know the aphorism, the egret said, 'Why do you humans plant such lies upon us? Just because you idiots can't separate between two shades of white, why do you pointlessly paint me in black?' But that was not the only reason for the egret's annoyance. He then suddenly took a big leap and asked, 'You don't even seem to have read the Jataka tales.'

'I may have read a tale or two,' I said, 'but what's the problem there?'

The egret got so upset that he immediately went into his meditation. In twenty seconds or so, words began to descend – just as little yellow leaves come down from trees when the wind blows. A darkish screen had spread across the water and whitish-grey letters had emerged on the surface, as if written in someone's hand. When all the words had descended, the story that I could read off the surface of the lake was this:

> There was this egret meditating on the lake. It was summer time and the water had begun to shrink. The egret, however, stood on one leg, meditating. A few curious fish saw him standing on one leg and went up to him and asked, 'O great one, why do you look so worried and lost in thought?' The egret came out of his meditation and said, 'O fish, I am worried thinking about your future. Summer doesn't seem to be in any hurry to depart, and the water has begun to shrink. It will become more and more difficult for you to find food. That's what I have been thinking about.' Asked the fish, 'What's the remedy, then?' 'If you listen to me,' said the egret, 'I will carry you in my beak one by one and drop you into that big lake there. There's good water there.' The fish were in a bind. They said, 'Can't agree, sir. Has anyone ever met a fish-loving egret since the world began? You may be planning to deceive us and eat us up.' The egret responded, 'It's true that egrets eat fish, but how can I play such a treacherous trick on you? If you have any doubt, I can carry a representative to the other lake. Let

that representative satisfy itself, and I'll bring it back. You will then believe me.' The fish liked the suggestion and sent one among them with the egret. The egret carried the fish, dropped it into the big lake, let it experience the benefits, picked it up and brought it back to the old lake. The fish related its experience to the others: there is, indeed, a big lake there and there is plenty of water in it. The excited fish then agreed to be carried over to the big lake one by one. The egret carried the representative first. But this time on reaching the lake, he did not head for the water; instead, he went straight to a tree on the bank, and there he ate the fish up and threw the bones down. His meal finished, the egret set off again for the old lake where the other fish were all ready and waiting. One fish after another, the egret brought over and finished off as he had finished off the first one. When the old lake had been emptied of every single fish, the only one left there was a crab. The egret addressed the crab: 'O crab, all the fish are living a merry life in that big lake now. Why should you then stay alone in this rapidly shrinking lake? You can come along too. I can put you in that other water.' The crab had been having doubts. How was one to know whether the egret had actually deposited the fish in the other lake? On the other hand, checking out that other lake wasn't a bad idea either. If the egret deposited the crab in one piece in the other lake in one piece, well and good; but if the fellow had other ideas, the crab would have to devise a plan to ensure that the egret didn't take away his life. So, the crab said, 'Brother egret, how will you carry me over there?' 'As I carried the fish: in my beak,' said the egret. At this, the clever crab replied, 'But for one, brother egret, I am too big to fit in your beak, and for another, I am so smooth and hard that you will not be able to hold me either. But my claws are nice and strong. I can easily hang onto your neck as you fly me over safely to the other water.' The egret liked this plan. Accordingly, the crab hung on to the egret's neck as the bird flew it over to the other lake. When he reached the lake, the egret began heading towards the tree, at which the crab exclaimed, 'Brother egret, the lake is over there. So why are you landing on the tree?' 'Just because I flew you over here hanging onto my neck, you think I am your slave? Look at the heap of fish bones below the tree. Your bones are going to join them soon.' The crab shot back, 'The fish were foolish, brother egret, so you could kill them, but don't you forget that you are dealing with a crab. It's not for nothing that I hold your neck by my claws. If I have to die, I'll take you down with me. Watch how I separate your head from your body.' As he said this, he began squeezing his claws round the egret's neck. The bird choked and the whites of his eyes began to show. 'O great one,' croaked the egret, 'please be merciful. Gift me my life. I shall drop you in the water.' 'All right,' responded the crab. The egret flew the crab to the edge of the water and lowered his neck to allow the crab to descend in the slime. The crab instantly broke the egret's neck, as if it were a lotus stem.

I had heard this tale, but I hadn't known it was from the Jataka stories. At least, I couldn't remember that immediately. The message of the story was clear: a crook meets a super-crook. The characters were clear too: fish foolish, egret crooked, and crab clever. I then understood why the egret before me was so upset. The storyteller told his tale with a limited purpose, and while his main purpose was served, the quality assigned to the *egret* got stuck to him forever. The storyteller had no intention of vilifying the egret, it is clear, but then, why would he have picked on the egret for vilification? Why would the egret alone have got into his head for assigning the quality of crookedness? Who knows how much of this crap keeps sitting in everybody's head? You keep hearing people referring to somebody as fox, egret, ass, and so on. So, because of the skill of these stories for sticking qualities on animals, have we begun to think of these animals being stuck to qualities? It may be true, too, but what does one tell the egret?

The egret seemed to have a lot of stories stashed away in his mind. I tried to reason with him. Arey, this is the story of one individual egret, that doesn't mean all egrets are like that. He is just a character in the story. And as far as I know, there are Jataka stories about bodhisattvas in the shape of birds too. Can't remember them right now, but there would be such stories. If I had stretched my persuasion strategy longer, it would have turned out hollow. For one, the egret knew many more stories than I did; if he had started on Sanskrit and such like stuff, my persuasion efforts would have looked hollower still. I did get into my strategies, nevertheless, and then the egret pulled out more words. Again they began floating on the surface of the lake, greyish letters on an indistinct black screen:

The egret gets into meditation,
But that is just a pretence to fool the fish
The daughter-in-law weeps for the mother-in-law,
But the feelings in the heart are different.

No point explaining the essence to the egret
That's tiring oneself without any purpose.
Tuka says that's how it is with teaching the sceptic,
It's only a waste of effort.

This verse of Tukaram I hadn't come across. For that

matter, I don't know most of his verses. So, anyway, Tukaram has also used the egret as a metaphor for a pretender – being one thing and projecting oneself as another. Every person has things to say under different circumstances, so we do use these metaphors while talking, don't we? There are references to the mother-in-law-daughter-in-law relationships in so many of these verses. Of course, this relationship has been settling into a cast over the ages, so maybe these verses reflect that; but how does one explain all this to the egret? And though I hadn't known of this Tukaram verse, I did know somewhere at the back of my head that the egret was used as a metaphor for a dissembler, like a person sitting in fake meditation, and so on. How all these metaphors came trickling automatically into my head, the egret knew its entire history. But then, many more things have been said about humans all along in stories and in poems. There's plenty of black and white stuff in them, exactly as the egret has said. But then the readers are human beings, most of them, so they would be doing this black and white thing on all the other animals with a great deal of alacrity, according to what suits them. But they don't simplify human beings according to this simple formula of black or white. Humans are left with some elbow room. I mean, when a person behaves strangely, they say, 'He's behaving like an ass.' And if they want him to behave decently, they say, 'Start behaving like a human being.' Hey rhinoceros, hey you buffalo, that lordship of an egret, cunning wolf, you have grown like a horse and still you don't earn a penny, a dog's tail can never be straight, we automatically talk in this vein among human beings. We probably talk on the strength of what we have observed, which is fine. The problem comes when we begin talking to other animals, nothing else to it.

If the egret had decided to give me a tutorial on all this, it would have been the death of me. And even if the storyteller or the writer had not intended to stick this quality permanently on the egret, it does happen that this one single meaning gets stuck in our heads, it does. When we call a person a dog or an ass, is it the implication of the word that pushes it deeper and deeper inside the head? I don't know. With such little knowledge, I couldn't have got into an argument with the egret. He could have separated milk from water, and I would have been all water. I'm just a human being.

I admitted as much, and the egret said, 'Why have you taken this so much to heart? Don't behave like a human being.' Finally, one has to say, the egret himself became quite understanding because he said, 'I talked to you because you had come with a reference from that teak leaf.'

My main interest was in listening to all that the egret would have seen from above as he flew across the world. The eyesight of birds is phenomenal, they can keep changing focal length with such ease, they say. I have no idea what lineage and what species of birds an egret belongs to. But if it can catch a fish with one snap of its beak, it must surely be blessed with terrific eyes. And then flying and landing after making such delicate calculations, all this has to be the work of a great pair of eyes, this we can see with the naked eye. Therefore, I had wanted to record all that the egret would have seen. Thus it happened that some of the information that the egret gave on his latest wanderings was recorded as given below. There were some details that the egret could not remember to perfection, but was able to recall them with some prompting; or some other words were suggested, which he accepted; there were some questions asked too; all this the reader will know when reading the text. This is how the text was written, the major credit is the egret's:

So many villages, spread everywhere. So many towns, spread everywhere.

Take that village. Looks so sad. Looks so tired. There are a few kids there who study tirelessly, this is the superficial information I could gather. It may be useful to you. There is this earthen cast lying at a place. Wax etchings are used. Then melted brass is poured into it. The wax melts. And the thing is ready. It's a cast for a hakum. Hakum you may not know. You'll recognize it when you see it. It's a musical instrument. This cast is broken. All labour gone waste. Nobody does anything here anymore, but there is somebody's cast lying here. Houses. Shingles. A compound fence of thick wood. These people have grown corn here, in the square next to the house. Two girls sitting there, with books in hand. They sit there to shoo the birds away from coming down on the grains. They were eating something. (What?) Probably wafers. (What were the books?) Oh, the books, I'm going to show them later. There's this pen for goats here. On the other side was a girl sitting on a cot with a sheet wrapped round her. About eighteen. (What was she doing?) Very interested in girls, aren't you, saalya? She just sat looking into space; a sheet of cloth wrapped round her, her knees drawn up and her cheek resting on them. Have you ever seen ducks sitting quietly, lost in a reverie, with their necks turned and their beaks tucked into their feathers? That was how the girl sat. She had tucked her neck into her covering and gone into reverie. (What was she looking at?) What do you mean 'what'? She had buried her eyes in that bamboo fencing in front. The hens were cackling away, but she sat on. Silent and melancholic, poor girl. Her hair slightly messy. The covering messy too. In fact, everything messy. The borewell in front also messy. That is, not fitted in. A cement square. A pump on top too. But there's no lever. Two cows grazing there. (But there would be some government board at the borewell). Board? Oh, yes. Yes. *Integrated Action Scheme. Arranging for drinking water. Under the scheme: Digging bore-well and setting up a hand-pump. Year 2011–12. Hand-pump water, guarantee of health.* It's a blue board. But why do you want the board, saalya? (A government board is a story by itself, egret, you will know by and by. What can I say here?) Well, yes, what you say is right. Now that we are talking of boards, shall I tell you about other boards near other borewells? (Yes, please.) There is a functioning borewell in another village closer to the town. There's a yellow board there with 'Jalswarajya Prakalp' written on it. There is the sketch of a flower done down there, with the petals carrying the words 'Pure Water', 'Complete Cleanliness Drive,' 'Women's empowerment', 'Adivasi development', 'People's participation'. One petal, one word. And then again: 'Jalswarajya', 'Pure Water Clean Village'. (See the story there, egret? How many stories sunk in this water! Cleanliness, women, Adivasi, people's participation, fuck it. Great.) Yes. Well, I have to tell you this. I don't get the slightest bit bored while observing these big and small things as I fly over them. It is a kind of habit, really. But if your readers get bored, well that's your problem. You are boring creatures, you humans. (No, rey, they won't get bored. I've put a few boards in my earlier novel too). Then they'll get bored for sure. (We'll see. And earlier, I had not elaborated upon it so much; so, this is in the same vein, more or less. You've read the novel. So then, why all this? And, anyway, if they get bored, then they get bored, it's all right. People get bored of water too, so does it mean they don't want it? Everything depends on need. You tell me what else you saw. It's a bigger need now). All right, so let me tell you about water. I told you about this good borewell in the village near the town. There are so many jeeps that drive off from there in different directions. Black jeeps. Yellow top and a yellow band in the middle. They're called kaali-peeli, black-and-yellow. So, here was this battered kaali-peeli, driving along with around twenty-two people loaded in it. There was this song playing: *'Aaj blue hai paani paani paani paani paani paani'*. (Oh shit.) Now what? (It's this song. I never used to like it, but I heard it so often everywhere that now I've begun to like it. Rotten singer that, Yo Yo Honey Singh. You can hear his songs across the entire country. That's how it is with us humans. Such things come up every now and then and become popular for a few days.) Yes, that's how it must be. But that jeep liked this song, I can tell you. Looks like it needed the song as much as petrol, that jeep. Water, water, water. The jeep was quite like your novel. Rickety. Went up to the village, picking up and dropping people on the way. Your novel likely to go that way? (Don't know. But now that the two of us have arrived this far, it may arrive too, perhaps. But you continue.) What more? I kept flying from the earth to the sky, oh, there's a lot. Tell you about this village. There, on the other side of the river there. There were these hardy soldiers of yours spread out across every nook and corner. A kilometre from the village is a tar road. There was a small bomb explosion there. They snapped to attention, guns in hand. They'll wait till it turns dark, and then set off. It's a seventy-odd house village. There are these mahua seeds spread out at a place for drying in the sun. The sun goes down and the seeds go inside. Have you ever tried mahua liquor? (No.) Behind, there, not in the village, in the village close to the town, a bunch of people had arrived. Journalists, social workers, a group of ten or so, they had mahua liquor, and were praising it to the skies for the locals. But let me tell you, the locals don't feel the same. I can't give you the finer details either, but whatever I can gather while flying. So, it looks like people get awfully bored and then they drink, that's it. Looks like they want to blank out the present. You should try it too. (Arey, I've had it a couple of times.) Why did you lie, then? You humans are such liars, that's why I don't like talking to you fellows. (Oh, please. It wasn't a lie, honest. Sorry. I sometimes don't understand your questions. You were talking about the soldiers, and I got caught in that. So, it took me time to reach up to understand this liquor message. Sorry, honestly sorry. Grovel at your feet.) No, wretch, don't get to my feet. You catch a being by the feet and hang it upside down, that's the kind of animal you are. (No, no, please. Sorry, sorry on behalf of everybody. Understand, please.) Well, all right, I have forgiven you already. That's why I talk so much. But next time I ask you a question, pay attention. So, yes, you wanted to know about the soldiers. Nothing unusual there. The villagers were used to it too. The headman had turned mute, true, but that must have been because of the fear of being beaten. The police had carried him away earlier, and because of the hammering he had received, the first finger of his right hand became limp forever. It could never be fixed back. The others were silent too. A child was crying. A dog was sleeping under a cot. A man slept on the cot. Trees, vines, all silent. The borewell is working nicely here too. Earthen houses, shingled. The houses in your village there would be shingled too, no? (Yes, but they've started collapsing.) What's your village? (Zirambvali). Why did you then come so far for your writing? (Well, got to understand how much geography there is. And then, I met you too, pal.) Don't give me that bunkum. (No, really. I had never known your side of the picture. But now, I suspect, I may not understand geography either from here on. That's why I sit by this lake.) Good that I came here, then. I got you right, saalya. (Yes, okay, now finish that soldiers' story.) So, those soldiers had spread across the village in every corner, standing so still, a fly wouldn't fly off their noses. Later in the evening, they went and sat in their camp there on the other side. A thick, stone wall with barbed wire on top. They had to spend the night inside there, and stay awake the rest of the time. So, well, here they stood glued to a single spot and there, in the jungles a few miles away, about a thousand people were emerging in groups. (What?) Yes, the people of an inner village had taken out a rally. Their demand was the release of their companions imprisoned in the taluka headquarters on the other side of the river. They had been incarcerated without any case being filed against them. The prisoners were many times more than the capacity of the jail. Not enough food, no medicines, no hearing of any kind, said the people. They had walked for the entire week to reach where they had reached. They planned to lay siege to the prison. They carried red banners that carried the demand for the release of all political prisoners, who are all adivasis. (Did the banner carry the name of the party?). No. If you are speaking of the Maoist party, there was no mention of it on the banner. But the police would have done their calculations. A give-away was the sheer number of demonstrators. The cops must have been flustered by the size of rally heading towards the town. But they did some hustling and blocked them at a certain place, and the senior officers reached there in quick time. Initially, not even one of the people was ready to talk. They were Gondi speakers and the officers understood no Gondi. Finally, a few people stepped forward and said, 'Our people lock in. No court, no food,...' (How long did this go on?) Not very long.

The people reached there by afternoon. Then the chief official started explaining to them. They could place their demands before them and start a dialogue, but it was not right to take the law into their hands and surround the prison. Their demands could be genuine, and they could place them before the authorities without breaking the law. The police persuaded them to go back the way they had come. So they began their week-long journey back, cooking their meals by the wayside. The tar road was traversed first, then, finally, their journey finished in their individual villages after traversing miles of jungle tracks. (What's this, going on?) You figure it out. You asked me to tell you, so I told you. There's a hell of a lot more to tell. I know all about your dirty businesses. Our people are spread across right up to Mumbai. News from there reaches us. It's you, then, who have to see what's going on. (But I can't see as much as you can.) Oh, well, forget it. We are very different from you. (I want to ask you something.) Yes, what? (What lineage and species do you belong to?) You don't know that? Then why did you ever begin to talk to me? Don't make me repeat the entire Ramayana all over again. (Oh, not for any purpose. Had simply wanted to know.) To hell with what you want. some other time. Night has begun to slide away. (All right, so?) So nothing! I'll be leaving in a little while. I talked to you about those people some time ago. The eyes of so many of them were like the eyes of that Lattakka you talked about in the novel. (Arey!) I've told you that I talk to you because you brought this reference from the leaf. Well, another reason is what you have written about that woman in the novel. (Arey pal, thank you.) Cut it out. I don't want your thank you and I don't want your sorry. (What should I do then?) What can you do? You couldn't write her story, you couldn't write mine. (I'm going to write yours. I'm going to write all that you've said. That was why I had wanted this talk.) But mine means whose? (Egret's.) Again, then, exactly which egret, no one would know. This is what had happened with the example I had given in the beginning. (Oh yes, of course, quite true. All this confusion happened because you guys have no names.) Good you understood this quick. (That's why I had been asking you your species.) How will that help? There are so many of my lineage and species. And like you looked at me and identified me as an egret, the other men are going to do the same. So how will anybody know that the story you told was mine? And look, it is for your convenience that I am using words that you people use. But about my lineage and species, how do I tell you in your framework? (Yes, that's quite true. So, what do I do?) What can you do? (Chyaayla. We have this saying: he who holds the lake gets to taste the water. That's how it is with us. So, we just maintain a lake of words.) Good. You've understood this at least. (But you seem to know everything: Sanskrit, Pali, Marathi, everything.) Isn't what I have told you enough? I'm not going to sit here giving you clarifications on everything. We'll see about it if we meet again. (You're quite right. And Lattakka at least is a proper noun, but you don't have even that, so your story will have to be told with a common noun: Egret's Story.) Hmmm, well, so be it. I don't mind. This fancy for names you guys have, we don't. (True.) There's another thing. You must have seen these big stones planted here. (Yes.) Forget us, so many among you humans too don't have their memorial stones planted like this after their death. There seems to be this custom of raising a memorial stone, but so many get missed out. I saw one such case of a small kid dying in a village a few days ago. Barely six or seven months of age, that kid. Looking at the age span of you humans it's nothing. I've seen that kid so many times while flying over that village. Its mother had two blouses, one yellow and the other red, and three saris. She wore mostly the yellow one. For company, they had a dog, which lived in the same house as them. The infant's neck had just about become stable. It had now begun to look around. For clothes there was no need. There's a rough tar road that goes past the village some three kilometres away, and there's a track that leads up to the road. There's a small stream that runs alongside too. To put it in a language you understand, the hamlet is not too much in the interior. You could say that it sits on the boundary between your government and the interior government. If you want more details, two houses there have a TV, and what you call a dish. (Any other details? Like a song you'd talked about earlier?) Song I can't remember, but I had once alighted on a watery place near the stream that runs behind the houses. There's an older boy in one of the houses. He used to go to school, but he's been sitting at home for the past six months. People tease him, calling him a compeeter. (Why?) Because he wants to buy a computer. (Which standard was he in when he quit school? You may have some idea.) Look, he should be about fifteen. I would have been able to tell you about the grade by looking at his books if he had ever stepped out with them, but I never saw him studying outside like the girls I earlier talked about. It wouldn't have missed my eyes. This boy now constantly stands in front of a pinkish mirror in front of his house and keeps doing something. Sings all kinds of songs, I can't remember any. The details, I can go on rattling them. (Please do.) I wanted to tell you about the death of that infant, and you find all this stuff interesting. (I understand. The death of that kid is not just a matter of one less person. You think I don't realize?) Hmm, so you do understand things a little bit.

Another thing, the mirror before which this boy does all his antics, there's a wooden door nearby, two feet away. There was a picture of an actress there on the door. (Which actress? I'm sure you know, come on.) Priyanka Chopra. (How do you know all this?) Told you just now I've got my relatives all over Mumbai. We don't go too close to houses, so I can't give you the details of the insides. Anyway, this picture was not a new one, in fact it was quite an old one. Thirty odd houses in that village. No electricity in most of them. People go to charge their mobiles to houses that have power. Some even charge money for the service. So, well, this kid had been growing up in this village six months. Once I had seen it – finger in mouth – staring unblinking at the dog. Another time it was suckling at its mother's breast. This woman is so thin, but the kid was nice and cuddly. Wasn't the crying sort either. Every time I flew over the village, the kid would either be staring at something or smiling. The mother would be working somewhere, but no crying from the child. It would shove its toes into its mouth or a finger, or just smiled. Once it started rolling over, it would just play around. So, the mother had gone up to the road for some work, carrying the kid with her. There were some cows and buffaloes grazing nearby, and we were with them. There was suddenly a very loud noise, how loud no point explaining because you won't understand. A jeep just took off in the air, caught fire and fell some distance away. There was a bigger vehicle standing there and there were people with guns crawling forward. When the blast came, we took off towards the sky. I saw the woman racing towards her house. Smoke was billowing behind her, by the side of the road. There was the sound of people calling out, interspersed with the sound of gunfire. This went on for about an hour and a half. By then, we had covered quite a distance.

But as I flew, I carried with me the image of that kid's smashed skull. (What?) The woman was quite far from the site of the blast, so she didn't get caught in the crossfire and survived. But as she was running, she tripped on something, probably a stone, yes, a stone; but such a small stone, she would otherwise not have fallen. Well, she fell on her face, and she banged her head against the trunk of a mango tree there. The kid on her right shoulder hit a big rock near the trunk and . . . (Stop, please stop.) I didn't hear that sound. Nobody would have heard it. How much sound can a small skull make against a rock? It just got drowned out by the sound coming from the road. How much blood would such a small fellow have? All of it flowed out, some got absorbed near the roots. The mother had taken a big knock too, so it took a little time for her to recover consciousness. Later, when she came to, she carried the dead kid to the village. I saw the kid's skull splitting, also saw the blood spill out. But after that we had gone. There would have been wailing at the village. Such a smiling kid. Gone in just a second. Without even getting a chance to cry. Dead, without even feeling the heat of the flames that were shooting up near the road. What do I tell you? I haven't seen any stone erected in its memory. Even the blood near the tree has disappeared. (What do I say?) I know there is nothing you can say. That's why I talked to you of the passing away of just one human being. No point in telling all the rest to you about the death of the rest of the others. The number of deaths I have seen, you won't be able to stomach it. Well, we eat flies and we eat insects, but that's a different thing. The other deaths you won't be able to stomach, either. Forget it. (Sorry, sorry. Forgive me). Who am I to forgive you? As a matter of fact, I don't even have any complaints. It doesn't happen this way with me. I've seen a lot of dead human beings. But when

I saw this kid's death, I felt sorry for this ability of our eyes to see so well. This was the first time it happened, and that's why I told you the story. My sharp eyes have helped me survive. My wings have helped me survive, and my eyes have seen a lot of deaths too, but that kid's skull refuses to leave my head. (What, friend, what's all this?) I'm telling you the truth. I'm off now. The sun will begin to creep out in a little while, and I have to go there to the other side. I won't be able to see how you have written all that I have said. The rest of your novel I have skimmed through. I know quite a bit about your subject too. (Hey, how's that?) Oh, forget it. You've got some paper? (Of course, here.) Tear out a couple of pages and leave them here. I am leaving now. When the sun comes up, and when the rays hit you, that's when you pick up the pages and go away. (All right. Thank you. How do I say it?) Don't say anything. Do what you can with what I have told you. We too keep the lakes, see if you can keep this in mind. See you then. (Okay, goodbye.)

There was a rustling sound in the water, and there was the egret flying away. Where it had taken off, small, concentric waves had begun spreading out on the surface of the lake, reaching out farther and farther. The egret dissolved into the dark. The last episode he had recounted refused to leave my mind's eye. Anyway, I tore out two pages from my notebook and kept them as per his instructions. Had no idea how many hours I had spent chatting with the egret. No idea when the dawn would break. That kid's episode had turned my head heavy, so tenaciously it sat inside. Time turned heavy as it had not been for so many hours that had slipped by. The chirping of crickets could be heard. How come the moon had disappeared altogether from the sky? After some time I stretched out. Blackness everywhere.

When I came to, the sun's rays had just about begun hitting the lake. There were those whitish-grey words that had come floating down to the dark surface of the lake during the night. Again, something came floating down on the surface. This time it was not words. With the arrival of the sunlight, two photographs, a little entangled, a little wrinkled, stood up on the surface. Looked as if they had references to the village the egret had described. They looked beautiful, those photographs floating on the water. As the sun rose higher, the photographs disappeared, and when the rays touched the papers by my side, my attention shifted to them. Those photographs appeared to have got printed on the papers. I attach these two photographs provided by the egret, along with all the memories attached to them, at the end of this chapter.

Note: The photographs show the History and Civics textbook of Std V and also a notebook for the same subject. The title on the textbook reads: 'Aapla Swatantrya Ladha' (Our Freedom Struggle).

Die-gram

A person lived within ten minutes of the place where the teak leaf lay dead in Ratnagiri. However much the people had branded that melancholic man a madcap, he was not all that much of a madcap. Enough evidence can be unearthed if he is subjected to a decent biographical study. His name, his surname, all these things may be necessary to sketch out his biography. You run into the surname Manvi in the region of Belgaum-Nipani. Why a person from there came over to Ratnagiri is another question that we come across while putting together his biographical sketch. Well, he worked at the Municipal Council, which was why he had come this way. He had got married too, but since he didn't have any children, his family had stopped growing. Where's his wife? Why should we care? People didn't have enough information on these questions, so they called him names. But if somebody's wife has left him, and if that person is good to us, why then do we need to twist things? And why go so deep into private areas? But that's not how people's perception runs, and consequently, except for a few, people said things about Anand. The vocal ones can sell dust; the silent ones can't even sell gold – you must have heard this saying. That was why Anand couldn't sell his wares to the world. He hadn't wanted to place them in the market either. He had got two of his novels published: one *Chalval*, meaning Movement, and the other *Valval*, meaning Restlessness. Both the novels carry the same tale forward. The first has as its background the stamping out of the mill workers' movement in Mumbai. A huge fabric is woven around a family, originally from Konkan, returning to their native place – husband, wife, a boy and a girl. The husband goes mad, and he sits at home muttering things and roams the streets muttering things. The wife tries to hold the family together, keeps doing all kinds of odd jobs, and finds a rented room for the family in Khalchi Ali area of Ratnagiri. The girl is married off. The boy falls in love with a girl, goes chasing her to Mumbai first, gets into drinking, comes back to Ratnagiri to witness his father's death, and stays home beating up his mother. This is where the first 250-page novel ends. The second novel is almost exclusively a description of this youth caught in the restlessness triggered by memories of his dead mother and the woman he had fallen in love with. It is only ninety pages long. The novel ends with this youth wandering around, drawing lines on the sand along the black sea beach (Mandvi beach).

Anand Manvi lived in a shingled house opposite the Ganpati temple. His house was full of books. When I told him about this novel, he gave me a sheet of paper and said, 'Whether or not you give me credit for this, do include it in your novel.' With the novel nearing its end, I realized the value of his paper. It combined well with the subject of this novel. There is no coincidence here either. Anand Manvi's subject and the subject that interested me were the same. It may even be said that it was because of him that I started getting interested in the subject, which was why I got to know him, chatted with him and exchanged a few books. Anand later died of a heart attack. I attended his funeral. I don't know where some four or five his relatives had sprung up from. But

I got to know of his passing away and I went, and I found a few persons already assembled there and the preparations had begun. Preparations for the last leg of Anand's existence: cremating him. He was cremated at the Mirya beach. The Anand with whom I had had long talks, both about this novel and about things in general. The white sand and the massive amount of sea water had spread there on the back side to bid Anand goodbye.

Ratnagiri has two beaches: the Black Sea at Mandvi with its black sand, and the White Sea at Mirya with its white sand. Mandvi has now become a regular Chaupati, while at Mirya there is place for a crematorium on one side and place for the fish on the other. Both these beaches are at walking distance from the place where Anand Manvi lived during his last days. Mandvi a little farther away, Mirya relatively close. It doesn't take half an hour to cover the entire distance. Between white and black lived Anand Manvi. ('White and Black' is also the name of a story he had written. This story is among the documents he has left behind – a clipping from *Lokrang*, the supplement of the Marathi daily *Loksatta*.) It was very rarely that he went to the beach. He liked going there, but the crowds were a disincentive; so he would leave the beach by half past four in the evening. Later, he stopped going there altogether.

Anand Manvi died quite young; I guess he would have been around forty-five. Two of his novels were published. He also wrote a few stories and poems, whose clippings he had preserved. A few days after he gave me the sheet of paper for this novel, he also gave me a polythene bag with a few clippings of his stories and some notes and jottings. They should be published some time. (The readers will get to read his remarks on despair in the next chapter.) Even towards the end, his efforts at writing had continued. There were hundreds of poems, most of them unpublished. His first novel had also received some award in Mumbai. There was a second edition of the first novel because of the award; the second one had just one edition. That's why his books are not seen in the market. The publisher of the first one was a small-timer from Mumbai, and the publisher of the second was a big player, again from Mumbai, but that didn't make any difference. All things put together, it did not happen that people around him could get to know about his authorship or realize his worth. He just wasn't cut out to talk about himself and let people know his worth. Things reached a point where he would even take insults without feeling upset about them. It's one thing to feel that one should not impose one's opinions on others, but quite another to swallow insults. You should have seen him to know what happens when you apply this principle. But after all his humility, people never cared for him, and that's sad. So many flaunt themselves, create their cliques, and feel thrilled at strutting around in their own little groups; why then should this have happened to Anand Manvi? In fact, I had thrown this question directly at him, to which he'd responded, 'But why should it matter? I'm not doing badly. Maybe it's a need for lots of people. Insulting somebody or being considered superior to somebody is as important for them as drinking water, so they do it. My need is quite the opposite, and so I behave the way I do.'

'All this is easy to say, but you can see for yourself how cliques are formed, can't you?'

'Who are you talking about? About writers and all?'

'That, of course, but look at the neighbouring temple. See what's happening there? Simply that people gather around somebody.'

'Aayla, that's a great example! Bang on the nail. They all work like temples. Must be out to deify themselves. So, let them do it too. That's not the job of a writer. And, well, a writer is not a god either, so why would he ever want to do that? But then, you decide if it suits you.'

I was thrilled to have come up with such a cracking example. Anand Manvi was right. A writer is not god.

'How then did you strike upon the subject of your novel? Because you had this allergy to god?' I asked.

'Can't say this with any certainty. Maybe you can. You've also thought up a similar subject, so you may have arrived at some hunch.'

'I don't know for sure, but you have lived for a much longer time with this. I asked because you had a better chance for a hunch.'

'Can't say with certainty, again, but it's possible. What do you think about man becoming god?'

'I simply cannot say anything about this. It was you who said it just now. It'll take my head some time to digest it. I mean, I can't say anything right now.'

'Hmm, but it's a good point. Quite true. Unless you turn into a god, it's impossible that people would present themselves uncomplainingly before you. You have to be at least a demon, if not a god. Don't know whether there is any difference between the two. They are strong, these people, aren't they?'

'Yes, but we seem to be making too much of this people business.'

'Meaning?'

'Meaning they and us, we are separating the two. Isn't that akin to converting ourselves to god? There can be a god around whom people do not gather too. You know that

Maruti temple in Khalchi Ali? People do not gather there, do they?'

'Hmm, that's there too. Like, when I say there's a crowd on the beach, that's the kind of conversation we have had about people; even if I know that the crowd's assembled because of me, I don't say so. But it's all very complicated. You'll probably get to understand only out of writing your novel. Or we could even have done this: that instead of talking this way on the subject, we could both have written our individual novels, that would have been a whole lot better. Or one writes and the other reads, this at least we should have done. That would have been a nice conversation. But now it's not possible for me to write, saala...'

'Why not?'

'The mood's gone. And I should have written it all when I was young. This break has messed me up. Can't manage it any more. The thoughts have disappeared from the head too. The kind of enthusiasm you have about the subject, you feel like writing about it; I haven't felt so for some time now. That's why I have given that piece of paper to you, haven't I? I don't have enough strength left either.'

'Are you joking? How can you call yourself old?'

'No, it's not that I've become old, but I don't have the strength left to stay with the subject. I don't mind telling you this straight. There are some reasons from my personal life too. They are another reason why I can't handle a subject of this kind.'

I had not wanted to ask about his personal life. If he had needed any support I would of course I have spoken on it, but it would not have been possible for me to broach the subject on my own. He didn't talk anything personal either. But he did say during the conversation that there were personal reasons for his not being able to write. He also said: 'You will also feel the same some day, perhaps. Or you may already have felt it. In fact, it is out of our personal reasons that we write, don't we? Maybe with you it is different, but whatever I have written till now, it has all been out of personal reasons. But there are times when we want to write on a certain point, that point gets so shaken up because of personal reasons that the writing drifts away from the main point to some other point. Not as if that's bad, but the main point still gets left out. This is how that subject got left out.'

I couldn't understand well enough, and I told him so.

He said, 'What do I say? Perhaps I couldn't forget my wife; that might be the reason. Or probably I didn't know for so many years whether to respond or not respond to what people said. How do I tell you what I feel? Look, when something has happened in our lives, when it's so messed up that there is no alternative to screaming, we fret, scream, get into fisticuffs, perhaps. I don't have anything to say about that. But if it's just somebody talking rubbish, or if somebody just refuses to listen, or insults us, is there any need for expression for such small things? And if such small things were to lead to arguments, then what about the really big things? What do you do with them? Look, whether everyone gets enough water to drink or not, this is a subject to argue about, talk about, and if the need arises, to fight about. But if I am insulted all the time, how much do I sit worrying about it?'

Anand, Anand, what could one say? He wanted to be heard, that seemed to be his need of the moment, and if I had not been able to do even that little bit, hear him out, what use would I have been?

So, he was saying, 'I don't want to bring this again to any superficial level. So, do I feel bad? Yes, I do. Earlier, I would respond. Then I began to think, why respond to such utterly trivial things? Earlier I would wonder: do I consider them trivial only because the matter is personal? Then I realized, it's not an issue of personal. At the personal level, if somebody attacked me with a knife and tried to take away my money by force, I would certainly hit back. I must, too, to the extent possible. But there should be a limit to how much offence a person should take about what people say. This taking to heart what people say, it is fundamentally wrong.'

'But there are bound to be people who have given answers to this question, na! Aren't there stories like: okay, you have abused me, but I don't want to be abused, so?'

'Well, yes, that's true. But they are stories with a pre-decided moral. There are things that don't finish till we die. Spending so much time explaining to oneself that there is a point here – I think this needs examining. Look, a chap utters a few words, meaning, he makes a sound, and the meaning of the sound he knows and we too know, and someone has given meaning to that sound well before we were born, so does one sit raising one's temperature on account of a third person's meaning?'

'But what you are saying is superficial too. When we see such things happening on the street, our temperature does rise, doesn't it? Suppose there is an old woman sitting out there, and if somebody shouts at her, "Hey, you whore, get aside," how're you going to feel? Likewise, we would feel bad if somebody said such stuff to us too, wouldn't we?'

'That's exactly why I can't agree with that conclusion. One gets upset because somebody says something to the old woman, so what's wrong in getting upset if somebody says something to oneself? But I believe – and this too I am telling you with complete honesty, all right? – that old woman and I, or that crow sitting out there in front and I, or you and I, or that coconut tree in front and I, what exactly is the difference here?'

'Arey yaar!'

'Hey, why do you say that? I'm going overboard, probably. Okay, wait. All right. I'll tell you about a statement of Marx's in *Das Kapital*. You might have read it too. Man sees himself as the same as somebody else before he identifies himself. For example, when Peter sees himself as the same kind of person as Paul, that's when he realizes his own identity. In the eyes of Peter, Paul embodies the entire humankind. In fact, he establishes his humanness in comparison with the person before him. I remember it well because of this Peter–Paul business. Have you come across it? The observation looks quite good to me, but there is much beyond that.'

Aayla, are Anand Manvi and I really drawn to the same subject or are our subjects fundamentally different? This question troubled me and I asked him. Then I said, 'Forget it, I'm getting tired of all this. We've really been talking randomly. What do the ordinary people have to do with it? That old woman sitting there – if that person does say something to her, what are we going to do? Come on, this is my subject, then.' I now feel that I went a little too far with this statement. It was a big mistake. Big as the ocean. Maybe he didn't take it to heart, but it was a mistake all the same.

But he was still sticking to the original subject. 'You are right,' he said, 'maybe our subjects are different. The statement I gave to you from *Das Kapital*, my subject is different from that. But you keep hearing something again and again, and you begin feeling the same too, so I went and read a bit of it. Maybe, to begin with, we do define our identity as humans being from the people around us. I mean I just talked to you about those abuses – that other people have assigned meanings to those words. Well, what meaning can those words – that is those sounds – have by themselves? I got to know the meaning that everybody had agreed upon through somebody. And that we have accepted. But once all this is over, when we look at it from the other side, when we begin to decide a person's humanness by comparing the person to ourselves, this is frightening. And it's not necessary that the being in front should be a human being. It's in comparison to ourselves that we decide a dog is a dog, an ass is an ass and a cow is a cow. We impose ourselves on others. Look, I am speaking with my feet on the ground now, I think. You talked about that old woman, this fits there too. If that man called her a whore, I would be angry because I have no reason to impose my thoughts on that old woman. If she thinks of it as an abuse, well then, she does. Of course, there is the question of how I should get to know what is in her heart. But we can always ask. Whatever lack of clarity remains, well, it remains. But I think her opinion in this episode is important. Give you another example. Here, close to the temple, a pair of dogs was copulating, and a couple of boys threw stones at them. The dogs yelped and ran away. I would now have to hear the dogs out and decide what I have to. The problem here is that here we sit talking, while so many people go and kill so many other people in this world. They are fucked. That is to say, we are fucked, I am fucked. In short, what I have to say is that we should hear the version of those who are dying. To hell with everything else like insults and so on. Let's wash all that away. We now seem to have finally arrived at the proper issue. Because there is no point in killing so many people who have decided to live. They want to live, and we impose death on them; it's not right. The USA dropped an atom bomb on

Hiroshima and a hundred and fifty thousand people died. What a fucking number! And yet, that alone is true. And as for the novel, let me tell you that the topic cannot be decided in this fashion. What we have been talking about is way beyond the scope of the novel. If the subject had been so easy to articulate, wouldn't I have taken a degree in it?'

Anand Manvi was a good friend of mine. But let me confess that I couldn't talk to him very openly about my novel. The way he was talking so openly with me, straight from the heart, I didn't lay bare my heart as openly to him. But it is also true that I do not register issues fast enough. After he died, I thought very often about the points he had made, and I think they started infiltrating into my novel automatically. It occurred to me that he had become a part of my novel, but I could not have been a part of his. The question isn't who was responsible for this. It could be that my subject was different, but I was not able to speak to him about it. He will understand. I can't even ask for forgiveness now. The day we had talked, I had asked him this too: 'So, what do you think is the role of a writer here?'

'Have you ever been there? That path that goes behind?' he asked.

'Oh yes, plenty of times.'

'There are plenty of teak trees there. There's a huge litter of leaves down there. Seen it?'

'Yes.'

'So, what do you feel?'

'You are quite right. That's exactly what I feel.'

Anand Manvi let out a 'litter' laugh. I too let out a 'litter' laugh. We both became litter. He must certainly have noted what he thought when he observed the leaves. What I thought I have written in this novel. I should look through his writings. And we both got attracted to the same subject; a lot of the credit for this should go to the teak leaves and the water there.

However, Anand Manvi should not have lost the power that was inside him. But then he spent his life here next to the seashore, and then he got into the habit of keeping on flattening himself. We can't expect the person before us to be all that understanding, can we? The person before us can be like a skyscraper, or a tower, or a person who desires to climb the Everest. So Anand went on flattening and flattening himself. It's a matter of great grief. The sea wouldn't be able to fathom my grief, you neither.

You can see the image of the paper that Anand gave me on the next page. If you found this chapter a little over the top, well, it will come flat down on the ground, down to sea level. That's why these sea waves are long, quiet, peaceful. The sand peacefully spread out. So, this is the atmosphere, and then this image. Around the end of the nineties, when Anand was very young, he was working in Gadchiroli. He had sat on the bench in front of the grand triangular buildings of the Municipal Council and sketched this image. He told me this when he handed it over to me. His handwriting was good too, poor chap. See the next page:

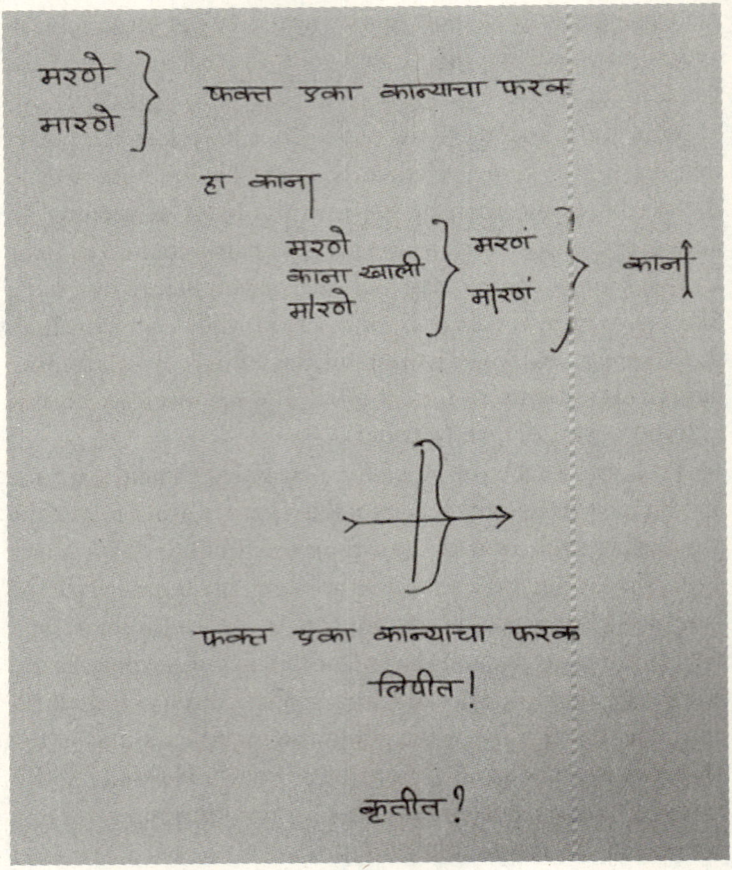
मरणे
मारणे
फक्त एका कान्याचा फरक
हा काना
मरणे
काना खाली
मारणे
मरणं
मारणं
काना
फक्त एका कान्याचा फरक
लिपीत!
कृतीत?

English rendering of the image:

मरणे
(means to die)

मारणे
(means to kill)

The difference is just of a single kānā, that is the vertical bar, for the vowel sound 'ā' after 'म'

This is a kānā:

मरणे
काना खाली
meaning: bring the kānā down or below the ear

मारणे
('kānakhāli mārne' means to slap)

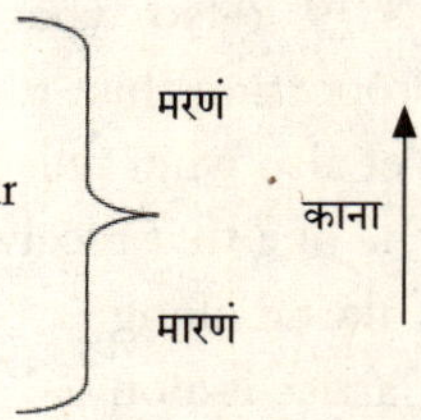

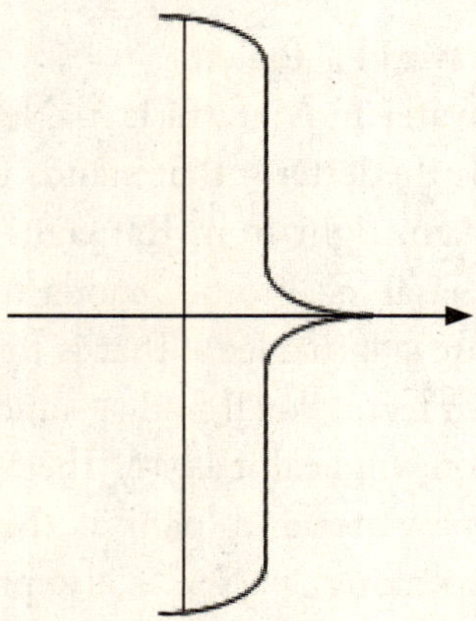

The difference of just a single kānā
In script!
In action?

Water

What spills out of the eyes when sad
Also what spreads across the earth in far larger proportion than the land
Yet also what falls from the sky in the name of rain
The one that receives the dead teak leaf
Takes it along –
Carries it along –
Keeps flowing –

That's why the world is fooled.

The word for water in Marathi is 'pāNee'. When written in Marathi, it uses the letter ण that stands for the hard nasal 'n', but when spoken, right from Ratnagiri to Gadchiroli, it uses न, the softer nasal 'n'. From Chanda to Banda, they say पानी (pāni), but write पाणी (pāNee). That is to say, if you search for it in the written form, you'll find पाणी and if you search for its spoken form, you will hear it as पानी. The Marathi dictionary says 'pāNee' means water and 'pāni' is the one who drinks water. But while speaking, 'pāNee' is also pronounced 'pāni'.

See how water moves in nature: frothing, meandering, stopping, springing, gushing, steaming, cascading.

It is the same with a story. Water itself is not watery. It is stored according to the needs of people: in a tank, in a bottle, in a bucket. What would happen to it if it is just kept? That's how it is with stories. The more open and unrestrained they are, the better. Sahir Ludhianvi has said, *'Ashquon sey jo paaya hai, woh geeton mein diya hai'* (I've expressed in my songs what I've received from my tears). If some stories emerge from such salty-open-mad water, what can one do?

Ever tasted tears?

They are salty.

Like sea water.

Seventy per cent of the earth's surface is sea. Therefore!

❖

Water is essential: from birth to death, from the orifice of the mouth to the orifice of the bum; for women and men; from mustard seed to cow.

Many people in the world have written poems on water. Two Marathi poets have written poems on water. Both poems, in large or small measure, deal with the caste system. One was a founder member of a militant dalit organization in Maharashtra. The organization collapsed in a couple of years. But it was an incident that got recorded in history. No one knows when historical records become available in the future. No one can say when this recording will be of use to someone somewhere. The recording of this organization's history helped Shridhar Hasure. An issue of his little magazine carried the story of the organization. The poet who founded this organization hopped from party to party till all his struggles ceased. But...

While this organization was still in existence, it rained in Worli. But the rain was not of the regular kind.

It rained, but it didn't rain water.

It rained stones.

A person was killed by one of the falling stones. It rained stones on a rally of the poets of the dalit organization, it rained on the dalit tenements of the BDD (Bombay Development

Department) chawl at Worli, Mumbai. It's an old incident. It occurred in 1974. Even after this rain of stones there was no flood of blood. The rains continued to visit the city even after this event. The organization turned watery thin later and faded away. And did the passion of the poet turn watery too? Maybe it did, but he got recognition. His death was reported not just by the newspapers but on TV too. It was also carried by the English newspapers. So many people knew of him, see?

It is clear that not many people know of the other poet who wrote a poem on water. The second editions of the two volumes of his poetry that had been published in the seventies came out in 2013, but they did not create any noticeable stir. This poet had also written poems on Karl Marx. At one time, he left Mumbai and went to Shahada in Nandurbar to participate in the adivasi movement. He suffered a blow from an axe on his right arm, but stayed on. Stayed on, with his left arm intact. Faced disappointments, but stayed on. Then he went to another city, a metropolis, where he stayed on. Perhaps because he now had a well-to-do family, but that's okay.

The resolution of the bread-and-butter question is also related to living. Poetry does not resolve the bread-and-butter issue. For one, the question is resolved by a political person, for the other, by some close relative. It may have been resolved differently for these two, but that is not what we are talking about. Our point is simply that both wrote poetry on water. Both these poets met each other occasionally and were friends. Water water water, where all it flows through. Influencing each other with the flow. So it is with words, whether of poetry or of water. So mixed up are they that they are impossible to separate. This flowing water, that is, words.

Everyone does not write poetry, but everyone drinks water

all right, uses it all right and this is awfully important. In the end, man himself is a poem written by water.

❖

Although Mahesh learns poetry in school, he doesn't write poetry, not yet. He lives in a village in Gadchiroli that cannot be reached by any motorized vehicle. You can reach it on a bicycle. He studies in the tenth grade in a charitable residential aashram school that is quite far from his village. He is good at studies, so one can hope that he will pursue further studies somewhere or the other. When he goes home for holidays, it happens sometimes that the Naxalite *dadas* visit his village and he is required to serve them water during their meetings. The dadas urge him to study hard but say that he should not join the police.

That's quite okay by Mahesh, not joining the police. But when the probability of their inviting him to join them increased, Mahesh began visiting home less often.

❖

At the other end, Vamu returned home. On the face of it, one can assume that he returned home on account of the water in his mother's eyes. Vamu passed the tenth grade and began moving with a Naxalite squad, a dalam. He even axed a person to death, used a gun too, and also experienced the respect that his villagers gave him. Vamu was convinced that outsiders were invading his adivasi culture, and he had got bored anyway, sitting at home. What else did he have to engage himself with? That was why he began moving with the Naxalites. It isn't as simple, of course, but his mother had been asking him to come back. He came back too. Tired of all the roaming around, he stayed on. His mother got him married too. Vamu had a wife at age nineteen, the daughter of a police patil whom the Naxalites had bumped off a couple of years earlier. The Naxalites had been upset with his family too. It was under these circumstances that a girl of that household came to Vamu's house as his wife. Bad scene. What if one of her relatives came visiting them here? The smart thing would be to clear out of the village. He let his house at the village stay as it was and moved out himself. Keeps visiting though. And it's good that he is not on bad terms with any party.

Vamu now works as a gardener for two thousand rupees a month, mowing grass, clearing weeds and so on. It's quite convenient. It's now been five years since he has been doing this. He is now learning bamboo handicraft from someone. Once he gets some expertise in it, that's what he will change over to. He doesn't get compensated in his current work for the effort he puts in, he thinks. But he has a wife, and he's had two kids in these five years. As of now, therefore, has no choice but to do what he has been doing right now.

❖

The way Vamu's mother's eyes water, Hemlata-bai's eyes used to water too. But now, if you ignore the layer of water over the pupils, her eyes do not get watery any more. It may happen that little by little an entire drop forms after some time and trickles down, but it isn't the regular, crying kind of water. Hemlata-bai has weathered a hundred monsoons. She's had water from countless villages. And she let plenty of water flow down her eyes. She was born in Bangladesh, but when she dies, it is going to be in a Gadchiroli village in India. When East Pakistan became Bangladesh, there was a war, a genocide; a number of people had to abandon their homes and flee. They fled to their neighbours, to the next-door state of West Bengal in India. From Kolkata to everywhere else. The then government of India rehabilitated them in the central part of the country. Gave them a little land too. People don't remember the government; Indira Gandhi gave them the land, they remember. She was the Prime Minister then, remember? That is how Hemlata-bai got the land where she has been living. But she had arrived in West Bengal much earlier. It must have taken her twelve years to reach Gadchiroli. One of her sons survived. As did stories she had heard and incidents she had seen. Saving one's life by going under the surface of the water and breathing through a lotus stem; swords being thrust into women's private parts; infants being tossed up and caught on the tip of the sword; women being stripped and dragged out into the open and then subjected to mass rape; pools of blood everywhere – these were the images Hemlata-bai still carried in her head. Little by little, her language faded out. Actually, she knew only Bangla and everybody around also spoke Bangla. There were some Madiyas in the village, but the Bengali population greatly outnumbered them, so she could survive with only Bangla. But that is leaking away too. She knows hundreds of stories which have made her audience cry. She just had her boy to begin with, then came a daughter-in-law, and then a grandson. Then the grandson's wife, and also a granddaughter. And now there is this girl of her grandson, about five months old. There's all this blood running in her arteries now. Many years to go before the great-granddaughter begins to menstruate; many years since Hemlata-bai menstruated last. Meanwhile, the water in the eyes. For most of the waking hours Hemlata-bai sits swaddled in her khaki-yellowish coloured quilt in the corner.

❖

Hemlata-bai came from the Bengal yonder; Siddharth Choudhury belonged to the Bengal on this side. He needs water to wash his headache pills down his throat. But why did his head ache so?

Because he would be wandering around Kolkata either on foot or by bus. And he had just returned from a job interview. Besides, a chap had further jammed his head by giving him unsolicited advice. The interview that he appeared for, let's see how it went:

Interviewer: *What's your age?*

Siddharth: I am just over twenty-five, sir.

You are a BSc?

Yes, sir.

When did you graduate?

1966.

Have you been idle ever since?

No, sir. I was in a medical college for two years.

What were you doing there?

Studying sir.

Only two years?

Yes, sir.

What made you gave up medicine? Did you suddenly lose interest?

No, sir. I lost my father.

I see... What's your aim in life?

Right now, it's to find a job, sir.

But the job you have applied for has nothing to do with medicine.

No sir, but I also did botany for my science degree.

Do you like flowers?

Not unconditionally; some I like, some I don't.

Does the term 'mitochondria' suggest anything to you?

It's a botanical term, sir. Mitrochondria are small, thread-like bodies in the cytoplasm.

Who was the Prime Minister of England at the time of independence?

Whose independence, sir?

Ours.

Atkins.

What would you regard as the most outstanding and the most significant event of the last decade?

The war in Vietnam, sir.

More significant than the landing on the moon?

I think so, sir.

Could you tell us why you think so?

Because the moon landing…you see, we weren't entirely unprepared for the moon landing. We knew it had to come some time, as we knew about the space flights, the great advances in space technology. So, we knew it had to happen. I am not saying it wasn't a remarkable achievement, but it was not unpredictable – the fact that they did land on the moon.

Do you think the war in Vietnam was unpredictable?

Not the war itself, but what it has revealed about the Vietnamese people, about their extraordinary power of resistance…ordinary people, peasants…and no one knew they had it in them. And this isn't a matter of technology. It's just plain human courage, and it takes your breath away.

Are you a communist?

I don't think one has to be one in order to admire Vietnam, sir.

That doesn't answer my question. However, you may go now.

The interviewer presses the bell under his table top to call for the next candidate and Siddharth leaves. As he is sitting for a cup of tea somewhere outside, someone walks along and feeds him a few doses of advice. Now, Siddharth is standing in front of a pharmacy. The shopkeeper brings out a strip of pills. Siddharth asks him for a single pill, which he gives. The man brings him water in a transparent glass. 'How many rupees?' asks Siddharth. 'Sixty paise.' Siddharth tosses the pill into his mouth and downs it with the water. The money was for the pill, not for the water. And one of the reasons for the headache was the need to earn money.

This attitude of Siddharth Choudhury one can encounter in detail in Satyajit Ray's Bengali movie *Pratidwandi*. The movie was released on 27 October 1970. We have seen just one of its scenes above. The screenplay is based on Sunil Gangopadhyaya's Bengali novel *Pratidwandi*, but the scene above has no equivalent in the novel, nor will you find the above dialogue there. Both the novel as well as the screenplay are written with Naxalite activities as the background. While Siddharth Choudhury wanders around Kolkata in search of a job, people like Bhaskar are trying to wage an armed revolution, with communism as their ultimate goal. Satyajit Ray himself wrote the screenplay and the dialogues, so it is fair to assume that the above dialogue, which does not occur in the novel, was Ray's contribution.

These were the times when a country called Vietnam had been split into two. The northern part contiguous to China was under communist rule, while the government in South Vietnam was under America's sway. In this conflict, the soldiers and citizens of North Vietnam made life hell for the American forces, and ultimately compelled the American army to withdraw in disgrace. This piece of history many know. Even in this distant state of Maharashtra, anyone who is a decent reader would know about it. Or put a search on the internet. Of course, it is not as if you can get to examine historical information in deep details on any part of the world any time. If you do sit examining, then your search for courage mainly meets with disappointment. So, more headache for Siddharth Choudhury. Remedy? Keep popping pills and keep downing them with water.

❖

But water... even if you don't have to take pills for headaches, you drink. When your train stops at a station, you want to run out and have water. 'Water, cold water,' blares the man selling water bottles up and down the train. He will quote whatever price he wants to, usually at least five rupees more than the printed price. Better then to carry your water with you. When it gets over, you can hop off at the next station and fill your bottle again. This is how a certain dark, heavily built woman felt. She appeared to be around fifty-five and wore a heavy mangalsutra. She, her daughter-in-law and three grandchildren were off travelling somewhere. When the train stopped at a station, the mother-in-law got down. There was a railway stall there in front. The lady took idli with chutney, thirty rupees for a plate of three idlis! The year was 2014, and even then it was a little steeply priced. The financial status of the lady counting out the thirty rupees for three slim idlis was delicate too; so she took just one plate and handed across the paper plate to her daughter-in-law through the window bars. She carried in tea in two paper cups for which she had paid seven rupees. That was when she realized that the water in their bottle had run out, so down again. She pushed the empty bottle to the person at the stall and said, 'Brother, please fill this up.' But filling water for clients was not a part of the rules for running the stall. The brother refused and advised her to buy a sealed bottle of water for twenty rupees. The thirty rupees for the idlis had already hurt the poor woman, and now another twenty for the water? There were three faucets for public use, but they were not functioning. So, what did one do? More headache. So she forgot the water and just drank the tea, and had a plate of idli with the daughter-in-law.

❖

It happens. Not as if it happens everywhere, but happen it does. There is water in the cow's eyes. There is such a cow in Jhirambavli, the author's village. It's housed in a shingled barn. The barn is an independent unit. The landlord pays a hundred rupees as additional house tax for it. His house there in front, and the cow's house is this barn. House No. 458. There is this government slogan on a metal sheet and nailed on the cow's door: *Small Family, Happy Family. Prevent AIDS.* The cow, of course, does not have a family. This cow is black. It's a cross between a native cow and a Jersey. Seventeen years of age, so it's got another seven or eight years to go. Its owner had bought it for two hundred and fifty rupees. It has calved seven times since then: one male died, and the owner sold off four. The two females too he sold off. Once it delivers, it gives plenty of milk for about eighteen months. To keep the milk flowing, it has to be seeded all the time; then it gets pregnant and delivers, and this has been going on and on. Poor cow. It is slim of build, but it is resilient. Big, black, round eyes, like big berries. There are all those berries that keep dropping off the tree on the other side, red-black berries. There's no red in the cow's eyes. But the water in her eyes has been flowing inside for years now. Cow, oh cow, little girl mine, the granny used to say. Does everybody's granny sit making quilts? Cow, how much will you cry?

❖

I had promised to offer to the reader an entry of Anand Manvi, so this is what I finish the chapter with. These were the lines on Anand Manvi's paper:

Neer is one more word for water, and *Aasha* means hope.

When water runs over hope, that is Neer + Aasha = Niraasha, which means despair.

Consuming harmless-seeming slices

Of such meanings
And turning fat
With such indulgence –
If, instead,
One lives
Free of hope
But whole
So, any problem, anybody?

Ah, well, that's been a lot of reading. Some water for you?

Epilogue

What can I say? I have nothing to say. I'm not in the habit of talking. I simply cannot talk. I understand, but expressing what one understands is not a part of our tradition. And forget tradition, I don't even have the language to talk to you, so how can I talk?

But this author has been bugging me for so a long time that I must talk.

If you have to talk, then language comes in. His language is Marathi. He says, just sleep for a night with her; by morning, she will be all around you.

But to sleep like humans is not our tradition. Forget tradition, we don't even have any need for sleep. So we are wide awake all our life.

That's exactly why he wants me to speak, as the author himself told me. It's out of continuous conversation with him that I have begun to know his language (and he mine). Talking to each other is a much better alternative for learning a language than all this business of sleeping with it, I would imagine.

Who am I?

I am a leaf –

A teak leaf.

That is, I am not a human being. And leaf would mean the same kind as the author was talking about in the beginning of the novel. Floating on water, the upper edge a little submerged in the water. The author was saying that he had seen the other leaf, quite identical in looks to me, dying at its place of residence. Quite possible, I said, what's new there? Lakhs of teak leaves fall to the ground across the world; so nothing special in his finding two looking so much alike.

Well, now that this author has become my friend, I have decided to talk. Besides, he had come with a reference from the other leaf too, so I have given him leave to talk. But there are some natural doubts I have. Things can be learnt in double-quick time too, but if I have to talk, there's this elementary natural doubt I have with regard to language. Your language is such a funny thing. Look, I am a teak leaf, that is, I am a neuter gender. And when a neuter gender speaks in the first person, what verb should be used?

If I had to use the masculine gender in Marathi, I would say 'Mee zhopto' for 'I sleep'.

If I had to use the feminine gender in Marathi, I would say 'Mee zhoptey' for 'I sleep'.

Being of neuter gender, what do I say? There's no verb in Marathi for me.

What can I ever know about grammar? It's out of speaking to him that I learnt the language; and my ability to learn is so many times more than a human's that once I decide, I understand all at one stroke. But he understands even less grammar than I do, I suspect. And there's no first-person verb for a neuter gender thing like me in his language. Funny. Makes me laugh. Ha ha ha ha.

I told the author, give me gender at least, verb at least.

You know, the author laughed too. Ha ha ha ha.

Then the author said, 'My grammar is not good either. So I placed this doubt before a friend of mine who has done his PhD on Pāninian grammar. But that friend too had no remedy for my doubt. Scanned through a couple of books too, but grammar has no answer to this doubt, or there is no grammar on this doubt. This friend who is connected with Pāninian grammar was a friend outside of all this. There was no grammar connection between us. I mean, the friendship didn't happen because of his subject of study. It happened independent of all that. For the rest, I have had nothing to do with Pānini and his grammar. How water and grammar sneaked into the novel, I just didn't register.'

But I don't have time to spend on grammar.

So, I speak now.

I speak, yes, 'boltey', the feminine form of the verb, and to hell with grammar. From here on, the verb for me in Marathi is the feminine one (although in English it isn't any different for the masculine one). The author hadn't realized all this, but when first person masculine is used in Marathi, it often needs an additional diacritical mark or an additional hyphenated word somewhere or the other. Since gender doesn't make any difference to me, why waste ink and paper on those marks? I'm not going to take this verb issue seriously anyway. I'll keep hopping from one to the other, and sometimes even try to cook up some neuter gender verb of my own. Actually, there are places where even Marathi speakers use neuter gender verbs, but this author doesn't seem to know that. (With this English translation, of course, the problem vanishes. So, that's settled.) Anyway I shall continue with what I have decided. Rather than grammar and language, what I have to say is more important for me.

There are serious things I want to talk about, and I haven't much time. I'm coming to my end. That I speak about such things all by myself, the author has advised me. I know a lot of stories. See, it's like this: geography is limited, but there are winds that blow past the tree from here to there, there are birds visiting, there are the rains, the clouds wandering from there to here. So, the stories I have got to know are so long and so many that it's difficult to decide what to talk about and what to leave out. My geography has extended automatically, and since I am open, I can learn things quickly, absorb them. For example, your language, your doubts about verbs, or the subject of the author, or that it is called a novel, I have learnt them in no time. I have some special ability, you may say. You won't understand this strength. The author hasn't understood it either, otherwise I would have let you know through him. All I can say is that I am open to all the stories of the world. So, if you are surprised at what all stories I know and in what all manner, keep it to yourself. You are bound to be human like this author. So, the more than justifiable confidence you have on your information, well, snip it some. You will then be able to pay attention to what I have to say, or feel like paying attention, you may say.

It was because I was paying attention that I got to know of the splashes of blood that burst out from the jeep that was blown up on that tarred road. Also heard the gunfire that followed the explosion. There were human voices floating in and out too. Got to understand everything that was happening. It was happening very fast, and it was all over in a short time. A large number of people arrived in a military truck, began taking photographs of those who had died, got into other investigations and talked on the phone.

'Who was going to surrender? This woman, right? Bitch. Began to flee.' This is what one of the men there said, looking at a body. It was the body of a young girl. Blood had congealed below her nose. The stuff she was carrying on her back had broken off and lay scattered there. Her dark green uniform was as it had been. There was a muffler wrapped round her neck. Her eyes were open, and there was a cut across her lips. She was stretched out straight, but one of her hands had bent crooked. From my tree here I have seen her pass by at least three-four times. Going by human age, she would be in her early twenties. Some dust had got into her mouth since she died. Some of the blood from her nose had settled on her teeth. She lay close to that tree in front. Her eyes were fixed on top of the aerial roots of that tree as she died. I lay on the water there. The military people left with her body. There were five other bodies scattered there. There was another one on the other side. A body lay there face down. 'Who could it be? A woman?' muttered the army people and went closer. Saw her face as they reached closer. It was a girl. One of her eyes looked grotesquely injured, the other was open. Blood had flown out of her neck and soaked into the earth. There was another body fifteen feet away. A very young boy stretched out absolutely straight. Younger than that girl. His trousers looked burnt white around his private parts. The muffler round his neck looked like it had strangled him. One leg looked completely broken; eyes, again, wide open. Ants were crawling over him.

The army people were checking out the bodies first. There was an hour to go before sunset, and it was necessary for them to inspect the bodies and carry them over to the camp. They were, therefore, busy. It was in the hustle-bustle of this day that I fell off the tree. Fell into this water. So many days have gone by since I fell. I am close to finishing up. No regret there. So many leaves around me on the same tree have fallen too. They will finish too. It's just because I happened to fall in this water that I get distinct glitters every day. The yellow sun rays glitter quite differently around me. My body will become one with the earth. But before that, I had to talk about the human bodies that I saw. It isn't that I would necessarily have talked about it. It was just that the author came with reference from another leaf, so I talked. I had to.

The writer was searching for the cause of people's death. Well, it's an old, old cause, I told him. During the rather short conversation, I couldn't know how much of history he knew. He gave the egret's reference too, and I also quickly read through the rest of the novel. But this much is not enough to understand a person. And I don't have that kind of time either. I can feel everything stopping bit by bit in every part of me.

It's not as if I saw people dying only during the bomb explosion. There have been a good three-four encounters between the policemen and the Naxalites. Some of the trees have disappeared from here too. That has reduced the number of encounters. But being right alongside the road, I could witness a few events. The day the jeep blew up, skirmishes kept happening. Couldn't get to know whose jeep it was, actually. The police don't roam around on jeeps here. The Naxalites have taught them enough lessons in this regard. But police action continues. They killed that girl who had wanted to surrender. Earlier they had killed two girls and three boys who were not in uniform. They were not carrying guns either. Thin kids. Once before too, another small vehicle had gone up in the air, all of it. It didn't belong to the police. The police don't roam around in jeeps here, at least not openly. It was just a taxi person. There were four others in it. No way they could have survived. Bodies drenched in red and black. The smell of burnt rubber stayed for a long time. Good I don't have a nose. The police then arrived and took the bodies away. This time the eyes of the corpses were not as they were the previous time. They were not the kind that would arrest attention. But from whatever experience I have of human beings, they were enough to bring tears to the eyes. Good I don't have eyes.

A few days later, there were some cows that were passing by here, with a few egrets accompanying them. The egret that appeared in the novel earlier was among them. I got to know from it about the infant that had fallen on the stone and died. Felt very bad. In fact, that was the main reason I agreed to talk. Otherwise, I have seen lots of people dying. But that kid smashing its head on the stone and dying, and the sound not even reaching anyone. Good I don't have ears either.

I have seen the deaths of so many other insects and birds. Have seen birds kill so many insects with their beaks. You may not get this fully, but since getting into this water, I have seen so many insects dying under cows' hooves. The tiniest of tiny insects, I've seen them die too. I have heard of the deaths of so many other things. I'm using these terms 'seen' and 'heard' so that it makes sense to you. The channels through which I understand things, your language doesn't have the words required to communicate the meanings of those channels. In any case, that's not our subject as of now. The subject is that of that infant. Don't know why, but I've not been able to find peace since I heard about the death of that kid. Well, I'm on the verge of dying too. But it was important, before that, to bring up the memory of that kid. The egret had to do it too. And there was the reference from that leaf, so…

Nobody accepted responsibility for that kid's death. The way the police came to inspect the other dead bodies, no such inspection was done for the kid. It didn't have to surrender either, so nobody called it a bitch or used any other abusive word. From the egret's description, I think that I've seen this kid at least once in the company of its mother. They had a dog with them too. There was a black mark on the kid's back. It hadn't even begun to straighten its palms, such a small kid. It wasn't even of an age where it would need clothes to cover its body. Nevertheless, its mother would generally wrap it in a pink rag when carrying it around. It wasn't required to be in any uniform or anything. It was just not big enough to wear the kinds of clothes that people are required to wear. It would just lie staring into infinity, always.

What happened was bad. I've understood lots of things in the course of my life, but I haven't understood why it got to be so necessary for me to bring up that kid's memory before passing away. Well, whatever it be.

The sun is setting, so I put a stop to my talking. I may or may not be here tomorrow. The memory of that kid's eyes will remain. It had a flat nose between its eyes. I couldn't read its death when I peered into its eyes either. It was a healthy kid. Quiet kid. Small eyes. There was no talk visible yet in those eyes. There was just water. That was why I decided to talk. And there was this reference from this other leaf, so, that's why…

Thus Ends

The golden sunshine has spread inside now. Some light clouds have also gathered. I've just finished reading this novel. Had been reading it for the last three days. I would find time for it in the middle of all the other work. I felt like making time for it. It's been raining heavily for two days too, washing away a number of engagements, so that gave me some more time with the book. The leaf that the author had seen in the prologue would have got washed away. Well, anyway, I could run through all the leaves of the book. I am Anand Manvi.

This writer is quite junior to me in age, but we've got to be good friends. He just vanished a couple of years ago and so contact with him snapped. And now, three days ago, I received this manuscript in a green folder, with a small letter accompanying it.

Dear Anand,

Sending you the novel as per our discussion earlier.

I've left one chapter called 'Thus Ends' unwritten. You may write whatever you feel as a reader in this chapter: a line, a page, whatever. But I think you should write in your own name because there is a person in the novel who bears the same name. My apologies if you haven't liked it. But you have always been the first reader of all my writings, and I thought of placing its memories within the novel. I am sure you would have recognized who that person is. I felt grieved at his death, so I wrote about him.

My request is that you write about the author's ending on behalf of the reader. Another request – write your piece the very day you finish reading, or as soon as you can.

Regards.

Yours,

अज्ञ

Amravati, 1 April 2015

I had expected he would contact me again after he stabilized somewhere, and that's just what happened. There had been no agreement between us that I would write the last chapter called 'Thus Ends'. We had, of course, decided that, as with his previous two novels, I would read the manuscript of this third one. There is a saying here in Konkan which, in essence, means: the dust has settled, but the particles are floating around. The author has let the dust settle for this novel and asked me to gather the particles. There's no point in stretching it too long. When the manuscript arrived, I didn't much agree with the contents of the letter. I felt that if I wrote here as a reader, it would influence the opinion of the later readers. It would prevent them from arriving at their own opinions. But again, saying this is being unfair to the other readers. Hence I have decided to express my opinion here in brief. In brief because I have read it just now and I haven't arrived at any settled opinion yet. This is just the first reaction.

Two things should be clarified at the outset. One: whatever

similarities or differences there are between the Anand Manvi of the novel and me, I shall not delve on that. (Though I should say that my wife does live with me.) Two: the author has indicated that I have recognized the real Anand Manvi. It won't be proper for me to comment on that either. As a reader, I should observe this decorum, I believe. However much we may be tempted to peep into the author's life, it's good to treat a novel as a novel. Outside the novel, we may write a thesis on the author, but here we shouldn't.

We live, we work, sex, food, cinema – and in the middle of all this, how would it feel if we were to be confronted with the body of a six-month-old baby with its head smashed? It would be horrendous. I haven't experienced the same kind of sorrow as the old woman Hemlata, Lattakka, Smita, and the others in the novel. I felt particularly guilty when I read about them. Some pieces were beautiful. Other parts of the book left me feeling that I should think a lot more. Although our direct or indirect relationship with violence is not new, the author has made a considerable effort at examining it. But on the other hand, towards the end of the novel, who is responsible for the tragic death of the six-month-old? The author doesn't come out clearly enough on this. It wasn't killed by any weapon. There are many reasons for jeeps blowing up; Lattakka tells us about one of them. Whatever the fear that had caused the mother to run with the infant, should that be held responsible? Or was it a completely natural accident due to her tripping on a stone and losing her balance? It's not as if he should necessarily have blamed the death on a single cause, but what could be the reason for not looking at that death as a part of a process? Does the writer not have the courage to withstand a process? Is that the simple answer to the question? I wonder. There should be no violence. If the answer has to be as simple as this, then who carries the responsibility for bringing it to a halt? It's upon those who have the larger number of weapons in the respective circumstances, would be one answer. It may not happen that way, though the first responsibility is theirs. There is the possibility, of course, that other readers would arrive at a different understanding of the affair. Harping on one subject, instead of talking passingly about it, could mean ignoring other aspects of the novel. But the author had insisted, so here I am. If it hurts him in any way, he will have to bear it. Be that as it may.

As it is said in the novel too, there'll be some kind of a hangover and other thoughts will stream in. But there's not much left for me to say as a reader. He had insisted that I write immediately after reading the novel, so this is all I can think of saying right now. I feel a little numb. My girl is in the fourth grade. Her immediate presence, my wife's presence and the presence of this novel, it is important to arrive at a balance among them. A novel, in the final call, is the writer's limitation. The world spreads well outside this limitation. But despite this limitation, I was quite overcome on reading this work. The true effect of this novel will be determined by what Smita, Lattakka, Rani, Sayali, Bhaskar, Ayan, the egret, the teak leaf, and all the other readers feel about it.

The golden sunshine is disappearing, the clouds are thickening. It may rain again today. The rains at Ratnagiri, don't even talk about them. It's like sheets of water advancing at you. You can hear the rains striking against objects here. Good if it rains today too.

About the Author

Avadhoot Dongare is a writer and a translator. He started writing fiction in 2007. He has published four novels in Marathi: *Svatahala Faltu Samjanyachi Goshta* (*The Story of Being Useless*, 2012), *Eka Lekhakache Teen Sandarbha* (*Three Contexts of a Writer*, 2013), *Paan, Pani Ni Pravah* (*Leaf, Water and Flow*, 2015) and *Bhintivarcha Chashma* (*Specs on the Wall*, 2018).

Dongare's first novel was awarded the Sahitya Akademi Yuva Puraskar in 2014. He has also published two tracts on the practice of translation: *Svatahacha Avakash Tapasatana* (*Probing One's Space*, 2017) and *Eka Shabdacha Pech* (*A Quandary about a Word*, 2021) and a book of short stories for children. He blogs at ekregh.blogspot.com

About the Authors

About the Translator

Nadeem Khan has been a teacher of English for fifty years. He was the founder–director of the Western Regional Centre of the Indian Institute of Mass Communication, a position he occupied for eight years.

Nadeem has translated Marathi and Hindi writings into English and English writings into Hindi. Among the many works of translation to his credit are three major novels of the well-known Marathi writer Vishwas Patil, including the iconic *Panipat*. Nadeem's translations of Avadhoot Dongare's *The Story of Being Useless* and *Three Contexts of a Writer* won the Valley of Words award for the best translated book of 2020. His translation of Dr Savita Ambedkar's autobiography, *Babasaheb: My Life with Dr Ambedkar*, has won acclaim among scholars and lay readers.

The HarperCollins–Ratna Sagar Translation Series

Ratna Sagar is an Indian publishing company founded in 1982; Ratna Books, its translations-only imprint, was launched in 2017. The aim of the Ratna Sagar translation list has been to bring acclaimed works written in the Indian languages to a wider readership in English translation, and the focus has been to ensure the quality of the translations, to provide the reader with a seamless reading experience.

Forty-two books have been published in the Ratna Sagar translation list so far, all in hardback. The books have been received well by readers and have met with critical acclaim from the media; many of the books have also won or been nominated for literary awards.

HarperCollins is proud to partner with Ratna Sagar to bring this list of high-quality translations to readers in paperback editions, publishing under HarperCollins's prestigious Perennial imprint.

READ MORE

Havan by Mallikarjun Hiremath
Leaf, Water and Flow by Avadhoot Dongare
Parthiban's Dream by Kalki Krishnamurthy
Prison Notes of a Woman Activist by Bellapu Anuradha
The Bells Are Ringing in Haridwar by M. Mukundan
Dukhi Dadiba by Dadi Edulji Taraporewala
After Yesterday and Other Stories by Appaduari Muttulingam
The Sixth Finger by Malayatoor Ramakrishnan
A Faceless Evening and Other Stories by Gangadhar Gadgil
If a River and Other Stories by Kula Saikia
On a River's Bank by A. Madhavan
Echoes of the Veena and Other Stories by R. Chudamani
Here I Am and Other Stories by P. Sathyavathi
The Rock That Was Not and Other Stories by Githanjali
The Story of Being Useless and Three Contexts of a Writer by Avadhoot Dongare
Mirror in the Hall and Other Stories by Prakash Bal Joshi
The Songs of Life and Other Stories by Vijaya Rajadhyaksha
Jalasamadhi and Other Stories by A. Sethumadhavan
Kadambari - The Flower Girl by A. Sethumadhavan
The Scent of Happiness by R. Vatsala
Asprishya Ganga and Other Stories by Kolakaluri Enoch
Alka and Other Stories by Goutam Das
If there is a God and Other Stories by Imayam
Ananta Jeevanam by Kolakaluri Enoch
The Stepmother and Other Stories by Laxmibai Abhyankar
Cracked Glass Jar and Other Stories by Chandra Latha
A Fine Thread and Other Stories by B. Jeyamohan
Forever Yours, Krishna by Indira Parthasarathy
Mayaloka by Poornachandra Tejaswi
The Go-Between and Other Stories by Ghanshyam Desai
The Masked Face and Two Other Stories by Vaasanthi
Vasudeva ... The Wanderer Prince by Sanghadasagani Vacaka
Randhi: Of Power and Desire by Kolakaluri Enoch

HarperCollins *Publishers* India

At HarperCollins India, we believe in telling the best stories and finding the widest readership for our books in every format possible. We started publishing in 1992; a great deal has changed since then, but what has remained constant is the passion with which our authors write their books, the love with which readers receive them, and the sheer joy and excitement that we as publishers feel in being a part of the publishing process.

Over the years, we've had the pleasure of publishing some of the finest writing from the subcontinent and around the world, including several award-winning titles and some of the biggest bestsellers in India's publishing history. But nothing has meant more to us than the fact that millions of people have read the books we published, and that somewhere, a book of ours might have made a difference.

As we look to the future, we go back to that one word—a word which has been a driving force for us all these years.

Read.